D1021764

THE IRON HUNT

"Marjorie M. Liu writes a gripping supernatural thriller."
—*The Best Reviews*

"From the imagination of one of today's most talented authors comes a mesmerizing, darkly disturbing world on the brink of apocalypse." —*RT Book Reviews* (4½ stars, top pick)

"Readers who love urban fantasies like those of Charlaine Harris or Kim Harrison will relish Marjorie M. Liu's excellent adventure." —*Midwest Book Review*

"A stunning new series . . . The mythology is fascinating, the characters complicated, the story lines original." —*Fresh Fiction*

MORE PRAISE FOR THE NOVELS OF
MARJORIE M. LIU

"Will charm, tempt, and surprise readers into coming back for more." —*Darque Reviews*

"Raises the bar for all others competing in its league . . . Readers of early Laurell K. Hamilton, Charlaine Harris, and the best thrillers out there should try Liu now and catch a rising star."
—*Publishers Weekly* (starred review)

"The boundlessness of Liu's imagination never ceases to amaze."
—*Booklist* (starred review)

"Nonstop adventure . . . A rich world with paranormal elements."
—*SFRevu*

"Liu is masterful . . . Fiction that goes beyond the boundaries of action-adventure romance or romantic suspense." —*Booklist*

"Fabulous romantic suspense fantasy that will hook the audience from the first note to the incredible climactic coda."
—*Midwest Book Review*

"Marjorie Liu seems to have an endless imagination for creating new and interesting characters and stories." —*Affaire de Coeur*

continued...

LABYRINTH OF STARS

MARJORIE M. LIU

ACE BOOKS, NEW YORK

THE BERKLEY PUBLISHING GROUP
Published by the Penguin Group
Penguin Group (USA) LLC
375 Hudson Street, New York, New York 10014

USA • Canada • UK • Ireland • Australia • New Zealand • India • South Africa • China

penguin.com

A Penguin Random House Company

LABYRINTH OF STARS

An Ace Book / published by arrangement with the author

Ace Books are published by The Berkley Publishing Group.
ACE and the "A" design are trademarks of Penguin Group (USA) LLC.

For information, address: The Berkley Publishing Group,
a division of Penguin Group (USA) LLC,
375 Hudson Street, New York, New York 10014.

ISBN: 978-1-937007-85-0

PUBLISHING HISTORY
Ace mass-market edition / March 2014

PRINTED IN THE UNITED STATES OF AMERICA

10 9 8 7 6 5 4 3 2 1

Cover art by Craig White.
Cover design by Judith Lagerman.
Interior text design by Laura K. Corless.

Para Junot
Entre nosotros, que siempre haya luz

In this brief transit where the dreams cross
The dreamcrossed twilight between birth and dying . . .

—T. S. ELIOT

I am the mother, yet the daughter is more,
she is everything that the mother was, and that
which the mother was not becomes great in her;
she is the future and the immortal past,
she is the womb, she is the sea . . .

—VARIATION OF 11.4 FROM RAINER
    MARIA RILKE'S *BOOK OF HOURS*

CHAPTER 1

I'LL be honest: I can't recommend having a demon as
your obstetrician.

Fight with them, live with them, feed their hungry stomachs all the M&M's, chain saws, and small artillery they
can handle—but when it comes to taking pregnancy advice,
avoid at all costs. Even *if* they've been delivering the babies
in your family for the last ten thousand years.

"Need ash," Zee muttered, pressing his sharp little ear
to my belly. "Volcanic. Hot. Fresh to eat."

My husband, sprawled in the grass beside me, started
laughing. I flinched. He was turned away from me, so he
didn't notice.

I took a quick breath, trying to stay calm, and focused
on the rich, delighted sound of his voice. I tried not to think
about how long it had been since I'd heard him laugh—and
I certainly didn't dwell on how starved I was for it. Instead,
I listened, listened with all the strength I'd once spent fighting demons—and suffered a panged mix of relief and joy.

I placed a hand on my belly. "Oh, sure. *You* think it's funny."

Grant turned his head and flashed me a grin. For a moment I had the crazy hope things might be getting better. But then the shadows crept through his eyes, and his smile turned brittle. He was trying, though, which made it all worse.

I clutched my cold bottle of ginger ale and took a long swallow, using it as an excuse to look away and wash down a wave of nausea. Grant rolled over on his side and placed his hand over mine.

Softly, he said, "Breathe, Maxine."

"You breathe," I grumbled, finishing off the ginger ale. I heard a hungry chirp and passed the bottle to the demon nesting in my hair, listening to glass crunch.

It was a warm night. Moon had already set. Around us, demons: Raw and Aaz, sprawled on top of my grandmother's grave, clutching teddy bears and gnawing on meat cleavers— dashing them with gunpowder, tobacco, to spice the metal. The scent put a burn in the air.

Zee leaned on my stomach, listening to unborn secrets. Playing doctor, nutritionist, making clicking sounds with his skinny black tongue and closing the second lid of his red eyes, as if in a trance. Dek nibbled my ear and hummed the melody to an old Pat Benatar song, "We Belong." Mal joined him: a soft trill, lilting into the night.

Oak leaves hissed, joined by the tall grass: waves and waves of those delicate dry hisses, rising and falling in the night with the wind. I listened to Grant's slow, even breaths—the rasp of scales and claws, my own heartbeat— all of it, together, something I tried hard to relax into. As if I could make them, with sheer willpower, the only sounds in the universe.

But nothing—nothing—could drown out the drums.

It wasn't a beat. Nothing as hollow as a human instrument. A throb, maybe a pulse: organic and wet. Accompanying it, floating like a loose thread, an eerie lilting chorus that sounded like a Chinese opera married to some ancient tribal chant. A melodic, thrusting sound that made the hairs rise on my neck.

I hated it. My mother was probably turning in her grave.

Because here we were—dead center in the middle of three thousand prime Texas acres—and somewhere near us an army of demons was *partying*.

"If I find out they're sacrificing virgins, I'm chopping off heads."

"Yes," Grant replied, and opened his eyes. "Do you smell blood?"

I waited a moment because when someone, anyone in my life, says they smell blood, it's usually *not* their imagination.

"No," I told him, and he closed his eyes again.

"It's the link," he muttered, sounding tired. "The Shurik are nesting inside that new herd of cows we brought in. It hit me, all of a sudden. The smell and . . . taste . . . of it."

It was like both of us were pregnant. Me, I had a human baby inside me. Grant had demons. Not just one, but nearly a thousand—more than half of an entire demon army. Bonded to him: through his heart, through his power. Which meant they felt everything he did. A pyramid of influence and dominance, trickling into every living Shurik and Yorana—keeping them under control. Otherwise, *humans* would be on the menu—and not a herd of cattle.

The price was that Grant could feel *them*, as well: the force of a thousand lives, a constant presence in his heart and head. Buzzing, burning, crowding. Voices that whispered, voices begging, voices that brought migraines that showed no signs of abating.

I knotted my fingers around the soft, loose flannel of his shirt, and tugged, gently. "I would do anything to help you."

"I know," he said, scratching the rough beard he'd been growing for the last month—a symptom of exhaustion rather than fashion. "I'm learning to cope."

"Liar."

"The other demon lords manage. Those bonds make them stronger."

"You're not a demon."

"If I can't do this," he said quietly, then stopped, flexing his big hands: all of him, big, warm, hurting. "Breaking the bonds will kill them. I can't do that. I can't sacrifice all those lives just to save mine."

"I can," I muttered. "You're not healthy, Grant. You're barely eating. You aren't sleeping. And when you do, you have nightmares. You're going to be a *father*, for fuck's sake. If we could talk to my grandfather—"

"Leave him out of it." Grant gave me an unexpectedly hard look, which only made the circles under his bloodshot eyes stand out like bruises. The effect was worse at night: his face hollow. "I'm done talking about this, Maxine."

He was being so stupid. Stupid and honorable, and courageous, and stupid. My *irritation* had irritation. Zee raised his head, giving Grant a cool look—even as Raw and Aaz jerked to attention, staring. Dek and Mal muttered something musical, and no doubt, vile—drew in deep breaths, rattled their little tails—and spat fire at him.

Grant yelped, rolling away. I laughed.

"Thanks," he said, from the shadows. But he was laughing, too.

⊰❊⊱

I'VE always had a good appetite, but being pregnant meant now I ate more like the boys—minus the barbed wire, engine oil, and occasional bomb.

Raw reached into the shadows, all the way down to his shoulder—fished around for a second—and then pulled out a small white cardboard box filled with two hamburgers smothered in cheese, what appeared to be a pound of fries, and a container of frozen custard that had the name of a famous New York burger joint written on the side.

I don't ask where, or how, they get these things. Not anymore.

I held the box in one hand—propped against the small, barely noticeable bulge of my stomach—and started in on the hamburgers. Grant gave me an amused smile.

"You should eat one of these," I said, and I thought he would refuse. But then, slowly, he reached over and took the second hamburger from the box.

We were walking down the hill, back to the farmhouse. Going slow, because it didn't matter that Grant was sort-of-a-demon-lord (and even without that title, *still* one of the most dangerous men on earth), he had a crushed kneecap that had never healed right, and he needed a cane to walk.

The music hadn't stopped. I kept checking the sky for helicopters, or police lights swerving up the long driveway.

"The odds are against us, no matter what we do," I said, around a mouthful of burger. "We've gotten lucky so far, and that's with mistakes. Nothing this *weird* is going to stay hidden forever, Grant."

Nothing this dangerous, either. For ten thousand years, an army of demons had been locked inside a prison just beyond our world. Until, three months ago, the walls had fallen, releasing the horde upon this earth. An army accustomed to hunting humans. An army that was starving. Starving to *death*.

Now those four demon clans were living on my dead mother's farm. Packed in like refugees. Eating cows, pigs, anything . . . meaty . . . our money could buy. And not particularly enjoying the taste, either.

"Alaska." Grant's hamburger was already gone: eaten in three bites. "We could buy land there. Or somewhere else even more remote, where no one goes. Parts of Canada. Detroit."

I finished the hamburger and handed him the fries. Again, he hesitated. I waved them under his nose, making "choo-choo" sounds. He snorted, still holding off, and Dek began humming "Sing for Your Supper," an old film song recorded by the Mamas and the Papas.

Grant narrowed his eyes at the little demon but gave in. After the first several bites, I thought he would puke—that had been happening more and more—but he swallowed hard, waited a moment, and reached for another.

Zee was prowling in the shadows beside us. "Need territory. Migration. Someplace wild. Far."

I tried imagining such a place. Maybe an island in the Pacific. Deserted. But even that wouldn't be entirely safe. Humans were everywhere. And there would never be enough food to sustain the demons.

"No such thing on earth," I said, finally.

Zee glanced at his brothers. "Then leave earth."

Raw and Aaz stopped tumbling through the grass. Dek's and Mal's purrs broke. Grant and I stopped walking and stared at Zee.

"Better to leave," he rasped, meeting our gazes. "Enter Labyrinth. Find new world. *Safe* world."

"Safe," I echoed, and a primal urge to dig, dig and hide, hit me—with dread. Because I knew instantly what he was saying, and it was the one thing I hadn't wanted to face. The very thing Grant and I had been skirting around for months.

It's hard, knowing what you have to do. And worse, not quite having the strength to do it.

"Safe," he whispered, giving me a long, knowing look. "For little light."

I exhaled, slowly. Grant took my hand. "You think our baby is in danger."

Zee continued holding my gaze. "Homes change. Or homes die."

I looked back up the hill at my mother's grave—at my grandmother, buried beside her. Grant squeezed my hand, but I barely felt his touch. I realized, suddenly, that I had expected to be buried beside them one day. Despite all the time that had passed since my mother's murder, and no matter how much I had to live for—that was the one grim promise about my eventual death that I looked forward to.

How fucking sad.

Grant suppressed a cough, then another—his thinning shoulders jerked violently. In the six years we'd been together, I'd never even heard him sniffle. Now he was frail.

Another coughing fit hit, this one more violent. I dropped the food, wrapping my arm around his waist as he sank into the grass.

"Sorry," he murmured, wiping his mouth.

"Don't be," I whispered. Our gazes locked. Remorse was in his eyes, and he wet his lips, which were suddenly dry, cracked.

"Grant," I began, but stopped, overcome with nausea. *It's the pregnancy,* I told myself, only this felt even more powerful than usual. In fact, I really thought I was going to—

I turned away, doubling over as I began puking into the grass. Nothing came up, but it left me shaken, dizzy. It didn't feel right, either. In fact—

"Maxine," hissed Zee. "Door opened."

Door opened. I knew what that meant, and dread spread through me. The only door Zee ever talked about was the door to the Labyrinth—that quantum highway that connected countless worlds. The last two times it had opened, I'd felt it—just like this.

Someone had come through. Or *something.*

"Hurry." I tried to stand, grabbing Grant's arm, hauling him upright. He struggled with his cane, found his feet. But he didn't run. He stood stock-still, head tilted as though listening. Raw and Aaz were doing the same, but looking in the opposite direction. Zee disappeared into the shadows.

My right hand tingled: pins and needles. No flesh around my fingers, palm, and wrist—parts of my forearm, lost— covered in a living, sentient metal, an armor that was quicksilver, dreaming. I could feel it dreaming now, dreaming itself to awareness, and it was not a good sensation. It was a warning.

Grant's hand stretched out, slowly, as if to push me behind him. I took his hand, instead—squeezing it hard.

A sudden lightness fell around my throat. Two demons are heavier than one—and in the space of a heartbeat, Mal dropped into the shadows of my hair and disappeared. I glimpsed, almost in the same moment, his reappearance on my husband's shoulders—

—just as a hail of darts whistled down upon us.

CHAPTER 2

I didn't think. I turned to my husband, ready to throw him to the ground and cover his body. But for once, he was faster. I squeaked in surprise as he tossed me to the grass and dropped on top of me. It only took seconds. My heart thundered, and his breath rasped hot in my face.

I heard the thud of darts in the grass. Grant flinched, whuffing out his breath—and not in a good, startled way. I knew what hurt sounded like.

I tried rolling him off me. He protested through gritted teeth, but I just pushed harder. He weighed more than he should have, and I saw Raw peer around his shoulder to look at me.

"Up," I snapped, and the little demon disappeared. So did the extra weight. I shoved hard, squirming sideways. Grant couldn't hold on to me.

The ground around us looked like a porcupine had exploded. Slender slips of wood wavered upright in the grass, not as long as arrows or as thick, but just about the length of a small chopstick. I stared at them, stunned. An unfamiliar smell hung in the air, stinging and vinegary. Made me sneeze—

—just as a spear the length of my mother's station wagon slammed into my chest.

Or tried to. Zee leapt into the air, taking the strike against his ribs. It was a thunderous weapon, and would have torn a hole in me the size of my fist—but the force of the impact didn't even make the little demon fly sideways. The spear broke around him, showering us in splinters. I heard more whistles, more spears raining down—Raw grabbed one of them out of the air and threw it back into the darkness. Aaz blocked the other from hitting Grant and ate the tip of it—a jagged, barbed shaft of iron that looked better for hunting whales than people.

Zee disappeared into the shadows. A moment later, I heard a deep-throated scream.

I'd forgotten about the demons and their music, but the drums stopped as soon as that scream hit the air. The silence was abrupt, complete. My heartbeat, Grant's ragged breathing—a faint hiss in my ear—were suddenly all that existed, more real, more substantial than flesh.

But not as substantial as the severed head that rolled past me down the hill.

It was the width of a tire, and I glimpsed a contorted open mouth, huge white eyes, and sloped skull that all together resembled the misshapen face of giant-sized clay Gumby doll. Even the skin looked green, but in this darkness I couldn't tell for certain. If my vision hadn't been as good at night as it was in the day, I would never have seen it at all.

A bone-chilling howl rose from across my land—a cacophonic shriek of enraged demonic voices so discordant I wanted to cover my ears. But even that didn't matter because I finally saw what was attacking us, and it was as terrible as I'd thought it would be.

Barrel-chested, bullish. All around us, shaking the earth—hulking, towering shapes more than five times our height, whose feet slammed into the trembling earth like pistons. Only at the last second did I catch impressions of details: naked, bloated, torsos; thick legs jiggling with fat and muscle, those startling white frog-eyes missing lids. I couldn't count them all, but their bodies blocked out the night, and their mouths were slick, wet pits. Big enough to chew on me.

No chance of that. Raw and Aaz tore through them like their flesh was made of butter, plunging headfirst into pale chests that cracked open and poured out blood. Zee darted among them, flying from shadow to shadow, and each second he appeared it was to slash his claws across a throat, with such violence and strength their heads tore off, sometimes hanging from a ribbon of flesh as their bodies crashed.

Grant shouted a single word. It sounded slightly slurred, but the power should have still been there. All the power he needed to possess these creatures and end this.

Only, it didn't work. The creatures, those giants, kept coming.

Mal nipped my ear. I whipped around, heart pounding, and swung my right arm. A blaze of light burned back the night. The creature nearest us bellowed, shielding his eyes. I didn't look at what my hand had become—I already knew. The armor had transformed into a sword: silver, serrated, growing out of my forearm with smooth perfection.

I could feel my hand, somewhere beneath the armor—but the armor was alive, the armor was part of me, and in that moment I was furious, desperate. I'd never been much of a fighter. Left that to the boys. But what I lacked in martial arts skills, I made up for in sheer dumb luck—a little bit of courage—and a whole lot of stubbornness.

I darted forward, dodging the whistling arc of a falling ax, then sidestepped again as the ax almost swung, blade first, onto my head. The creature was moving too fast to predict his movements—and while distance would have been safer, Grant was behind me, on the ground and still struggling to rise.

Fast, but not strategic. Not even a little. The next time

the ax came down, I lopped off the hand that held it. His wrist was thick as a tree trunk, but I felt no resistance in flesh or bone: I could have been tearing silk with my bare hands. The creature reared back, roaring in pain, and I slashed my sword across the only other parts of him I could reach: his knees.

His lower legs toppled sideways from his body, and he toppled with them—Zee appearing at the last moment to knock him backward, so he didn't fall on me and Grant. His screams were cut off seconds later.

We were no longer alone. Mahati warriors swarmed the remaining three giants, slashing flesh with their razor-sharp fingers—and accompanying them were the Osul, who climbed those swinging bloated limbs like big cats wrestling with writhing trees. Some of the crimson-skinned Yorana had come, but they hung back like it was a spectator event, watching and smiling—smiling even more when they saw Grant still struggling to sit up. I wanted to kill them.

Instead, I fell on my knees beside Grant. Sitting still made me dizzy, and my heart pounded too fast. I hadn't fought anything in months, and battling the unfamiliar—being ambushed—was even worse. Although nothing was as bad as seeing my husband on the ground, grimacing in pain—his lower leg covered in blood.

He had his hand up, trying weakly to fend off Mal, who was licking his face. An old human woman crouched over him, too: Mary, her white hair thick, wild, sticking out at electrocuted angles like some Einstein wig. No fat on her body, just leathery brown skin that covered more hard muscle than a starved wolf. She gripped a machete in her wrinkled, leathery right hand. In the other she held three darts, blood on their tips.

"M'fine," Grant told us, but he was having trouble keeping his eyes open. Mary sniffed the darts—and her lips peeled back in disgust.

"Poisoned?" I asked her.

"Badder than," she muttered, and threw the darts away.

Rummaging around the big pocket of her housedress, she pulled out a clear plastic bag of fresh cannabis leaves, tore it open, and tried to stuff a handful into Grant's mouth.

"Come on," he said, still slurring his words—but obviously not that out of it. "Mary."

"You gotta be kidding," I said. "What are you doing, Mary?"

She ignored me, finally stuffing the leaves into his mouth. "Chew. Swallow."

"Mary," I said sharply.

"Antidote." Mary poked Grant hard in the chest. "Hurry."

I'd known the old woman for years, and while my opinion of her had transformed over time—from homeless, crazed, drug addict to a wiser-than-she-looked-even-when-she-sounded-crazy otherworldly assassin—she was *never* a fool.

Two other things that had never changed: her devotion to Grant—*and* her devotion to marijuana, in *all* its forms. In fact, I'd pretty much decided she needed weed for some biological function given that I never saw her when she *wasn't* eating it, sniffing it, or cooking with it. Now I wondered if there was another reason why she was so paranoid about keeping it close.

Grant grimaced as he chewed, but when he finally swallowed the bundle of leaves, Mary shoved more into his mouth. He didn't protest. In fact, he looked stronger.

I let myself breathe again and looked around. We were surrounded by giant corpses, all of them covered in blood, leaking blood, in some cases still spurting. The air smelled rotten. The dead stank, no matter what species they were.

Mahati warriors perched gracefully on top of bloated stomachs, examining bodies, poking at the heads. The Osul were sniffing the remains, tasting blood with the tips of their tongues and growling with satisfaction. The Yorana had already disappeared.

The sword still covered my right hand, absorbing the blood covering its blade like roots soaking up water. *Time to sleep,* I told the armor. I could almost hear its resistance in my head—just one presence out of many floating inside me—but the metal receded, shimmering in a soft light that revealed my hand. Mary watched the transformation and grunted with approval.

Zee and the boys pressed close. Raw and Aaz were grinning, each dragging a bloodied baseball bat behind them. I didn't think they'd had this much fun in months. Zee, on the other hand, looked troubled.

I was terrified.

Too late to run, I thought. *We've already been found.*

CHAPTER 3

THE thing about demons is that they never lie.
They'll hunt you, torture you, eat you—but that's nature and habit, a particular need to consume the pain of others. Biology, really.

Also, they're just assholes.

But they do have rules, a code of honor, and even though I should have slaughtered every single one of them when I had the chance (Zee and the boys being the exception—because it's like that, with family), it was their honor that kept me from making that final, destructive decision.

Honor means dignity. And dignity is that common dream that seems to unite our disparate species.

Blame sentience, Grant once said. *Blame hearts, blame the possibility that the universe, no matter how vast, doesn't allow for a true separation of spirit.*

All of us, *one,* in some way.

Which is a real pain in the ass.

❦

"SO," Grant said, staring up at the night sky, "this is awkward."

"You're my hero," I told him, in total seriousness. "Now, can you stand?"

He could, and he did, picking up a dart in the process and smelling the tip. I took a whiff, too. Same stinging, vinegary scent—only ten times stronger. I sneezed again.

"You recognized this," Grant said to Mary, holding up the dart to Mal, who ate it.

"Old weapon. Old, but effective. Doesn't kill. Just scrambles mind." The old woman tapped his head with a gnarled finger. "Keeps you from focusing. Makes you normal, with normal voice."

"Permanently?" I asked, trying not to show my horror that something like this could exist.

"Maybe, sometimes." Mary kicked at some of the darts with disgust. "Poisoned many Lightbringers before we knew what happened. Poisoned them, stole them, studied them. Aetar could not have won war without it."

I risked a glance at Grant, who had reached inside his shirt to touch a pendant that had belonged to his mother—and his father. His father, whom he had never known. His father, who was not of this world, just as Grant's mother wasn't—or even Mary. Their world, gone, destroyed in a war with the same immortal creatures who had made my bloodline and fought the demons.

Grant's world had been the *first* world, the only world, where humans had ever existed. Same world on which humanity lost its freedom, to become the slaves and playthings for the Aetar—who then proceeded to seed countless worlds, including earth, with human DNA.

We weren't alone in the universe. Not by a long shot. We were the stuff that Aetar dreams were made of. The giants dead around us had been grown from the same genetic material. Countless other creatures in the universe could claim a similar ancestry, even if they didn't know it. Only demons weren't related. Something else had made *them*, even if it was just nature and an accident.

Grant said, in a strained voice, "So. They want me alive."

"Alive, harmless, so you cannot kill them. Last of the free Lightbringers," Mary said, running her thumb over the tip of her machete. "New flesh to play with."

My husband glanced at me and my stomach. No, he wasn't the last. Our daughter would have his gift. But that just made the Aetar even more dangerous.

"How did you know marijuana would be the antidote?" I asked Mary.

A strange expression passed over her face, oddly guarded. I'd seen her fierce, delighted, crazed—but never secretive.

"Recognized it," she muttered, as if she was confessing something terrible. "Same plant was on our world."

I frowned, sharing a quick look with Grant.

No chance to ask. Dek chirped at me, and I turned to see the demon lord of the Mahati clan striding toward us, his hands bloodied but with a glint in his eye that was quietly, deeply, satisfied.

"Young Queen," said Lord Ha'an in a soft voice; giving Zee a nod, as well. Raw and Aaz were prowling around the dead giants, poking them with their baseball bats.

"Hey," I said, craning my neck to look at him. He was so tall, his people had been forced to cut the low-lying branches of the trees so that he wouldn't keep knocking his head. Ropes of silver hair fell into long, knotted braids, braids woven into silver chains of chiming hooks tied like armor around his bull-like broad chest—also the color of silver. His fingers were as long as pitchfork tines, longer than my forearm. Just as sharp.

The polite reverence in the demon lord's expression faded as soon as he looked at Grant. It wasn't with hostility, but uncertainty—the kind reserved for those freaky unknowns:

like my husband, who looked harmless but could kill Ha'an and his people with nothing but the sound of his voice.

I could kill him just as easily, but I was more demon than human. Funny, how that could put some folks at ease.

"Lord . . . Cooperon," Ha'an greeted Grant, awkwardly. "I smell human blood. You are wounded?"

"Nothing serious," he said.

A frown touched the demon lord's mouth. "Show me where you are hurt."

Grant hesitated, then bent to pull up the ankle of his jeans. I did it for him. The darts had pierced his bad leg, and leaning on his cane made it awkward to reach down.

Lord Ha'an crouched, licking his long fingers clean of blood. I hoped he wasn't going to touch Grant, but he did, using his knuckles to gently press the skin around the three holes in my husband's calf. No fresh blood oozed out, but he'd lost enough. Zee sniffed the wound.

"Should I be worried about something else?" Grant asked.

"I do not know," replied Lord Ha'an, rising gracefully to his full height. "As one who holds the bonds of the Shurik and Yorana, you should be healing faster. But you are also human. I cannot know if that affects the bond you have with your . . . clans."

"The bonds are hurting him," I remarked, before Grant could say again that he was fine. I ignored the irritated look he gave me.

Lord Ha'an's frown deepened, but instead of pushing deeper, he said, "I do not recognize these creatures though I smell the Aetar in their flesh. Are we at war with them again, young Queen?"

War. What a word. I wasn't even sure I knew what it meant except that it would bring more death and fear, and uncertainty. Then again, if it was fight or die . . . fight, or lose my family . . .

"If it can't be avoided," I told him, "then yes."

"War *is* coming," rasped Zee, dragging his claws along

his arms, striking sparks that floated against my skin. "Blood for blood."

"Can you track who made these creatures?" I asked him. "Do you know where they're from?"

"Track, yes," he rasped, but wariness entered his gaze. "But follow back? Unwise, maybe."

It was stupid, that's what it was. I just didn't know if I'd have a choice.

"Maxine," Mary said, touching my arm. I turned, and what I saw made my stomach drop hard.

Red and blue lights flickered in the distance. Two cars, roaring down the driveway. My vision blurred.

"Shit," I said.

⊰⊱

THE neighbors might not have cared about the music, but they sure knew what a killing field sounded like.

My clothes were covered in blood. So were Grant's. Raw and Aaz pulled new jeans and a fresh white T-shirt from the shadows, tossing them at my husband. For me it was a pair of shorts and a long-sleeved shirt that covered the dried blood on my arms. We made sure to pull off the tags.

Doesn't take much to look normal. Acting normal can be a little more problematic.

The police were already parked and walking around when we reached the farmhouse. Two men, both white, swinging their flashlights across the barn and inside the window of the old parked station wagon. I knew some of the demon children liked to visit sometimes—I hoped they weren't around or had the good sense to hide.

The third cop was different, and that was because he was possessed by a demon. I could see it, plain as day—and that thunderous black aura was so violent, so encompassing as it roiled around his uniformed body, I couldn't imagine how other humans didn't sense it. But that was the danger of

those demonic parasites: They were good at hiding, good at
slipping under the skin and feeding off a person's pain. Or
worse, forcing that person to make *others* feel pain.

For years, those were all I hunted—parasites, possessing
humans—exorcising them, feeding their spirit bodies to the
boys. They'd been the only demons haunting earth until the
prison had split open. Easier times, now that I thought about
it. More straightforward.

The demon in front of us, though, wasn't like the rest of
her kind. Only one parasite had that aura.

The possessed cop was waiting for us beside his SUV.
The others began approaching but were still too far away to
hear us.

"Blood Mama," I said. "Fancy meeting you here."

Blood Mama, the lady lord of the parasites, and the old-
est, slyest nemesis of my bloodline. She'd ordered my mother's murder and the murder of so many of my ancestors; and
yet, we had a truce. For now.

"I heard there was a disturbance in the Force," he replied,
but in a particularly sultry, feminine voice that totally did
not match the gray stubble, beer belly, or the tattoo of Bugs
Bunny on his forearm. He might have been in his fifties,
and I sort of recognized his face from trips into town. Definitely the sheriff. Blood Mama didn't slip into the skins of
anyone who didn't have beauty, wealth, or power.

"You," he said to Grant. "I hoped you might be dead."

"Ha," replied my husband, dryly. "That never gets old."

He scowled, but the two other officers were finally near
enough to hear us. Up close, they weren't just white—they
were pale as ghosts and looked shaken, scared. Maybe even
traumatized. I didn't think it was anything they'd seen here,
or else they'd be talking—but something bad had happened.
It made me even more nervous.

But no one mentioned anything. Blood Mama—or whoever
she had possessed—proceeded with the official questioning.
In front of the others, his voice didn't hold a trace of her charm:
It was gruff, deep, masculine. *The neighbors reported strange*

sounds. The neighbors heard screams, even though they lived miles away. What were you doing tonight? Could the men look around?

I kept quiet for the most part. Grant spoke, using his voice—his real voice—and I felt the shimmer of his power on my skin as he soothed the other two police officers, twisting their minds, making them believe we were harmless, taking away their fear. I saw it happen in their faces—a slow relaxation of their jaws and shoulders, a better light in their eyes.

Dangerous, manipulative—and necessary. If Grant hadn't been such a good man, if I didn't have such faith in him, I would have been forced to take his life years ago.

My mother wouldn't have waited at all. Keeping a man alive who could alter the fabric of any living creature's *soul* was not what she would have considered *wise*. Maybe the fact that the boys and I were immune gave me the distance to have a different perspective.

"I think we're done here," said the sheriff. "You boys go home. I'll finish up."

No argument. In less than a minute, the other patrol car was ripping down our long driveway. And Blood Mama was back, smiling at us through her stolen lips.

He ran his hands down his body, a caricature of seductiveness, and gave me a slow wink. "Do you *want* me like this?"

"I've had enough trauma for the night," I replied. "I suppose you heard?"

"Of course." Blood Mama leaned against the SUV, examining the thick, rough hands of the body she'd stolen. Raw crept out from beneath the vehicle. Aaz was already perched on the hood, carving something into the metal. The sound his claws made was hideous, but no one said a word.

"You're both fucked," added Blood Mama, and smiled. "This should be fun to watch."

"You don't think you'll be affected?" Grant asked, in a cold voice.

"Pfft. Spare me my life." Blood Mama glanced down at Zee, who crouched beside me. "My old wretched King. You don't have the army to fight the Aetar. We didn't have the army before, and we were a million strong. Even the Light-bringers could not save themselves. You think this will be any different?"

Zee gave the other demon a long, steady look. Blood Mama, after a moment, flinched—and glanced away. "Fine. As you wish. I have nothing more to add except that my children do not know where the Aetar are hiding on this world—if they're here at all. These creatures they sent through the Labyrinth to attack you and Grant . . . it might have just been the first poke, to see what would happen, and test you." Blood Mama's gaze found mine, then dropped to my belly. "They'll poke again, Hunter."

My jaw tightened. Blood Mama opened the SUV door and climbed in. Before pulling away, though, the window rolled down, and that thunderous aura spilled out around the sheriff. "Have you decided what to do with those dead constructs on your hill?"

I frowned. "What do you mean?"

"Will you let your army eat them?"

"No. That's disgusting."

Blood Mama looked at me like I was a fool. "You refuse to let the demons eat the flesh of humans because it is 'wrong' . . . but these creatures, and any the Aetar send, are your enemies. If you wish your demons to think of them as such, as *prey*, then you must give them that flesh to feed on. Give them that pain. Give them the hunt. There must *always* be a hunt. If you want any chance of surviving, you must remember that." The demon's smile was cold, mirthless. "You, who are the Hunter, with the old wyrm inside your heart."

I didn't say anything, and that smile widened into something close to a silent laugh.

"What is so funny?" Grant asked. "You're dying to tell us something."

"You can see *that*, but you cannot read my mind. How delightful." Blood Mama blew him a kiss. "Your night is far from over. I would conserve your strength if I were you."

And before any of us could say another word—or, more importantly, before Grant could, and compel her to stay and talk—that SUV roared away in a cloud of dust and fumes. Aaz, still clinging to the hood, leapt off and landed on top of Raw. Dek and Mal, who had been hiding in the shadows of my hair, poked their heads free and started humming Bon Jovi's "Runaway."

I took Grant's hand. "Tell me everything is going to be okay."

"Everything is going to be okay," he said, and drew me close for a long tight hug. "Breathe," he whispered. "We're still here."

I exhaled, slowly, and it almost hurt. I looked down at Zee, trailing my fingers through his spiked hair. The little demon leaned against me.

"How about you?" I said to him. "What do you think about all this?"

He hesitated. But before he could say anything—*if* he was going to say anything—my cell phone rang.

"Don't answer that," Grant said.

"I don't want to." I reached into my back pocket for my phone, not taking my gaze off him. "Hello?"

"Find a television," said a quiet, male voice on the other end of the line. Byron, the most serious, grown-up teenager I'd ever met. "You need to see something."

Dread spread through me. Zee sighed, and once again pressed his ear to my stomach.

"Ash," he murmured. "Fire, for dreams."

CHAPTER 4

PEOPLE had to die, of course. I always knew that was how it would start. I only hoped we would have more time.

The first murder—we got lucky. Single male, no family, driving a pickup truck that police later found in a ditch at the side of the road. The demons were so hungry for human flesh they didn't leave a speck of blood. The man might as well have walked away from his life. Which is what the authorities finally concluded.

The second time made us sweat. A grandfather, fishing along a secluded riverbed. Four days after he was supposed to come home, a park ranger found a fishing rod—and four wrinkled fingers.

That caused a stir. But the investigation didn't go anywhere. Bodies couldn't be found, and no one was arrested.

The third time, though . . . that's where it blew the fuck up.

Frat boys and their girlfriends out for a weekend of crazy partying. A cabin in the woods. No one around for miles.

Like, the worst cliché ever. Right down to the massacre—
and the bodies eaten to the bone.

Some kids were still missing. I knew they wouldn't be
found.

In the first twenty-four hours, commentators speculated
it was the work of a religious (cue: Satanic) cult. Or someone
gone high and crazy. Maybe a drug cartel (one of the dead
students was from Spain, the TV announcers repeated
endlessly—as if there were any cartels in Barcelona). Ter-
rorists were on the list, some new order of Cannibal Jihad-
ists, by way of *crazy* and *oh, fuck*.

And there it might have ended. If the tape recorder hadn't
been found.

Someone had set it up in one of the bedrooms, probably
to record the girls getting naked.

Instead, it captured a lot more than that.

⊰⊱

BLOOD. I could smell it, thick and bitter behind the smoke
from burning fires: pitching red light, hot light, across the
encampment.

I could have used another hour without that death scent.
Hell, I could have used a whole *lifetime*. I didn't need any
of this right now. I had enough problems.

My land had become a refugee camp, split into four quad-
rants, one for each of the clans. Right now I was in Mahati
territory, and all around us were small structures built from
canvas and wood, bits of scrap: tents, in the roughest form,
with small sleeping pads and fires burning. Little of anything except the living. Little of *that*, as well.

Every demon in front of me was broken, physically. I'd
never seen the ravages of starvation before the Mahati.
Never faced it, with all its terrible desperation and consequences. No adult had all his limbs. Elderly Mahati showed
the most damage: missing arms, legs, long chunks of flesh
cut from chests and backs. Prison food. Feeding the young

from their own bodies. Cannibalized so others could survive.

But here, tonight, cows had been slaughtered. Cows—and the giants that I was going to let the demon clans carve up for supper. Something I wasn't going to think about. Ever.

Right now, though, I was only looking at cattle. Mahati children eagerly crouched over bulging bovine bellies that had been split from throat to tail—each of them bouncing with excitement as they removed intestines with their long, delicate fingers, while others collected blood. Adults squatted on the other sides of the huge beasts, skinning them with razor-sharp fingernails and serrated blades—a careful process that wasted nothing.

I imagined human bodies sprawled in place of the cows.

"Fuck," I said. "No humans. That was all I asked."

I heard a slow exhalation—a little too controlled, a bit too careful. I knew that sound. I breathed like that when I was angry. I breathed like that when I needed to calm the fuck down. Which was all the time, lately.

Lord Ha'an shot me a hard look. "I believe the temptation for a taste was too great."

I met his gaze with more calm than I felt. "Every single Mahati is bonded to you. Guided by your heart. Maybe *you* hunger too much for humans."

His fingers stilled, his stare faltered.

I walked away, furious—and panicked out of my mind. I hoped I was hiding it, but cold sweat trickled down my back, and my legs were unsteady. My hands, curled into fists, felt weak as water. I'd fought demon armies, traveled through time, gotten the shit beat out of me more often than I could count—but this was the first moment in my life I felt close to losing my nerve.

I didn't know what to do. Bad enough the Aetar had sent constructs to attack us, armed with drugs that would specifically neutralize Grant. *Now* I had to deal with public exposure of the worst kind.

Enter Labyrinth, Zee had said. *Find new world.*

And leave this one forever. Yes, in a simpler time, maybe I could have dropped the demons off on some random planet, given them a push, and said good-bye—but even so, chances of finding *my* earth again would be slim to none. And if I was so lucky, it might be earth a million years from now. The Labyrinth was a maze of time and space, an endless road between countless worlds. Never straight, never predictable. Even with a guide.

Movement caught my eye. Far to my right, in the camp. A Mahati child, darting around the trees, light on his feet—barely a wisp of skin and bone. Chest heaving, smiling with excitement, so much like a human boy I almost forgot he was a demon. His long fingers were wet, smeared red; he held the entire heart of a cow, dripping with blood.

The child collapsed in front of an old wrinkled male with no legs and only one arm. Even from a distance, I could hear the quick murmur of a soft young voice and watched him offer the heart to the elder Mahati. The old demon didn't say a word, but a grim, satisfied smile touched his mouth.

I glanced away, but not before Lord Ha'an saw what had caught my attention.

"A'loua," he murmured. "The child is alive because his forebear fed him his own flesh. And now the child repays him."

"I know," I whispered.

Lord Ha'an gave me a long, piercing look. "Our Kings who are bonded to you, young Queen . . . all the blood they have spilled while bound to *your* heart? What does that say about *your* hunger?"

"It says I'm a monster." I stopped walking and pointed. "Are those cats drunk?"

I was staring at an area outside the encampment, thick with shadows that gathered beyond the ring of campfires. Mahati warriors crouched in the thick grass, long fingers sunk into the dirt: anchoring themselves into preternatural stillness, every inch of them tense, taut, starving.

And then there were the demons from the Osul clan.

As a kid on the road with my mom, we'd stay in strange hotels in strange cities, and the only constant I clung to (besides Zee and the boys, and my mother's sharp smiles and guns) were the Saturday morning cartoons. Those were my religion—and each series was a different god.

Voltron, Transformers, even the fucking Smurfs. But nothing, I mean *nothing*, was better than She-Ra. And after She-Ra, there was He-Man. Along with his trusty sidekick, Battle Cat. Who *wouldn't* want to ride a giant green tiger into battle against the Forces of Evil?

No one would be riding the Osul—not unless they wanted to be eaten—but those demons certainly made me feel like a kid again every time I looked at them.

They were sprawled on their backs, in the most undignified poses imaginable. Muscular legs stuck lazily up in the air. Serrated claws jutted from flexing paws, and scales glistened beneath ragged silver pelts. Long tails rose and fell against the grass, a slow, thudding rhythm that was way too relaxed to make me comfortable. One of them yawned, revealing fangs almost a foot long, curved like scythes.

"I do not know the meaning of 'drunk,'" Lord Ha'an replied, somewhat dryly. "But if you intend to say that battling Aetar constructs, tasting their blood, and smelling their agonized deaths makes them want to contemplate breeding, then yes, they are drunk."

I gave him a long look. "Why are they here?"

"They are acting as . . . guards," he replied carefully, and I choked down a terrible, inappropriate laugh. "There was a rush on the flesh when these human bodies were first discovered. Some of it was distributed before I became aware of the deaths."

A rush on the flesh. Something the size of a golf ball threatened to rush up my throat. Nausea from the pregnancy or total disgust, it didn't matter. This was my fault. Humans were dead because I'd gone against my upbringing—and chosen compassion instead of genocide.

I could still make it right. Lord Ha'an stood beside me:

flesh and blood. Kill him, and his people would die. All their lives, bound together. It would be easy.

But the demon child and his cannibalized elder were right behind me; and they weren't alone. Death and murder, compassion and love. Right here. Right here, amongst these demons.

Kill *that*.

"Fuck," I muttered again.

I could almost see the dead humans in the grass. They couldn't have been here long. I'd learned about the cabin massacre less than an hour before, but according to the reports, those murders had taken place a full night before. Somehow, the authorities had managed to keep it quiet until now. FBI were involved, God only knew who else. The two survivors, boys who had been having sex in the locked basement, had called 911 once the screaming started. Otherwise, it would have taken days for the bodies to be found.

I was certain, as well, that the tape of the Mahati had not been intended for public release. Something that big, that powerful . . . it was too much. Someone had leaked it. If I had to take bets, that someone had been possessed by a demon. Probably Blood Mama. Just to fuck with me.

The Mahati warriors didn't so much as twitch as I approached the second killing ground, but the Osul stiffened and rolled onto their stomachs. No longer relaxed. Not even a little. Shoulders hulked forward, muscles and bone shifting until the demons appeared, from my vantage, to be little more than big toothy heads attached to a solid, impressively rippling wall of scales, fur, and claws.

Growls rumbled in their chests. Lord Ha'an moved between us, making a guttural warning sound, but the Osul ignored him. He wasn't their lord. And I didn't have time for this shit.

"Zee," I said. The little demon had been drifting in and out of the shadows but reappeared at my side, coalescing from between blades of grass. His ears pressed flat against his skull, and his gaze, as he looked at the Osul, was cold, narrow, and disgusted. Which should have been enough to shut them up. Unfortunately, they didn't seem to notice—which meant they were blind, or just very stupid.

Dek and Mal poked their heads from my hair and began humming the theme to *Jaws*. Lord Ha'an glanced at them and took a slow, careful step away. He couldn't have been familiar with the movie, but apparently the music of imminent death translated well across the demon-human cultural divide.

I didn't stop walking toward the corpses. One of the Osul bared its teeth, rolling its eyes at me, white and huge. The demon half lunged, just a feint, a bluff—and a heartbeat later, it was slumping sideways into the grass. For a terrible moment I thought it was dead—but no, its ribs still moved. Punched the hell out, was all.

Soft giggles. A hiss. Raw hopped on top of the unconscious Osul, dragging his claws through its thick silver fur. He'd jammed a Red Sox baseball cap through the spikes of his hair, but it was stained with old dried blood, perhaps from the earlier night's fight. The other Osul shrank away, ears flat, tails dragging—staring at him with contrition and fear. A toothy grin touched his sharp mouth—all teeth, all black tongue.

I kept walking. It was easy. I'd had years of practice at pretending I was hard. Lord Ha'an caught up with me in one long stride.

"They are very young," he said, quietly. "Born inside the prison, with no memory of their Kings."

"They'll remember now," I said.

The area where the humans had been murdered was tidier than I expected. Flapjack ribbons of skin were folded in a neat pile, while bones had been set aside—heads carefully detached. I was sure it was the missing kids from the cabin—it made sense the rogue demons would have brought fresh meat home for their clan.

I counted six people. Blood everywhere, blood on my boots, pooled and sticky, and hot. The scent was wild, bitter.

Made me dizzy—or maybe that was the boys, slipping in and out of shadows like smoke and wolves. Close, careful. Guarding me.

Aaz approached the dead, slinking low on all fours, nostrils flared. Zee crouched near me, eyes closed to slits, ears pressed flat against his skull.

I watched him, wary. "What?"

He was silent a moment too long, head tilted as though listening. Aaz tore a spike from his spine and used it to poke a flap of human skin, carefully, as if it might resurrect sans bones and muscle, and attack. Dek and Mal hissed to themselves, breath scalding hot against my scalp.

"Do not know," said the little demon, softly. "Something . . . wrong. Something . . . strange."

I saw Grant limping across the encampment toward us— let my gaze linger, taking in his gaunt frame, hollow eyes— and turned to Lord Ha'an. "Tell me what happened."

Lord Ha'an's broad chest rose and fell against the armor of his thick braids and silver chains. "These humans were brought here and killed. Supposedly, I was told, so that the rest of the clan could share in the spoils. Those responsible tried to escape my punishment. We captured all but one, and she is still missing."

"Great. And the ones you caught?"

"I ate their hearts."

I glanced sideways at him. Lord Ha'an noticed and studied me. "Do not tell me I should have offered mercy?"

"No," I replied, simply. "I was just wondering how you are."

I felt his gaze on me—intense, searching. I pretended I didn't notice. "Are you losing control over your people?"

His silence lasted longer this time. "They believe I have failed to protect them. And I have, young Queen. I have. Nor does it help that they see me obeying a human. A human who has done little to earn their obedience. Besides killing them," he added, after a moment. "You inherited power, yes . . . but what is that?"

"Nothing. I never wanted to be anyone's Queen."

"But the mantle falls upon you . . . and for you we sacrifice much. Perhaps we will sacrifice even more if the Aetar must be fought again." Lord Ha'an looked at his hands, those thin, deadly fingers. "My people hunger for the hunt. That is something I *cannot* control."

I thought about what Blood Mama had said. "I won't let them kill."

"And yet some of my warriors did just that." Bitterness touched his voice. "It would have been wiser to allow them a controlled hunt of your world's undesirables. To sate their desire."

"Playing God," I muttered. "No."

Lord Ha'an gave me a sharp look. "And those of my kind who have been killed because you considered us your enemies?" He leaned close, ignoring the warning hisses coming from my hair. "I can forgive those deaths. But you risk too much, you risk us all, when you ignore your own power. You have a God *inside* you, young Queen. Respect that. Fear that. I do not know how you have resisted being consumed, but your freedom cannot last." He looked at the encampment, and in a soft voice added, "I remember the feeling of its power inside our Kings, inside us, as it controlled our hearts."

"Ha'an."

"It is not a merciful God," he whispered, and darkness stirred inside me, deep below my heart. A slow awakening, a fullness that bloomed within my chest and rose into my throat.

There is no mercy in hunger, whispered a sinuous voice, curling around my mind until it rested far behind my eyes. *No mercy when you are past the size of dreaming.*

I pushed that presence away, pushed hard, ignoring its quiet satisfaction. But the air was suddenly too hot beneath the trees: on my face, in my throat, inside me—burning, suffocating. Lord Ha'an leaned away, watching my face with narrowed eyes. I could smell the fresh human blood surrounding us. I could taste it, the spice in the air—wet and soft, and warm. My mouth watered.

The armor on my right hand flared to life: the heat of it sliced through me like a sword, from crown to belly. I felt that jolt, and flinched, sucking in such a sharp breath it was almost a gasp. My cheeks were hot. I felt naked to the bone.

No, I said to the darkness. *I'm not yours.*

You have always been mine, it replied. *This is our dance, and it is sweet.*

The dance is over. But it was like pulling my will from the jaws of a dragon—my soul stretched until it was rubber, until there was no more give—but I kept pulling, hearing myself cry out in pain—

—until I tore free.

Free, and the terrible hunger was gone. I wiped my mouth.

"Young Queen," Ha'an murmured, bowing his head. I couldn't look at him. My eyes felt wet. Fear hammered my heart, but I swallowed it down, down where I felt soft laughter—nothing but a vibration against my ribs. The sleeping God, the darkness and its slow coil around my heart. That slow, tightening coil.

I felt Grant near me. I turned and found him standing near the bodies, leaning hard on his cane—knuckles white, face gaunt, eyes too dark as he watched me. He needed a haircut, I thought idly. I needed to run my hands through his hair and hold him close. He was slipping away, right in front of me. Maybe I was, too, in a different way.

I touched my stomach and walked to him. Dek and Mal were quiet, squeezing my ears between their claws until it hurt. Zee watched me from the shadows.

"You okay?" Grant asked, as I reached up to rub the heads of the two little demons coiled around my throat.

"You tell me," I replied, and the corner of his mouth softened as his gaze flicked over me, reading my aura, my light. His gift, and his curse.

"Still beautiful." His mouth relaxed into a gentle smile.

"Sorry it took me so long. I had to settle my demons. The Shurik were disappointed they missed the fight, and the Yorana were . . . same as usual."

"Assholes?"

His smile widened. "Divas."

"Some of them were there when we were attacked. They didn't lift a finger."

"I know." Grant took a deep breath. "They all heard about these dead humans."

"I bet they wanted some."

Grant grunted and opened his shirt.

"Fuck," I said.

A maggot the size of a hot dog clung to my husband's chest. Several of them, in fact: one on his rib cage, and the other pressed tight to his shoulder. All of them were the corpse color of zombie white, glistening with a snakelike sheen and pulsing with such violent force I half expected them to launch right off his body.

Dek and Mal extended their heads from my hair and let out a hungry chirp. The maggots immediately went still.

"I'm never having sex with you again," I said.

"They understand you."

"Good." I pointed at his chest. "Are you insane?"

"I'm trying to teach them not to crave human flesh."

I loved my husband, but I was going to kill him. I hated the Shurik. Their previous lord had been a malevolent, giggling . . . turd . . . and I had killed him with deep and probably disturbing pleasure. I didn't feel much better about the rest of his people, and I wasn't a big enough person to find any kind of connection or redeeming value in slugs that burrowed inside living creatures and ate them from the inside out. They certainly weren't worth more than my husband's life.

I pointed to the mutilated corpses. "Close your shirt, please, and let's focus."

Grant shook his head—still smiling—and covered the pulsating little demons. As he did, he looked down at the mutilated corpses. The smile faded. And then he swayed, so far to the right I thought he might fall.

"Hey," I said, reaching for him.

"Don't touch me," he said, still looking away.

I froze. He managed to straighten, with an effort, and murmured, "Look at them, Maxine."

I almost didn't. I wanted to drill holes into his head and find out what the hell was going on with him. But instead I knelt, running my gaze over the corpses. Bones, blood, and skin. Heads. Hands. I saw jewelry. Gold glinted on the left hand of one body.

I blinked, and looked again at the shredded faces of the dead. No real identifying features, but they all had hair. One in particular: long and smoky white, even with blood soaking the ends.

White hair. A wedding ring.

"These people aren't teenagers," I said, and wanted to be sick all over again. "They aren't from the cabin the Mahati massacred."

"No," Grant replied, finally looking at me. "I don't know where they came from. But it's worse, Maxine. They've been tampered with."

"Tampered," I repeated.

"They were human once," he said softly. "Just not when they died."

CHAPTER 5

$\approx$ _____

PRIORITIES. There was still a lone Mahati on the loose, and I needed to find her before someone else did. Like a cop, or some upstanding citizen armed with a shotgun and supernatural aim. Which pretty much described the entire population of Texas.

I also needed to stop the Aetar from attacking us again. Which seemed pretty much impossible. Not that I hadn't seen something like this coming. I'd just wanted to pretend we'd have more time. A chance to breathe.

Stupid me.

"Find out what you can," I said to Grant. If the dead weren't human, we needed to know in what way because the parts the Mahati *hadn't* eaten seemed pretty damn normal to me.

As for *who* was responsible for transforming a human into something *else* . . . that was no mystery at all. It made me feel surrounded, hunted—watched.

"I will," he said, and finally looked at me; but his gaze was tired and drifted down. I found myself touching my stomach and stopped—slowly, as if I might be burned. I'd always been so reckless, but it wasn't just me now. I had a light to carry. Another light to protect.

"Be careful. You don't have much time until dawn." He grazed his fingertips across my cheek. I didn't know why he hadn't wanted me to touch him before, but right now I was hungry to close the distance between us. I needed not to feel so alone.

Lord Ha'an knelt to sniff the remains. His long-fingered hands hovered in the air above those decapitated heads, and his nostrils trembled. "I can scent it now, the bitterness in their blood. If I had not been looking for it . . ." He stopped, shook himself, and rose to his full height. The top of his head brushed a tree branch.

"A trap," he murmured.

I thought so, too, but didn't want to say it out loud.

I touched Zee's head, my other hand already closing into a fist, armor oozing white-hot. Raw and Aaz bounded close, hugging my legs. Dek and Mal curled tight around my throat, burying their heads in my hair. My boys, warm around me: family, protectors, friends. Five hearts, connected to mine, bound to each of my ancestors: a line of women who had borne the burden of being hunter and hunted, mother and daughter—lives lost, to time. Just as I would be lost, one day. Lost, except in the memories of the demons at my side.

I looked at Grant one last time, and dread rippled through me. It was just an illusion, it had to be . . . but for a moment his gaze seemed flat, empty as death.

And then the link between us—the very real bond that kept him alive—flared golden hot. Grant flinched, blinking hard—swaying a little. Like watching a man come awake; I could almost see his heart rising to the surface of his eyes, with sadness, and too much pain.

I slammed my armored right hand against my thigh and fell backward into the void.

From Texas into oblivion. Dropping, like Alice into her

rabbit hole. Only, there was no Wonderland at the bottom, no bottom at all, just an endless darkness where nothing existed. Not even my own body. Barely my mind. Reduced to some fluttering, desperate flicker. If there was any place that could eat a soul, it was the void *between*.

Mahati, I thought hard. *Now.*

The void spit me out.

I staggered, drawing in a deep, wheezing breath. After the void, the sensation of air on my skin felt too raw; the hard surface beneath my feet as solid as mountain rock. I could have been standing on a mountain at the top of the world; the feeling of weightlessness, of just touching down, was the same.

No real mountain. Just a hard, flat sidewalk. It was still night, but barely; in my bones, I could feel the sun, and the horizon held the pale wash of a dangerous light. Too much light: that dim city glow, rising from streetlamps; falling from the electric, rising rush of distant skyscrapers.

Less than thirty minutes until dawn, and I stood on a long street that looked like strip-mall hell. Nothing but parking lots and battered signs, and miles of concrete cut into blocks separated by roads and scrawny bushes. Some cars in the road, but not many. Skyscrapers glittered in the distance, but what caught my eye was a familiar-looking diner just down the road, windows lit.

House of Pies. Practically a landmark in Houston, open all night. I'd been here before, while my mother was still alive. The endless roads and cities, all the violence, always took a breather when we were in a booth, with pie. It was one of the few times I ever saw my mother relax. Which meant I *always* wanted pie.

I started walking toward the diner. If the lone Mahati was in this area, she'd be close to people. It wouldn't just be the temptation to hunt—curiosity would pull her in, a need to be near other living creatures. The Mahati had been locked away for ten thousand years in a dimension that made the Gobi desert look like an oasis. Coming to our world was like living your whole life in a mud hut, only to discover *Blade Runner* outside.

Raw and Aaz prowled through the shadows beneath the parked cars, dragging teddy bears behind them. Zee closed his eyes, tasting the air with his long black tongue.

"Fresh," he rasped.

"Find her," I said. "Hold her for me."

Zee dragged his claws against the concrete, sparks flying. Raw and Aaz bared their teeth in a hot grin and disappeared from sight, taking the bears with them. Zee stayed with me.

I could see inside the diner. This hour, not too many warm bodies in the booths, but there were some men, and two teenage girls. No one was talking. Their gazes were locked on the television hanging from the ceiling in the corner. Even the waitress was watching, clutching the front of her blouse. Her face was so pale.

She was also a demon. Possessed by one, at any rate. I could see the shadow of her aura flickering like a storm above her head.

I looked, too, at the television. It was terrible. One image, replayed over and over. My heart died a little.

"Good times end," Zee whispered, as Dek and Mal hummed the melody to Bon Jovi's "Story of My Life."

"I was the idiot," I told him, as a tremor raced through me: bone-deep, teeth-rattling chills. "Believing they could act against their natures."

"All at fault." The little demon touched my hand, and the sadness in his eyes made my heart break again. "Us first. Us, their Kings, who made them."

Nothing I could say to that. It was true. *Demon* was a human word, steeped in religion: a mythic depiction that had nothing to do with reality. My demons, those demons living on my land, were not from hell. They were from another world. A collection of worlds that had harbored different species of sentient life. Peaceful worlds. Peaceful people. Where no one ever hunted each other or ate their own flesh to survive.

Until war had come, destroying it all. Those who survived were forced to change. Lives, generations, altered to become killing machines. And the dark entity that had remade them—long ago possessed by Zee and the boys—was now living inside me. Making me an unwilling part of this legacy, in more ways than one.

I looked again at those people in the diner. The news program cut to commercials, and everyone's shoulders sagged. I imagined my mother in there—both of us—and I could see the booth we'd sat in, years before. When life, as well as the killing, was so much easier.

The possessed waitress tore her gaze from the television and stared through the window—directly at me. Normal human eyes couldn't see me—too much glare from inside. But demons, especially the parasites, had better instincts. They knew when something was around that wanted to kill them.

I waited for a moment, and the waitress tightened her lips and walked to the counter, out of sight. I kept waiting.

Five minutes later, she appeared from behind the restaurant. Her gait was tired, unsteady, her stolen human body bulging at the seams. She smelled like grease, not pie, and her aura flickered like a caught bird when she neared me. Zee bared his teeth. Her stride faltered.

"We're fucked," she said, stopping ten feet away, an old pickup between us. "At least, you and the others are. The humans never did pay attention to us."

"Congrats," I replied. "Once again, the rats survive."

"Despite your best efforts. How many thousands of years did you women slaughter us? And for what? We shall still inherit the earth."

"Now you sound like Blood Mama."

"Mother knows best." The demon gave me a tight smile. "Are you going to kill me?"

"I should." I also smiled tightly. "But it seems a little useless now, doesn't it?"

"Poor Hunter Kiss. Being a Queen isn't what you thought

it would be, is it?" Her gaze flicked to Zee. "Not if you don't have the stomach for the old ways."

Zee leapt over the truck bed. The demon staggered, bravado disappearing—and a soft cry escaped her throat as she disappeared from sight, dragged down to the concrete. I walked around the truck, found her sprawled flat on her stomach. Zee sat on her shoulders, claws gripping her hair—pulling her head so far back her breath wheezed. I knew he wouldn't break her neck—hosts were innocent. But the demon wouldn't be able to leave its human without Zee snatching it up. And the boys always liked a good snack.

I crouched. "You didn't come out here to chat. What message did Blood Mama pass on to you? I've already seen her once tonight, but I thought she was holding back."

The demon's aura, wispy and black as smoke, shrank from me and Zee until it was nothing but a dense, tight ball. "She was only aware of the massacre at the cabin. She didn't know about the humans who died on your land. Our sentinels didn't see them until it was too late."

"I don't care. And I'm sure that's not all she wanted you to tell me."

Tears leaked from the demon's eyes. "You're the last, Hunter. You are the last of your line. That's what she wanted me to tell you."

Cold splintered down my spine. Dek and Mal jerked from my hair, snapping their jaws at the possessed human's face. She couldn't even flinch—Zee's grip was too tight.

"Is that so?" I whispered.

"The Aetar will never allow the child of a Lightbringer to live. Not a child who also holds your power. They'll destroy this world first before that happens."

Zee and I shared a quick look. It was true. I knew it. The Aetar were made entirely of sentient energy, capable of possessing and manipulating human flesh with the ease of a thought. They could be anywhere. And yes, it was easy to kill their mortal shell. But it was impossible to kill *them*.

Unless you were Grant. Or me. Which meant we had

targets that could probably be seen from the moon painted on our backs.

But our daughter would have the boys as her protectors and guardians. An entire Reaper Army at her feet. The same army that for millions of years had razed and destroyed Aetar-controlled worlds.

And she would have the power of her father. A Light-bringer. The last of his kind. Born with the ability to heal, to harm, to twist and alter the very fabric of a soul, with nothing but his voice. His voice, which could manipulate the deepest, smallest, bonds of all the energy that consumed, and created, life. The same energy that gave the Aetar life.

Our daughter. One strong girl. And very dangerous.

But still . . . we had pretended that our secret was safe.

In the distance, I heard police sirens. Zee tilted his head, listening to something else.

"Cutter," he said. "Mahati."

I let out my breath and stood. Zee released the possessed waitress, and she slumped into the concrete, breathing hard.

"Thank you," I said. "Save me some pie."

"Go fuck yourself," she whispered. "All of you are going to die. The humans will find your . . . *army*. And if by some miracle they don't . . . you know that the Aetar already have."

I needed a ginger ale, bad. My mouth tasted like shit. My heart felt worse.

I didn't look back as I walked across the parking lot, taking no precaution to hide in the shadows. I breathed in the grease-bitter exhaust pumping from the diner's kitchen, along with the lingering scent of strong perfume—probably from one of the teenage girls eating pie. I wanted to go inside and sit down. Order some pecan, or lemon meringue. Maybe peach, which my mother loved. It was so normal in there. Another world.

Behind the diner were two Dumpsters and a parked van with HOUSE OF PIES emblazoned on the side. No perfume here. Only the scent of rot. Dek licked the back of my ear.

Mal slithered down my arm, winding around it like armor. I crossed between dried-out brown bushes, into the parking lot of a strip mall that looked like a bomb had hit it sometime back in the seventies. The police sirens got louder.

I heard another noise, too: a low, chopping motor, coming from the sky. Helicopter.

I walked faster.

Raw and Aaz peered over the edge of the strip mall's roof, waved their half-eaten bears, and gave me little thumbs-up signs. Seeing that didn't cheer me up in the slightest. The sky above them was giving way to light, and the heavy, unrelenting pound of the helicopter rotor shook the air. I could see it coming, half a mile away and closing. Whoever was in there probably had binoculars with a long-range camera.

The sirens were equally grinding. Maybe the possessed waitress had called the cops, but it seemed more likely that some human with sharp eyes had seen something. Right now, people were probably paranoid enough to take potshots at their own shadows.

I glimpsed a flash of red and blue at the intersection, heard the squeal of tires as a squad car turned hard, speeding toward the strip mall. Maybe it had nothing to do with us—and maybe there weren't two demons hanging off my neck, humming "Jive Talkin'" at the tops of their lungs.

"You love this," I muttered to Dek and Mal, and tapped Zee's bony shoulder. "Are we being watched?"

He was silent a moment, head tilted. "Only eyes us. But quick."

"Quick" meant we might only have seconds. I tapped my right hand against my thigh and slipped into the void.

A heartbeat passed. A lifetime. When I reentered the world, it was almost in the same spot I'd left—except I was thirty feet higher, on the roof of the strip mall, and the sun was going to rise in less than ten minutes.

My skull rattled with the helicopter's approach; the churn of the rotors made my entire skeleton vibrate. The siren wail was just as earsplitting; the police car pulled into the parking lot beneath us.

I started running across the roof. I didn't know if I could be seen and didn't care. My focus was on the demon kneeling in front of me: the Mahati, head bowed. I glimpsed breasts beneath those massive coils of silver chains; and a bloodstained dagger strapped to her arm.

She looked up at the last moment. Her pale eyes were wet with tears.

I slammed into her and carried us into darkness.

CHAPTER 6

M Y mother once warned me about this sort of thing.
I was seven. I'd just seen a man beaten into the
ground, pulverized like a side of beef. He was sprawled at
my feet, knees broken, out cold, bleeding from a head wound
that had caved in half his skull. Regaining consciousness
would require a miracle.

My mother stood over him, a crowbar in her tattooed
hand.

"This is what happens to men who try to lure you from
the car while I'm in the gas station," she remarked, in a
deceptively gentle voice. "As you can see, sweetheart, he
wasn't possessed by a demon. He was fully human and fully
himself when he attempted to kidnap you. Therefore, I'm
allowed to kill him."

My mother always got very formal, and incredibly polite,
when it was time to murder, pummel, or otherwise terrorize
"normal people." As a small child, I found this . . . reassur-
ing. Until I got old enough to realize that most mothers did
not beat people to death like it was a hobby.

Which it was, for her. In the most righteous way possible.

We were parked at the end of a dirt road that had petered out in the middle of a dusty, dead cornfield. No one around. Not even a bird in the clear sky. We'd started out twenty miles away, at a small truck stop off the freeway. My mother was good at stuffing people into the trunk of the station wagon, and she had an instinct for remote, invisible places.

She led me back to the car, leaving the unconscious man in the dirt. "Just because a demon isn't involved doesn't mean a person is safe. You have to watch for that, baby. You have to watch *yourself*, too." She held up her hand. Zee's crimson eyes stared at me from her palm, the rest of him distorted in a tangle of tattooed scales and claws, and lines of muscle.

"We aren't invulnerable. The boys protect our bodies, but it's up to us to protect our hearts. We're monsters enough without becoming the real thing." She stood back and gave me a long, contemplative look. "But sometimes when the darkness calls, you have to answer. You have to become someone else to do what's right."

Becoming someone else sounded scary to me. I was just a kid. I didn't understand. But you don't argue with the woman holding a bloodied crowbar. Especially when she's your mother.

She put me in the station wagon and closed the door. The windows were rolled up, but I still heard bones snapping, and the hard, wracking thuds of metal meeting flesh. I read a book while she finished the man off.

We drove away.

And I remembered what she said.

·✦·

BUT I was still afraid.

We spilled into cold air. I hadn't had a destination in mind—just, *away*—and the armor obeyed. We were far from the strip mall in Houston, so very distant there was snow beneath us. The sky was crowded with stars, no hint of light on the horizon. I fell away from the Mahati, arms pinwheeling in a fight to stay upright as my feet broke through the ice-encrusted surface, sinking me to my knees. My skin froze, my breath hitched in my lungs.

The Mahati was more graceful, but Raw knocked her sideways, pinning her in the snow. Both demons disappeared in a tangle of limbs and ice. I crawled to them, Zee and Aaz pulling on my arms to help me stand. It was so cold. I saw the black edge of mountains in the distance, and all around us the tall, jagged teeth of trees.

I had good night vision. The Mahati sat in the snow, covered to her waist, with clumps and drifts hanging from her needlelike hair and bare shoulders. In another world, another life, someone might have called her a snow queen; covered in ice and night and starlight, she had a look of some snow-blooded creature who would exist in a fairy tale.

She was still weeping. No sniveling or hysterics, just the grief of a statue, with the same still, stoic, façade. Her hands betrayed the rest of her emotions: razor-sharp fingers clenched tight together, knuckles glistening silver, and her forearms trembling. Scar tissue covered her body: long strips on her thighs and biceps cut away; deep canyons in her flesh, cannibalized. Young warrior, or else she would have been missing limbs.

All the fight had burned out. She stayed sitting as I slogged close, her head tilted down. Long fingers kept trembling, and that tiniest movement made the silver chains dangling from her ears, across her chest, chime. I knelt in the snow in front of her, while Raw and Aaz draped themselves against my arms and chest to keep me warm. It didn't work. The chill settled through my legs, up into my stomach.

Zee crouched close, quiet and ready. I wished he'd tell *me* what to do. I'd made this speech before, when two other Mahati had broken my rules and gone hunting for humans— but this time was different, somehow worse.

"They are not cattle," I said, though the words sounded hollow, like I was some right-wing fundamentalist preaching fire, brimstone. "The humans are not meat."

The Mahati's gaze flicked toward mine, then down to her scarred thighs.

"*I* was meat," she murmured, each word delicate as floating ash.

I closed my eyes. Zee brushed his claws over my hand. I hated myself in that moment. I hated the Mahati, too—for not being alien enough that I could pretend this one was a parasite, something beneath me, that lacked humanity, or even a soul. A year ago it would have been easier. Five years ago, I wouldn't have hesitated.

Except too much had changed.

We are all meat, I thought. And in my heart, a shadow moved: a twisting rope of power, gathering itself with hunger.

Hunter, it whispered. *Will you kill one of your own for following her nature? When you yourself hunger for death?*

I shook my head, shook it like I was trying to knock away a cloud of flies. "Tell me about the six humans you killed on my land."

The Mahati flinched. I said, "Those humans weren't with the young ones you murdered."

She trembled, maybe with the cold. "No, my Queen."

"Where did you find them?

"We . . . did not." Her gaze flicked to mine, then away. "They were waiting for us when we returned from the hunt."

"Waiting." I drew that word out, staring at her. "On my land."

Her trembling grew more violent. "Like tribute. As it used to be, for the armies of the demon lords and Kings. That is what the others said."

"And did these . . . tributes . . . say anything to you?"

She shook her head, shivering. "They knelt and bared their throats, and did not cry out as we killed them."

I sat back in the snow, feeling every grind of ice in my

bones. Dek and Mal slithered across my shoulders, resting their heads on Raw and Aaz, who had gone very still. It was so quiet in this place, the thud of my heartbeat the only drum in the world, throbbing, pulsing in my chest, and ears. My pulse, too quick. My pulse, aching with fear.

"Zee," I said, and my voice was strained, barely louder than a whisper.

He raked his claws across his arms, creating a trail of sparks. "Flesh, free and given. Old ritual. Dead ritual. Meant to appease. Stall our hungers."

And it was familiar. Someone had known and used it to lure in the Mahati, those to whom the rules were still the same, no matter how many thousands of years had passed.

Zee swayed into the Mahati's face, and she went very still, like a rabbit trying to become invisible. He grabbed her chin, claws digging into her gaunt cheeks.

"I was born inside the prison," she rasped, as if he'd asked a question I couldn't hear. "I had never eaten human flesh. The older warriors said I must, I must, before I was fit to fight."

"Fight we had," he rasped. "Tonight. Your Queen, attacked, and you did not come. Too busy eating unfit meat."

Tears rolled down her cheeks. "Yes, my King."

"Open," he commanded, and she opened her mouth wide. Zee leaned in, nostrils flaring. I couldn't ask him why he smelled her breath, but the spikes of his hair jerked once, twice, and muscles rippled across his back. I watched, imagining this demon—this trembling, ashamed demon—dying at my command. And it hurt, made *me* feel ashamed. I wasn't sure I had the stomach to kill her. There had to be mercy, sometimes. Second chances, every now and then. The world wouldn't fall apart, would it?

Just one mercy.

"Zee," I said, ready to call him away from the demon. He glanced back at me, just as the Mahati made a strange sound: a cough, a gag.

He jerked away as she vomited.

Raw and Aaz hauled me back. I let them drag me, stunned. It wasn't the vomit, but the violence, as though someone was stabbing the demon from the inside.

What poured from her mouth was dark as blood, the scent the same as rotting meat and shit. She covered her mouth with such desperation, she gouged her face, blood streaming down her cheeks. Her chest heaved, her entire body rising from the snow as she tried to stop.

The Mahati toppled sideways, hands falling limp as she began convulsing. Vomit trickled from her mouth. Or maybe it was blood. Zee and the boys held me so tightly their tiny hands burned, but I didn't say a word. I wanted to feel the pain. It grounded me, and I needed that as I watched the Mahati go still, and die.

I turned away, holding my stomach, breathing through gritted teeth. Dek and Mal licked the backs of my ears. Quiet, so quiet. In the distance, there was a glow: morning rising, slow.

"Sweet Maxine," Zee murmured.

I was going to be vomiting next. "Seen anything like that before?"

He shook his head, expression troubled. "Smelled sick. Poisoned. Tasted it on her breath."

"Fuck. It was those humans. That's what the Aetar did." I tried to stand. Raw and Aaz clung to my legs, ears flat against their sharp little heads.

"Maxine," Zee said again.

"Hide her," I said, focused only on getting home, warning Grant. "No one can find her body."

"Maxine," Zee said, and this time the urgency in his voice made me look at him—and follow his gaze to the dead Mahati.

Her head was half-buried in the snow, but her eyes were wide open. I stared, confused, because I'd just seen her die. I could feel her death, knew with a certainty that her life was over.

But those eyes were very much alive.

A whisper floated on the air, a slow exhalation that went on and on, becoming a sigh, a hiss. My skin rippled with that sound.

"Hunter," breathed the Mahati, sprawled so still, still as death in the snow.

Nothing of the demon moved, not even those blood-stained lips. I thought it might be my imagination, except Raw and Aaz were stiff with tension, and Zee had planted himself in front of me: crouched, quivering. Dek and Mal wrapped themselves so tight around my throat it was hard to breathe.

Her eyes convinced me. Though the rest of her body was still as death, her eyes were filled with a different kind of life: a burning, calculated focus that was ruthless, cold, and utterly, magnificently ancient. Not the eyes of the young demon who had knelt before me and lost her life. Not *her* eyes.

Something else. Something I recognized. I knew that look. It didn't matter that the flesh was Mahati. Some things transcended the physical. Some things could *possess* the physical. And only one race of creature, one race of *alien*, had that terrible, immortal gaze.

Only one race of creature could tamper with a human and make its flesh poison. Or make a giant who killed. I thought of that demon waitress in Texas, everything she'd told me, and my blood got even colder.

"We see you," whispered the Mahati, and the voice was distinct, too: cultured, faintly crisp, like chipped ice. Her mouth contorted: a crazy, grotesque shape, dribbling blood and saliva. Took me a moment to realize it was a smile.

"We see what you hide inside your belly, what it is, what it will become."

I lunged. Zee beat me, gripping that head between his claws. Raw and Aaz prowled close, baring their teeth. Dek and Mal loosened their coils, hovering away from me, smoke pouring from their nostrils.

"Kill you," Zee rasped. "Make war. Destroy your worlds, again."

That terrible gaze flicked again to mine. I did not flinch. But I couldn't speak, either. My throat was too tight.

"Your daughter is already dead," she said, and a dull ache thudded hard inside my lower left side: a heartbeat, a pulse.

I stopped breathing. That monstrous smile widened.

Zee snarled. Bone splintered. Skin tore. Blood oozed as the little demon crushed the Mahati's head. Light escaped, a haze that had all the shimmer of a borealis—the shadow of an Aetar. I watched, unable to move, drifting inside a chill that washed through me from heart to bone, settling so deep I didn't think I would ever be warm again.

The pain in my stomach worsened. I'd never felt anything like it, as though a hook were inside me, yanking. The sensation felt hot. Wet.

I was wet.

I reached between my legs, rubbing my jeans.

My fingers came away bloody.

CHAPTER 7

MY knees buckled. Raw and Aaz caught me. I heard Zee speaking—a snapping snarl of words and growls—but his voice was far away. The entire world dimming to my stomach, and the heat, and the blood. I had read everything I could on pregnancies. I knew about miscarriages.

By the time the bleeding started, the baby was almost always dead.

"No," I said, holding my stomach, panic rising thick and bitter in my throat. I tried to breathe, but my chest felt heavy, paralyzed. I pulled at Dek and Mal, still coiled around my neck, and their soft keens broke apart as they fell from me.

But I still couldn't breathe. I couldn't breathe.

I slammed my right hand into the snow and fell into the void *between*.

Between space. Between stitches of reality. Between dreams and sanity, and breath and death, a place of infinite, crushing emptiness, stripped of sight and sound and touch— anything that reminded me of being *real*. Nothing existed in the void. I wasn't even sure that I did. Just a scattering of thoughts, held together by nothing more tenuous than my own will. I would fly apart if I stayed too long. Fly apart, lost in an endless scream.

I could only enter this place because of the armor encasing my right hand—armor made from a metal mined in the heart of another impossible place: a network of quantum roads called the Labyrinth—a nexus outside time and space, linking countless different worlds. Cross the universe in a heartbeat. Bend time. Bend yourself, *across* time. Anything could happen there. The Labyrinth was made of possibilities.

But the void was not the Labyrinth. And while the armor let me travel across earth in less than a heartbeat, I'd always been terrified that one day I would find myself trapped there, *between*.

I was still terrified. But for the first time, something else scared me more—and there was a fantasy in my head, a split-second wild notion, that if I stayed in the void, if I *didn't* leave it, my baby would be fine. That I could just float there forever, even if it meant losing my mind.

We all think crazy things when we're desperate.

⋅≈⋅

I fell from the void to a cracked linoleum floor.

Daylight had arrived. As soon as I slipped free, the weight of the boys settled on my body like a fine black mist, a sheen of warmth that spread over every inch of me except my face: between my toes, fingers, legs; beneath my nails; against my scalp. I glanced down at my bare arms. In that dark, cold place, there had been pale skin. Now I was covered in tattoos: coils of mercury and shadow, fine lines of scales and claws. Red eyes stared, unblinking: Dek, stretching down my arm; and Mal, his face resting in the crook of my elbow.

My boys. Imprisoned on my body until sunfall. Protecting me with their flesh.

Except, they couldn't protect me from everything.

Blood was still warm between my legs. I felt the heat and weight of it on my jeans, against my skin. I could smell it. I'd had a little bleeding in the last four months. That was normal in a pregnancy. This wasn't.

I shook so hard my teeth rattled. I couldn't even lift my head. I heard a harsh intake of breath, a scrape of metal, and the creak of leather. I also smelled chocolate baking: a warm scent, the one anchor I needed. I clung to it. I inhaled as deeply as I could. It reminded me of my mother. Strength and comfort, and heartache. I should have gone to a hospital, but instead I'd come home. Home to the farmhouse in Texas.

I rolled onto my side. I saw feet in front of me, bare and familiar. Odd, the body parts that you recognize. Stubby toes, the arch of a foot, even the delicate bones of an ankle. As distinct as a fingerprint. A cry of home.

My gut lurched again, but this was heart-borne—followed by a wail in my throat that I swallowed down and kept swallowing.

"Mom," I whispered, and those feet suddenly became my mother, my crouching mother, my mother who was dead, my mother who had chocolate frosting on her tattooed fingertips and who knelt on the floor to look at me with shock and horror, and concern. Her hair was black and glossy, and fell past her pale face. Her eyes so blue. So beautiful.

"Oh, hell," she whispered, her gaze lingering on my gently protruding stomach—and the blood on my hands.

Oh, hell, yes. I had traveled in time. Again.

Wasn't the first, wouldn't be the last—but I had no control over how or why, or when. The armor always chose: that fragment of the Labyrinth, with its wiles and impulses, and utter disregard for all those silly human rules about time and space, and how we were stuck moving in one direction, forever. Because time didn't work like that. Time was fluid, and we were fluid in time. If you only had the right key to unlock that particular door.

And I did. Even though I never ever wanted to use it again. Nothing more dangerous than time. Nothing with more potential to fuck you up.

But I was still happy to see my mother.

"When?" she asked sharply, grabbing my hand. "Maxine, *when did this happen?*"

I tried telling her, but all I could whisper was the month. I was fading. Or maybe the armor was taking me from her. I felt so far away, and I began to fall, fall backward into the floor, deeper and deeper, and my mother tried to hold me, screaming *hold on hold on hold on* but her hands slipped from my wrists and I called out or tried but my voice was gone—

—then, so was I—

—and I hit the floor again.

Face-first, on my stomach, exactly as I'd arrived in the past only moments before. Except now, beneath me, was a bloodstain that I'd never quite been able to clean. Blood, from my mother's murder.

Home, again. Home, in my proper time. And I wanted to go back. Being with her, only for a moment—was I supposed to be grateful for that? It was torture, and I was a kid again, a little girl who needed her mother more than she needed air to breathe.

I sensed movement around me, a frightened hush.

"Grant." My throat hurt, as if I'd been screaming. "Someone find my husband."

No one answered me. I rolled over on my back and stared through tear-blurred eyelashes at half a dozen young, inhuman faces; red and silver, or covered in fur; staring at me with huge eyes and chocolate batter around their mouths.

They were pushed roughly aside. Mary leaned close. She took one look at me and grabbed the nearest demon child by the throat, dragging him close. "Fetch the Lightbringer," she hissed, releasing him with a shove. He stared at her with terror and ran.

But Grant was already coming. I felt him, a bloom of warmth inside my chest: a golden thread of light, pulsing with frantic urgency. I could almost hear his thoughts, a wisp on the surface of my mind, but mine were too scrambled, panicked, to let him in. Nothing was getting in to me. I heard Mary giving other orders, but her voice faded into a muffled burr that suffocated beneath my pounding heart.

Zee and the boys writhed over my stomach, down between my legs. Once, years in the past, they had sealed my mouth and nostrils with their flesh to keep me from drowning; I didn't know what they were doing now, and I didn't care. As long it kept my baby inside me. Inside me.

A little corpse inside you, came the errant thought.

I heard a cane tap—felt the vibration in my back—and tilted my head just enough to see Grant's boots, that terrible shuffling limp that was almost a run. I tried to sit up. Mary held me down—or tried to. She jerked back, cradling her hands—burned. I felt the heat on my shoulders where she'd touched me. The boys weren't letting anyone close.

Except Grant. I heard the rumbling *om* of his voice, so strong it surged against my skin like thunder. A cold thrill of hope shuddered through me. Maybe, maybe, we could fix this.

Dizziness hit. I shut my eyes and felt pressure against my skin; the boys, gripping me in their dreams, holding me close with their tattooed claws. I almost thought I could hear Zee's voice, whispering to me in a language I didn't understand: growls, against the surface of my thoughts, soft sighs. I clung to that. I clung to the click of the approaching cane—tap, tap—echoing my heartbeat until it stopped dead beside me, and a large, warm hand touched my head. Grant's voice surged around me: wordless, full of power. I waited for the pain in my stomach to disappear, for the hot, trickling flow of blood to stop—but nothing happened.

I knew why. But I wanted this time to be different.

Grant's voice broke—and then broke again. I could almost see the pieces falling like shards of light. He tried again to sing, but it didn't last. His silence horrified me.

"Don't give up," I whispered, unable to look at him. I was paralyzed, terrified of moving, as if that would harm my child more. His cane hit the floor, and he collapsed on his knees beside me, his breathing ragged and hoarse. Trying not to cry. Trying. I was trying, too.

"She's immune to me. Just like you," he said.

"No." I dug my fingers into my stomach. "No, Grant."

"She's dying," he whispered. "I can see it."

Our baby. My girl. Dying.

Dying inside me, and I could not stop it. I could destroy the world. I could unleash hell on this planet and a million others. But I could not save the one thing that mattered most to me. Funny, how that could happen. Funny, how someone you didn't know, who wasn't even fully formed, could matter more than life. Funny, how fast that could slip up on you.

I closed my eyes. I could see the boys inside my head, as real as if they crouched before me. Zee, raking his claws over his arms; past him, Raw and Aaz, who hugged teddy bears to their chests, stabbing them with spikes torn from their backs; Dek and Mal, heavy on my shoulders, growling.

I'll do anything, I said to that imaginary Zee.

A hush fell. Even my heartbeat slowed. Between my thighs, a sluggish drip: hot and inevitable.

One way, he whispered, finally. *One way. But, a price.*

"Maxine," Grant croaked out, but my head and heart were already too far away to listen. All I could see was Zee. All I could feel in my blood was him and the boys, and ten thousand years of mothers and daughters burning through me, like love.

And with that love, something else: an awakening, beneath my heart; a familiar alien presence that uncoiled in a surge of terrible, aching power. It slithered through me, pouring through my pulse, and I looked down at my arms and legs, half-expecting to see my muscles and bones displaced, shoved aside for a spirit ripped from the heart of night: darkness, alive and breathing, and trembling with impossible hunger.

A monster. A God. Passed down from woman to woman—biding its time in dreams. Until me.

I had resisted its presence for years. Fought its destructive possession with all my strength, and won. Again and again, I had won.

Young Queen, whispered a soft, sibilant voice.

Grant reached out but stopped a hairsbreadth from touching my hand. I was glad. So glad he didn't touch me. It would make me remember him and think about consequences—and I couldn't do that. I couldn't.

I closed my eyes, took a breath. *Whatever you want. Just save her.*

A sigh passed through me, deep and hideous with pleasure, sliding like smoke into my throat. My mouth curved into a smile, but that wasn't me. It wasn't me at all.

Yes, whispered the darkness. *It is done.*

I didn't ask the price. I already knew it would be horrible. No bargains with the devil ever turned out good.

But the bleeding stopped. So did that tugging pain. Inside my belly, heat coiled around and around like a sun-warm snake making its nest, and the sensation only grew and strengthened, weighing me down until my back sank into the old linoleum, and the floorboards creaked. Sparks lit behind my eyes, sparks and stars, rushing at me: a torrent of light, as if my mind were traveling through space.

This is the path, I heard a quiet whisper. *This is the promise for your child's blood.*

Then, nothing. No stars. No presence. No heat in my stomach. Gone as if it never existed. I felt light as air, and my hand groped the floor, as if I could stop myself from floating away. Grant grabbed my wrist, held on tight. It didn't help.

What brought me back, what finally anchored me, was a new sensation. A tickle in my belly. A hum.

"Grant," I whispered, hoarse, my voice sounding far away. "What do you see?"

It took him a moment. When he spoke, he sounded old and tired, and broken.

"Light," he breathed. "A strong light. She's okay, Maxine."

I smiled.

Little light, I thought, touching my stomach with a hand that felt heavy as death. *I feel you, little light.*

I thought about my mother.

And passed the fuck out.

CHAPTER 8

MAYBE there's a God. I don't know. What I'm certain of is there are plenty of pretenders. No bigger con in the universe. No stakes higher. Power is the measure by which they live or die. But even so, they aren't that different from humans.

Gods love. Gods kill.

And then there's me.

WHEN I opened my eyes, I found an old woman sharpening her machete against my arm. Sparks popped, and the grind of the metal against those obsidian tattoos was soft and cold.

"Mary," I said, slowly.

Her smile was lopsided, eyes a little too bright, too intense, to be completely, absolutely sane. "Teeth need sharper blades."

"Some other time." I pushed myself up. It wasn't hard.

I was strong. If the memory of what had happened weren't still horrifically real inside me, I would have thought it was nothing more harmless than a nightmare.

I was on the couch, soft pillows piled under my knees. Naked beneath a light sheet. The front door of the farmhouse had been propped open, letting in a warm breeze that I felt only on my face. I heard chimes tinkling, and young, inhuman laughter, like a growl tickling the air.

A strong, familiar hand appeared in front of me, holding a glass of water.

"Glad you're awake," Grant said, quietly. "Mary, go outside."

The old woman tilted her head, studying him. She was wearing a housedress embroidered with poodles, a wide leather belt cinched tight around her nonexistent waist. Weapons hung from it: knives, two hammers, and a second machete. The dress was too large; the neck gaped so much I could see her breastbone, and the flat, circular stone embedded there in her flesh.

It was engraved: a knotted tangle of lines that had no beginning, no end. Same emblem as the pendant Grant wore around his neck: a mark of his family line.

"Must be strong," Mary murmured to him. "Lightbringer. Inheritor of blood."

Father, I thought. *Still a father.*

Grant's gaze met mine. He'd heard my thought, I was sure of it. And I was glad.

Warmth crept into his eyes. He did not look away from me as Mary slid the machete one last time over my arm and stood. I didn't look at her either as she walked from us on the tips of her toes, gliding gracefully through the open farmhouse door. Her voice hummed a tuneless, eerie melody.

"Move over," Grant said.

It was an old couch, wide and deep enough for several families, *and* their demons. I scooted sideways, and my husband lay down heavily beside me, using both hands to pull his bad leg onto the couch. We lay together, me on my side, him on his back. My head rested on his warm chest. I could feel his ribs beneath his flannel shirt but pretended not to notice. My arms were bare against him, black with the bodies of the boys, who slept soft and heavy. I stared for a moment. I always stared because it was always new.

My skin was not human. Not during the day. My skin was made of scales and muscle, and veins of organic silver that glittered and pulsed and threaded over me like rivers of deadly light. I was untouchable, like this. Not heat or cold, nor nuclear fire, could break me. Not a fall from a million miles. My fingernails were black, capable of cracking stone or tearing holes in steel. I used them now to grip my husband's shirt and hold him tight.

Because immortality didn't mean shit. Not when you still had a human heart.

Grant gave me silence. He gave me himself. No questions. I was so grateful for that. I didn't want to talk, or remember. I might start crying again, and there was nothing worse, nothing, not when I already felt cut, torn, clawed open. Tears had no place here. My baby was alive. Keeping her safe was all that mattered.

But finally I talked. Everything that happened after I left him, even the conversation with the possessed waitress. Each word hurt.

"The Mahati was dead, and the Aetar still possessed her body. When the attack came . . ." I stopped, and his arms tightened. "I didn't even know until it was too late. The boys and I . . . we couldn't do anything to stop it."

"I should have been there with you."

"Don't. That's an impossible regret."

He tapped my head with his hand. "Don't tell me what I should regret. I've got enough emotions inside me that aren't mine. What I feel . . . what matters to me . . . it's the only way I'm holding on to my identity."

That was a new revelation. A hundred different responses

pushed through me, most of them involving death to demons. I closed my eyes and swallowed them all. "The thing inside me . . ."

"Yes," he said heavily. "I know."

He didn't ask what the price would be for saving our daughter. No use, no need to complicate that one simple acknowledgment. I'd made the bargain and sealed it on our baby's life. What needed paying would be paid, with no regrets, no negotiation.

"We're sitting ducks," he went on. "We have to fight, Maxine. Any minute, we could be attacked, from any direction, any *thing*."

"So we find the Aetar, and what then? There are too many, and they're scattered across the universe. We kill the one who's bothering us now, and another will come. And they'll keep coming, and we'll be in this same situation again and again."

"And if we run?"

"Maybe," I muttered. "But then we'll always run. And even that might not save us."

Grant sighed. "Those six humans killed on our land were poisoned. Dead too long for me to get a strong read off them. I can't tell you how they were altered, except the Mahati and Osul who ate parts of them died. Looked like something out of *The Exorcist*. But you know that."

I pulled at the collar of his shirt, examining his chest for any stowaway slugs. "I'm surprised the Shurik and Yorana didn't take bites out of those humans."

"The Shurik burrow into the living. Corpses aren't their thing. And the Yorana . . . prefer seduction before the hunt." His jaw tightened; so did his hand on my back, fingers digging into my shoulder. "Zee was right. We need to leave, Maxine. We've known from the beginning. We waited too long to face it."

It was hard, hearing him say those words. Made it too real—and that choice was full of unknowns. It didn't feel safe.

But it could be safer, I thought. Zee and the boys had never steered me wrong. They were family. All of us, together.

Grant squeezed my hand. "Maxine."

"I'm scared," I said, thinking about my mother.

"Me, too." He kissed the top of my head. "We'll figure it out."

I placed his hand on my stomach and held it there. "We need help. We need it now."

No response. Grant was a former priest, and far too polite to say, *"No fucking way."* But I could practically hear it in my head.

"I need to find my grandfather," I said.

MEN have never existed in my family. No records of their names. No mention of fathers. You'd think we could clone ourselves—and given how closely all the women of my line resemble one another, that might be the case.

At any rate, my ancestors, those who could read and write, kept journals—and while not many of those survived (most of them stored in a lockbox in New York City), what did keep always made it clear: The Kiss women stand alone.

No family but mother and daughter, and the boys. No friends, no allies, no connection. No talk of love. My mother certainly drilled *that* into me, again and again.

But it was a lie. Maybe the biggest of all the lies she ever told me.

I could not be the only one who had rebelled against that family law. Surely some of us had tried—*tried* to have a normal life. It would have been difficult, yes, but not impossible. Even my mother had fallen in love—loved deeply—although the circumstances of that union were so strange and tragic, I refused to let myself dwell on it. I couldn't think about my father.

My grandfather was another matter entirely.

Old Wolf. Meddling Man. With eons of blood on his hands.

And yet I loved him. Maybe from the very beginning, when I'd first seen his photograph with my grandmother, and all the vast possibilities of what he and I could mean to each other were still fresh in my head. Before I'd learned the truth of what he was. Before a lot of things. I was so young, then. Desperate to have some part of my mother returned to me. My grandfather was the perfect surrogate.

But that's what happens with family. Sometimes you love what you should hate. Sometimes you trust when you should suspect. My mother probably would have been smarter, more careful with her heart—she was the true warrior. Always perfect, always strong. I was nothing but a pale imitation.

But that's the way it is with mothers and daughters.

Someone is always being left behind.

⊰⊱

IT was lunchtime in Texas, the sun blazing hot. The void spat us out into a world that was sweaty, blinking with electricity, and smelled like the seat of a dirty toilet. It was also night—and the boys woke right the fuck up.

It was like being drowned in a vat full of acid and fire. No beginning, no end, just the slow peel of my skin from my body, every inch from my fingernails to between my legs. I staggered, already disoriented from the void. Hitting night like this was the worst. At least with sunset, I had some warning. I could prepare myself.

Tattoos dissolved into black smoke, flaying me from my toenails to the roots of my hair. I could not breathe. I could not make a sound. My *mother* had never made a sound. Just smiled, and laughed, so that I never knew the truth until it was my turn. I realized now the strength of her sacrifice—how she'd saved me a lifetime of fear and dread by making me think this shit would be easy.

Don't ever let anyone tell you that immortality—even the half-ass kind—doesn't come without a price.

The boys ripped free, a sliding, terrible heat that felt as though their sinuous bodies were petals hot with lava. Claws scraped. Whispers pattered. In small pieces, the pain eased. But I still shook, and when my vision cleared, I was on my knees. Dek and Mal clung to my shoulders, humming Sting's "Every Breath You Take."

"Maxine," whispered Zee. "Sweet Maxine."

"Hey," I said, mouth so dry I could barely form the word. I glimpsed movement at the corner of my eye: Grant's feet, and the bottom of his cane. His hand came down, and I grabbed it, hard.

He pulled me up into his arms. His breath was warm on my neck, and I kissed his throat. His skin tasted hot, feverish.

"We're in Taiwan," he said, pulling away. "Taipei. Been here before when I was young."

I looked around. We were standing inside an unlit street so narrow I could have stretched out my arms and laid my palms flat against each opposing wall. Electric wires and other thick cables hung above our heads, along with laundry and birdcages. Raw and Aaz clung to the walls, claws dug in and hanging upside down. Both of them reached into the shadows and pulled out hand grenades. They yanked out the pins, and shoved the live explosives into their mouths.

Grant blew out his breath and looked away. "We better get moving."

I touched Zee's head. "We need Jack."

But the little demon didn't move, except to lean in and press his ear against my stomach. A tremor passed through him, and in moments Raw and Aaz gathered close, also leaning in for a hard, close embrace. I wrapped my arms around them, sharing their weak relief, and reverence. My heart, thick in my throat. Dek and Mal licked my ears, and Grant slid his hands against them into my hair. His brow pressed to mine.

"We're okay," I whispered.

"Yes," Zee murmured, against my belly. "Her dreams still sing."

Grant pulled me closer. I leaned against him, vision swelling in a slow burn that blurred the shadows with tears. Zee reached out and covered our joined hands, those claws soft as silk. Small sighs filled my hair.

"Family," Zee rasped. "Strong as, deep as."

"Family," Grant echoed softly.

"Mine," I said, but it didn't make me feel better.

CHAPTER 9

I T was a bad night to be out. Hot, wet, with mountain-kissed thunderclouds and humid winds gathered thick over a red-light market slum in the heart of Taipei. We were far from home.

Tourists spilled into the narrow road. Grant and I skirted the crowd, listening to gasps and camera clicks, and uneasy laughter. My heart tightened into a painful knot when I peered around them and saw a little girl, no older than eight or nine, grab a cobra from its tank and slip a wire noose over its head.

No fear on her face. Just focus: cold, unrelenting. Little hands pulled hard on the cobra's writhing tail—straightening that long, muscular body with an ease that would have been only slightly less disturbing if she hadn't been dressed like a ballerina, wrapped in a ratty pink tutu with bows in her braided hair.

A middle-aged man stood beside her. He held a curved blade, fake rubies glittering up and down the hilt. No costume. Just bloodstains on his pants and a smile on his face as he gazed at the gathered crowd.

Demon. Possessed by one, at any rate. I saw the shadow thick as ash above his head, flecks of darkness snowing down upon his shoulders.

His gaze found mine. His smile slipped. I made a gun sign with my hand and pointed it at his face. Grant shook his head, and the demon took a step back, placing himself behind the child.

Grant and I shared a quick look but kept walking. We weren't here for him, or any girls who weren't our own.

We moved fast. Grant's breathing became labored though his pace didn't slow. His color wasn't good—too pale, but with a flush high in his cheeks that looked like a fever. I wasn't feeling well, either. Sweat poured down my back, between my breasts. So humid it was difficult to breathe though I'd never had a problem before with heat. My body felt hollow, weak, heart pounding so hard. I blamed it on the near miscarriage, but there was a part of me—very small— that kept seeing that Mahati demon vomiting to death: blood and bile staining the snow. I couldn't shake the dread.

I touched the sinuous bodies coiled tight around my throat. Scales soft, warm. Dek and Mal loosened their holds on me, making it easier to breathe. For the first time in my life, I wasn't worried about anyone seeing them on my shoulders. We were past that now. It was all too late.

Zee slid through the shadows beside me, nothing but a sliver, a glimpse, a glint of red eyes. Raw and Aaz glided above the street, leaping between the neon lights that covered storefront windows and the signs hanging vertically from cracked, aging buildings. I felt them, close as my skin, close as my heart, racing quick. Little kings. Little family.

Tourists thinned. So did the light. More locals now, men dressed in house slippers and limp white tanks and slacks; several teen girls in miniskirts, smoking cigarettes and drinking bubble tea, giving us bored glances. Just more foreigners, overdressed for the heat.

Two old women stepped into our path: short, compact, hard lines etched into their sharp chins and cheeks. Small feral eyes, glittering. Hands flashed; for a moment I thought they held knives or balls of light. Their auras were full of demonic shadows. More of the possessed.

My first instinct was to kill them. Not the human hosts but the demons inside. My entire body tensed with the need—and I had to tell myself, had to remember, that things were different now. We were all on the same side. More or less.

The demons gave us wary looks and waved the flashlights they held, pointing the beams at a narrow metal door squeezed inside an alcove barely wide enough for my shoulders.

"He's on the top floor," one of them said with distaste, as though the words were shit in her mouth. Or maybe being forced to help us made her ill. I didn't like it, either. Seemed against the natural order of things.

"You've been watching him?" Grant asked.

"Blood Mama made us, all these months," replied the possessed woman, while her friend looked past us and gave some tourists a toothless grin. "The Wolf can't be trusted."

I started to walk past her, and she stopped me. "Our mother says you didn't listen."

"Listen?" I thought of that waitress in Texas. "I listened fine. The message just wasn't worth shit."

The old woman stepped forward, deliberately ignoring Grant. "You should have let your baby die and made another, with a different father. *That* was what you should have heard in her message. Your attachment to the one in your belly will fuck us all."

I grabbed her throat, and the woman squawked like a flattened chicken. The tourists who were passing us—a slight, elderly white woman, and her equally elderly black husband—gave us startled looks and kept on walking, fast. The demon's friend also backed away—right into Raw, who appeared from the shadows with a snarl.

"I'm going to kill you," I told her.

"Let me do it," Grant said.

I glanced at him, an unpleasant thrill in my gut. His eyes were so cold, so grim, I didn't recognize him. Truly, for a moment, it was as if another man had stepped into my husband's place. Even his face looked different: thinner, longer, lost in so many shadows he seemed to exist between *here* and *there*.

He looks like a demon, I thought.

Until, suddenly, he was my husband again. But that was almost as frightening.

The possessed woman's eyes bulged; she clawed at my hand. Zee flowed from the darkness and grabbed her leg. She went totally, completely still.

"Little light is our light," he whispered. "Cut her, we cut you. Cut you *all* dead."

"Traitors," she rasped. "False Kings. You reaped worlds and would lose this one to a child and a Lightbringer."

Grant made a sharp, slicing sound with his tongue—I felt it scrape against my skin like a razor blade. Both the possessed women stiffened, dark auras tearing straight up—invisible hands ripping them from their stolen bodies. I imagined a tearing sound—but that was just the women sucking in their breath through their teeth, inhaling and inhaling, standing on their toes, rising as high as their stout, stolen bodies would take them. Backs arched. Bones cracked.

My husband spoke again, and those demon auras snapped free of their hosts. Zee leapt up, grabbing one of them. Raw took the other, holding that struggling wisp in his fist. He grinned, sharp teeth absolutely hideous—and stuffed the demon in his mouth. Zee did the same, swallowing with grim pleasure.

I had already released the human woman's throat, but I touched her again, this time to hold her up as her knees buckled. Grant grabbed her companion, but he only had one hand free and she half fell to the sidewalk with a grunt. Zee and Raw were already gone, lost into the shadows.

Demons, parasites. For years, I'd called the hosts of these things *zombies*. Humans with weak minds, possessed by demons who fed on their pain and the pain they caused others. An old demon could possess absolutely. A weak demon was just a hitchhiker, influencing from the shadows of the unconscious. But either way, the host was always screwed. I'd known men and women forced to commit terrible crimes against their wills—and after an exorcism have no memory of it. No memory, but forced to live with the consequences, forever.

Both women were touching their heads, babbling to each other in Chinese. I didn't understand a word, but Grant began humming, a soft melody that skimmed across my skin like a feather. The women calmed, staring blankly at each other.

I pulled Grant toward the apartment-building door. His hand was clammy. I said, "That wasn't like you."

"Does it matter?" he asked tightly.

I forced him to look at me. "You're not a killer."

He paled but stayed silent. I didn't know what else to say except take his hand. I kissed the back of it, briefly pressing his palm against my cheek. Willing him to feel my concern.

I'm changing, whispered his voice inside my mind.

I caressed our bond, savoring the light and heat of it. *You're a father whose daughter is being threatened.*

Grant drew in a sharp, pained breath. *It's more than that.* And then, carefully, gently, he pulled his hand from mine.

We went inside, blinking at the dim, buzzing fluorescent lights, which cast the world in a sick greenish gray. I heard televisions, shouts in Chinese, but tuned it all out, listening to my heart pound as I ran up the stairs two steps at a time.

Grant couldn't keep up, but said, "Go on."

So I did. Zee uncoiled from the shadows, dropping on all fours to race ahead of me. His claws left deep gouge marks in the stairs. He looked over his shoulder, hair spikes flexing with agitation.

"Maxine," he rasped.

"Find Jack," I said. "I've got Dek and Mal."

But Zee did not leave me. Instead, he moved closer, so close I could reach out and touch him as I ran up the stairs; and I did, my palm skimming his sharp hair and the tips of the spikes jutting from his back. Comforting, having him near. I needed the reminder I was not alone. Even having Grant with me wasn't reassurance enough.

We reached the top floor. No one was in the hall. I heard men speaking Chinese behind closed doors, a dog whining. My boots scuffed the stained tiles. I smelled hot oil, garlic, and something rotten, like the lingering vapor from a dirty toilet.

We stopped at the second-to-last apartment. Door was already cracked open, Aaz just on the other side, peering out at us. His eyes were huge, sharp ears pressed flat against his skull. He clutched a half-eaten teddy bear. Not a good sign. My heart dropped, and I pushed inside.

It was night; I expected darkness. But the apartment I found myself in felt worse than dark. I could taste the desolation, sickly sweet: plates of rotting food on the table, the buzz of flies, the oppressive ovenlike air so thick I could have been pushing through solid matter. I waded into that apartment, stomach churning, letting my eyes adjust to the shadows and faint neon light streaming through slivers in the blinds.

"Jack," I said, and then louder: *"Jack."*

Zee fell into a shadow—slipping in and out of this world through the gloom—and then reappeared on the other side of the room, beckoning me with a flash of his long claws. I followed, Aaz staying close, chewing on his teddy bear's ear. I skirted books, paintings; a tall vase that I nudged with my shoulder and almost knocked over.

A smell hit me: more rot, but this time of the living; and I saw the rounded curve of a back, so hunched and still that at first I thought it was another piece of furniture. But no, there was an arm, pale and thick with muscle; and I heard,

I felt, a slow exhalation. I took a step closer, and choked. The air was rancid with filth. My shoes stuck to the floor.

"Meddling Man," Zee whispered.

I moved sideways and found the little demon crouched on top of a small table, his claws digging hard into the wood. All the spikes on his head flexed in agitation. Raw was there with him, and Aaz made a small, distressed sound. Dek and Mal coiled tighter around my throat.

A crystal skull was on the table.

It didn't resemble anything human. Wide cranium, protruding crests at the cheeks. Thick jaw, filled with teeth as sharp as dagger points, like a piranha's mouth. I could see the lines of that thing, all those spectral curves, as if a light were in my eyes, or its eyes, and it made me dizzy for a moment. I touched my stomach again, which felt warm. My right hand tingled, the armor encasing my skin coming alive.

Zee and the boys stared at the skull. If they destroyed it right now, I would not be surprised. That . . . thing . . . and twelve other similar artifacts were responsible for channeling the power that had been used to imprison my five little demons upon the body of my ancestor—and bind thousands of demons more into a prison outside this world.

My grandfather had been one of the prison-makers.

I watched the old man. It had been months. I barely recognized him. For a moment, I wondered if he'd found a new body to inhabit.

But I looked longer, harder, and all those rough edges were the same: cheekbones, nose, that broad, lined brow. His face was barely visible behind his matted beard and crusty shreds of silver hair. His shirt was rotting off him, filled with holes and stained yellow with sweat; and his boxer shorts were hideously filthy. He smelled like sewage. Made my skin crawl. Just standing there, breathing the same air: lethal.

He sat so still, eyes open, unblinking: staring at the crystal skull. I didn't want to imagine how long he'd been like that. Long enough, maybe, to kill a normal human. His lips were crusted with blood.

Grant entered the room behind me. "Oh, my God."

I ignored him, stepping in front of my grandfather— blocking his view of the skull.

"Jack," I said.

Nothing. For a long moment I was sure he wouldn't stir, that whatever had captured him would continue holding his spirit and flesh. He was in a coma, he was paralyzed, he was already gone from that body.

But just as I was about to call down Zee, the skin around his eye twitched. So did his hand, resting on his knee. I held my breath, waiting. I held my breath, so I wouldn't vomit. Sweat rolled down my back. I thought about home and wanted to reach past the filth and shake my grandfather awake.

He twitched again, a jolt that ran from his feet into his legs. His fingers flexed, and his shoulders hitched with a sharp breath that wheezed into his lungs like rattling leaves. I heard popping sounds. His mouth cracked open. I expected him to speak, but instead his tongue emerged, and it was grotesque: shriveled, dry, bleeding.

I snapped my fingers at Raw. "Water."

The little demon dropped his fist into the shadows; he pulled a bottle of water free, ice-cold and perspiring. I popped the cap, held my breath against the smell, and pressed the bottle against my grandfather's broken lips. His eyes were still open, unresponsive. He stared right past me.

He didn't drink at first. Water filled his mouth and spilled down the sides. I stood there, waiting. Dek and Mal pushed their heads free of my hair and slithered down my arms, peering at my grandfather's face.

Grant stepped close, a low hum pouring from him, a heavy sound that made the air vibrate.

That did it. My grandfather choked. Water sputtered from his mouth over my hands, but I held his jaw and the bottle, and when he managed to swallow, I gave him more. He drank and drank, and when that bottle emptied, Raw put another in my hand. At some point, his eyes closed—and then at some point, his eyes opened—so that when we were at the end of the third bottle I realized he was looking at my face. And this time, he was seeing me.

"Hey," I said, trying to smile.

My grandfather raised a shaking, filthy hand and touched my wrist. It happened to be my right wrist, covered in armor, and the organic metal reacted to his touch with a ripple. The old man shuddered, and leaned away from me. His gaze fell on the crystal skull. I moved sideways, blocking his view.

He closed his eyes. "Sweet girl. How long has it been?"

"Months since I saw you. But I don't know how long you've been . . . like this."

"Too long." Jack opened his eyes and looked at me. "Thank you for finding me. I was . . . not in my right mind."

And then his gaze fell down to my stomach.

"Ah," he said. "Time *has* passed."

I frowned. "Can you walk?"

He didn't seem to hear me. He tore his gaze from my stomach, then looked slowly around the room, as if seeing it for the first time. I thought for sure he'd already noticed Grant—given that my husband was standing right in front of him—but when my grandfather finally looked at him, directly, a bolt of tension ran right through his jaw, down into his grimy hands. He stayed like that, unblinking. Until, finally, I realized he wasn't really seeing my husband at all.

"Jack," Grant said sharply. *"Focus."*

No reaction. Zee made an impatient sound and grabbed the old man's wrist. I had never seen the little demon touch him, and the contact seemed to startle my grandfather almost as much as me. He recoiled, trying to pull free, but Zee was relentless.

"Meddling Man," he rasped, eyes glowing. "Be here. Be *now*."

Jack stared at him, then exhaled sharply. "What has happened?"

I glanced at the skull. "You tell me."

He still looked dazed. I almost touched him but was afraid of catching a disease.

"Can you walk?" I asked him. "We need to leave."

Jack didn't move. His gaze flickered back to the skull.

"Fuck it," I said, reaching for him. "Let's go."

My grandfather held up a trembling hand, stopping me. "Don't. I'm not an invalid. Just old and stupid." He slid forward on the chair, and that small movement released an odor that made me stop breathing. Grant bent his head and covered his mouth.

When Jack stood, his knees wobbled. So did the rest of him. I gritted my teeth, held him up. My skin crawled, but I didn't let go. He felt so frail. My hands softened, and so did my heart.

"Hey," I said, in a gentler voice. "Grandfather."

Jack closed his eyes and swallowed hard. "Have you ever called me that?"

"I can't remember." I looked at the skull. "Anything I need to know?"

"Of course not," he said tersely, then hesitated. "We should leave . . . that . . . here."

Zee gave him a doubtful look. Jack said, "Yes, yes, you're right. We'll bring it."

I opened my mouth. My grandfather shook his head, confusion marring his grizzled face. "No, that's wrong. It's safer here."

Even Raw and Aaz stared at him. Grant frowned, studying the skull with an uneasy glint in his eye.

"It's alive," he said, quietly. "Full of light."

"What does that mean to us?"

"I don't know." He tore his gaze from it, blinking hard. "But it can't just be left behind."

I wouldn't have left it, anyway. I took a deep breath—through my mouth—and looked at Zee. "Find a box to put it in."

My grandfather's shoulders slumped, but he didn't argue. Or agree.

Zee reached into the shadows beneath the table. I heard a clank, scraping; he pulled free a metal box.

Jack said, in that same terse voice, "Why are you both here?"

I almost snapped at him but swallowed hard at the last moment, kept my voice steady.

"We couldn't hide forever," I told him, which wasn't what I intended to say at all. But Jack stared at me, and in a heartbeat he was fully himself, fully present, and he straightened up and grabbed my hand.

"Maxine," he said.

I squeezed his fingers, and all the pain, fear, and dread that had been hovering just outside my heart, hovering on the cusp, spilled into me and kept spilling.

"Jack," I said. "They tried to poison Grant. And kill our baby."

"They," he echoed, but it wasn't a question. He knew to whom I was referring. He was one of them, after all.

"It almost worked," Grant said. "Too close, Jack. Too damn close."

"Well," replied my grandfather, sounding shaken. "Well, now."

Zee gestured at him with one long claw. I didn't know if it was a threat, but there was certainly menace in his glinting gaze; a bitterness that gave way to something old and calculated, and devastatingly fierce.

"Meddling Man," he rasped. "Choose now, or never. Choose, who."

I had never thought to ask that question. It hadn't occurred to me that I'd need to. But Zee had known my grandfather at his worst. He had known him, battled him, been imprisoned and tortured by him. Yes, he would ask. Yes, he would doubt his loyalties. I should have, too.

A preternatural stillness fell over my grandfather, deeper and quieter than death. For a moment, he seemed erased—as if, though I was looking at him, smelling him, he ceased to exist.

Jack said in a soft voice, "There's no choice. Not any-more."

I felt oddly vulnerable, hearing those words. I should have expected them. He was my grandfather, after all. But Jack was unpredictable. Jack had his own way. And some-times that had nothing to do with my own notions of safety, or with loyalty.

I went to the table. The metal box was open, but Zee was looking at the crystal skull like it might burn him.

Behind me, my grandfather cleared his throat. "I'll do that."

He sounded a little too eager. I glared at him. "Just got you *out* of a coma."

"Maxine," Grant warned.

"It's okay," I muttered, already reaching for the thing. I couldn't help myself. I kept thinking about the *maker* of this weapon, this tool that had caused so much harm and damage— and contributed to my existence. I felt no wonder or longing. Just frustration, aggravation. My mother had inspired these emotions, once upon a time. Now, so did my father.

I stared into the cavernous eyes of that carved, inhuman skull—and touched the crystal.

Why did you give this to them? I thought, hoping my father could hear me, wherever his spirit resided in the Laby-rinth. *I need your help, too, you know.*

But nothing happened. That was how it worked with these things—never, ever, predictable. I was ready for that. For anything.

Except for the image that passed through my mind, sharp and clear as memory.

It was me. I saw myself. Gaunt, hollow-eyed.

Being dismembered by fire.

CHAPTER 10

TEXAS. It was still daylight.

I had never actually seen the boys lose their bodies in the sun. The transformation always happened too fast. Maybe, sometimes, if I watched closely at sunrise, I might glimpse the edges of their bodies shred into some unnatural haze. But that was rare: a blink, then gone. Far easier to fall into prison than out of it. Which didn't seem fair.

I felt their weight settle on me as soon as we slipped from the void. My boys. Imprisoned on my body until sunfall. Protecting me with their flesh.

Jack stumbled, shielding his eyes against the light. Corpse-like, all bone, so starved and dehydrated it was hard to look at him. His beard and wild, matted hair stuck out at crazy angles—which, alone, wouldn't have drawn my attention. Except that something seemed to be *moving* in there.

"Yes?" he said. His beard twitched. Grant coughed and looked away.

So did I, scanning the farmhouse and the dusty, long

drive. I half expected to see more police, or neighbors with pitchforks, burning torches, and shotguns.

Mary opened the front door and stepped onto the porch. An Osul child pushed past her, looking like an extra big tiger cub—puffy fur, big eyes, even bigger ears—the kind of face that had a certain amount of *awwww* built in. Right behind it was a very young Mahati, naked, with a soft round belly and some chub in her cheeks. Good eating at the Kiss house.

"Old Wolf," Mary said, and spat at him. The young demons craned their necks to look at her face and backed away.

"Yes, Maritine. It's lovely to see you, too." Jack folded his arms over his chest. "Although you might refrain from spitting at me in front of the young ones. We don't want them learning bad habits. Or seeing bloodshed."

"We *like* blood," said the little Mahati, with absolute seriousness—and the Osul nodded furiously, letting out a fierce squeak and lashing its tail around.

I looked at Grant. "That's superadorable, right? Not just my hormones?"

"No, darling," he said. "I also want to *squee*."

"Ha," I said. Except for a few Osul crouched almost out of sight in the pasture—acting as guards—nothing else moved other than some birds that flitted over the rail of the old, sagging fence. I smelled cows, but the herd was gone.

A chill raced through me, a shiver. Grant bumped his shoulder against mine, and I leaned on him. He hadn't asked what I'd seen in the skull, and I couldn't speak of it.

But I remembered: the fire and blood, the sound of my flesh tearing, and the horrified, cutting scream ripping from my throat. No boys, no protection. My pregnant belly exposed.

"My dear," said Jack in a mild voice, and I twitched, giving him a look I hoped wasn't too wild. He paused, studying me, cradling the metal box under one arm. "I expected a nuclear arsenal. Commandos with guns. At the very least, some reporters. There isn't even a helicopter, or a barking dog."

I gave him a dirty look. Grant said, "Blood Mama's parasites are helping us. They've possessed enough police and investigators, and media, to keep this thing as controlled as possible. Which won't be enough, but it might buy us time."

Surprise flickered through Jack's eyes. "You both sanctioned the possession of humans?"

"Temporarily," I said, ashamed.

Temporary or not, it was wrong, all of it. I'd hated the gleam in Blood Mama's human eyes as I'd called her back for help—compelling *more* possessions, violating *more* lives. That should have been the line in the sand, one I'd never cross. But I had, without more than a moment's thought.

Because there was another line in the sand. Humans on one side, demons on the other. And God if I hadn't made a choice that I still couldn't face, or speak of out loud. It wasn't shame I felt every time I sided with the demons—it was self-loathing.

Grant squeezed my hand. I kissed his shoulder, wishing I could just stay there, leaning up against him for the rest of my life. Instead, I nudged him away. "We'll meet you in the camp. Lord Ha'an has to be warned that Jack is coming. The other clans will have to prepare, too."

Demons might want to eat humans, but there was no hate involved. Jack, on the other hand, was one of the architects of the prison. He and his kind had committed atrocities against the demons. Fought them in a thousand-year war.

This was not going to be cute.

Grant didn't smile. I wasn't sure he could. I realized right then how tired he appeared, and his dry lips were close to cracking. He still had that odd flush in his cheeks, which stood out against his pale, drawn skin.

I regretted I'd said anything. "Never mind, it can wait. Come inside. You shouldn't be alone, anyway."

He shook his head. "It has to be done."

"We'll get Mary to do it. She needs to take the kids back anyway."

Jack squinted, staring hard at my husband. I wondered how awake he really was because he seemed to have trouble focusing. But when he did lock in on Grant, all the considerable lines in his face seemed to get only deeper, and harder.

"My dear boy," he said. "You are being *cannibalized*."

Grant flashed him a hard look. "That's a bit dramatic."

I stared. "What?"

Jack scowled. "I knew there would be consequences to those bonds. I had hoped otherwise, but you, lad, are no demon. No matter how powerful you are. You were not *made* for the burden you bear."

Grant shook his head and limped toward the power-charged six-wheeler parked in front of the porch: the only vehicle that could transport him around the full three thousand acres of our land.

I blocked his path. "Jack," I said, holding my husband's gaze. "Talk."

"He won't die," said my grandfather, still watching him with those piercing, searching eyes. "The bond he shares with you won't let him. But the bond with those demons is different. He's not . . . taking. He's only giving. And that's not the way it works."

"How do you know?" Grant snapped, but all that anger deflated as a coughing fit hit him, and he turned away, bent over, covering his mouth as his entire frame rattled. It was an ugly, wet sound—and when it eased, I wanted to check his hand for blood.

"Lad," said Jack in a gentle voice, "I spent a thousand years studying these creatures. I had to because we were trying to kill them. What you are doing will leave you a walking corpse. I can see it. Surely others can, too. I'm surprised your . . . *people* . . . haven't warned you."

"Grant," I said.

"Another hour won't turn me into a zombie, Maxine. Let it go."

"This has to stop."

"How? I can't cut the bonds. Even if I could, we *need* them now. We need these demons."

"We never needed them before."

"You're being stubborn." Grant leaned in, dropping his voice. "I know you. I know how afraid you are of losing me . . . losing all of this . . . but there has to be a better solution than just letting the ax fall. You *know* that."

"Whatever." I poked his chest with my finger. "I know you, too, and you're too smart to let yourself be . . . abused . . . like this. You're not acting like yourself."

He closed his eyes, mouth tight—but it was all pain, and weariness. "Of course I'm not. The things I hear inside my head, what those demons make me *feel*—"

Grant stopped and went very still. It wasn't just physical. I felt him draw inward, shutter down, put up the walls: like a door slamming in my face. I couldn't remember a single time he'd ever done that to me. Usually, it was the other way around. I was the one who hated being vulnerable. I was the one who was defensive with my heart.

"Don't think for a moment I won't make the hard choice," I whispered. "You might never forgive me, but our daughter will have a whole, healthy father. I can live with the rest."

He still wouldn't look at me. "Murder is always your answer. Kill first, ask questions later. I don't want to be like you, Maxine."

I stood back, stung.

Grant limped to the six-wheeler. I watched him toss his cane into the passenger seat with such violence it almost careened out the other side. Mary was already there, helping the demon children into the back. They all stopped and stared at him. Mary, with disapproval. He didn't look at her, either.

She pushed his cane aside and climbed into the passenger seat. One hand on her machete. Guard duty, protecting Grant. Just as she had protected his mother and father—or tried to, on another world, in another age. The Labyrinth had torn her out of time—just as it had torn Grant's mother, who had escaped the war, pregnant with her son. All of them hurtled millions of years into the future, until they'd fallen here, on earth.

He drove away and didn't look back. I kept hoping he would. As if it would be some kind of apology.

Don't let him go, I told myself, watching the Osul hiding in the grass rise up and run after the six-wheeler. *It's not safe.*

But I didn't move.

Jack shuffled close. I was so distracted, I barely noticed the smell. The sting I'd felt was only getting worse.

"Grant didn't mean it," said my grandfather. "That man worships you. He's simply afraid."

I thought about the demon he had just killed in Taiwan. How quickly and ruthlessly he had committed that execution. This man, who wouldn't hurt a fly. Who had fought me for years, refusing to treat demons as I treated them. Grant was the one who had shown me they were more than parasites. He was the one who had made me realize I was *more* than just a killer—and that it was okay. It was *okay* that I had broken with precedent. It was okay I had stepped off the path the women before me had made.

I had become my own person, with him.

Not my mother. Not my grandmother. Just me.

"He's right," I replied. "My first answer *is* usually violence."

"And? Is that so terrible?" Jack forced me to look at him. "You women were made in a different age, your bodies compelled to be the homes of the five most dangerous creatures my kind had ever encountered. Violence, survival, war . . . that is in your blood. But that is *not* who you are. You broke with that. You made something new."

It was as if he'd heard my thoughts. He stepped back, a grim smile touching his mouth. "My sweet girl . . . you would have destroyed the world by now if not for your good heart. It's what has saved you, and us, again and again. Never doubt it."

I swallowed hard. "I don't like fighting with him. It feels wrong."

My grandfather made a rude sound. "That's because you're both disgustingly in love. If you actually disagreed like *normal* people, you'd have kicked his arse and been done with it. And it does need kicking, my dear. Not *just* for what he said to you."

"Jack," I said, but he waved me off.

"Enough. You didn't bring me here for this." He scratched the bridge of his nose, and a black flake of crud fell off. "Although, do you think I have time for a bath before the invasion? I haven't been this filthy since I was a gong farmer cleaning out cesspits in old London."

"Jack," I said, again.

"Every day," he went on, scraping the inside of his ear with a long yellow fingernail, "buried to my chest in human excrement. I did not allow myself to be born again in Britain for another three hundred years after that experience."

"You're sounding awfully peevish for a man who was in a *coma*," I remarked, walking toward the farmhouse. "What were you doing, anyway?"

Jack's jaw tightened. "Meditation."

He was lying, of course. But there was nothing productive in berating an immortal for the truth. All I'd get in return would be more enigma, more confusing riddles, and that oh-so-wise-man secretive smile that always made me want to throw a magnificent tantrum.

"It looked like torture," I said, simply.

There was no air conditioner in the old farmhouse, but inside felt cool, and smelled like chocolate. Mary had just been baking. It reminded me of my mother, and her face flashed in front of me, fresh and startling. Less than a day ago, I'd seen her alive in this kitchen.

God, that hurt.

I let the rest of the house soothe me. Shadows and pale edges, reflections of light from the windows, formed soft lines that relaxed my eyes. I heard a hum of music—just a radio set to a classical station—but it made me think of Grant.

The television on the counter was turned to the news. And, of course, *that* video was playing. It was totally silent, volume turned down. But it wasn't just the television that was muted. The kitchen, the house, the world. I could hear my heart beat.

My grandfather stopped, staring. I turned my back to the television and walked to the kitchen sink. Got myself a glass of water.

Jack made a disgusted sound. I didn't turn around.

"Congratulations," he said. "The apocalypse has arrived."

"Which one?" I asked.

"And millions are now convinced that demons are real," he added, ignoring me. "Although . . . just as many might believe this is a hoax."

I finally looked at the television. It showed a still shot from the recorder, and though the image was somewhat blurry, it was clear enough: What had killed those frat boys and their girlfriends did not look human.

I'd seen a lot of *humans* who didn't look human. Disfigurement could do that. Women's faces melted to the skull from acid burns, men caught in explosions that ripped their bodies to shreds. Too much plastic surgery had the same effect. To be human was one thing, but retaining the *appearance* of humanity—that required a superficial, very fragile, balance.

This was different. What I saw in that still shot was tall, gray, and lean, with arms and legs that were little more than ropes of sinew and leather. Narrow faces, blade-sharp cheekbones, chins that narrowed to points that resembled spearheads. Chains and long braids of silver hair that looped around chests gaunt and hard with bone. And those *hands*: massive, striated with muscle, each fingertip as long and deadly as a pitchfork tine.

But the eyes staring out of that photograph made every-thing else seem like a cheap trick; stare too long, and it felt the same as being shoved naked into a night blizzard: repulsed with bone-raw cold, a heart-flinching *fuck you*. And that was how *I* felt—knowing what I did—being who I was. I couldn't imagine how the rest of the world was tak-ing it. No one had been rioting in Taiwan, but that was halfway across the world. Here in Texas, in America? I was too insulated on the farm, in this business of death. I didn't know what people looked like anymore.

"Folks see that and have to be shitting themselves," I said.

Jack raised his brow. "This is the age of the horror movie. Photoshop, computer hackers, makeup artists. Special effects. What is *real*, my dear? Absolutely nothing."

I did not relax. "They'll run tests on those remains. Check for saliva, study the wounds—the fucking teeth marks on the bones. Someone is going to sit up and pay attention to the *possibility*, Jack. It doesn't matter how many possessed people we use to run interference."

"Of course," he said, and even beneath the grime his knuckles were white around the metal box he still held. "You should have killed the demons when you had the chance."

I expected bluntness, but hearing the words hurt. Because wasn't I still thinking the same thing?

"Even their children?" I stared out the kitchen window at the empty pasture, which ran up against a heavy line of trees. Something lean and silver flitted just beyond those pale trunks—a glimpse, a hint.

Jack was silent a moment. "Yes."

I looked down at my stomach, at my hands touching my stomach. For a moment I felt very far away from that part of my body, as if there were a million miles between my head and the area below my waist, a million miles that I could not cross, a million miles that would never be mine, which already stretched in front of the life inside me and the life that would grow inside her, and again, and again, descending through blood and demon until we outlasted this world and others, until we outlasted life itself, until there was nothing but the road.

Maybe that was what it felt like for all mothers. I didn't know.

I turned and looked Jack dead in the eyes. "Will you help or not? I can't handle both the Aetar *and* this. It's too much."

My grandfather leaned against the table, hugging the metal box against his stomach. He studied me, then the rest of the kitchen—slow, methodical, thoughtful. Until his gaze stopped on the old bloodstain in the cracked, linoleum floor. His fingers stopped moving. His expression never changed, but his eyes lost their focus. I didn't worry it was another relapse. I knew what the bloodstain meant—to him, and me.

"Jolene," he murmured, then, after a long moment: "Why does it still hurt?"

I swallowed hard. "She was your daughter. Maybe the body you made her with is dead, but she was yours." My voice dropped to a whisper. "My mother was yours."

Jack drew in a deep, shuddering breath, and looked at the television. "The Aetar have not attempted to contact me."

"But they know how to find you?"

"We have ways. The same way we know when one of us has died." He sighed and glanced at me. "I always knew this day would come."

"They'll try to kill Grant."

"No, my dear. They'll want to *study* him. A far worse fate."

"They used a poison on him."

"Of course. I'm familiar with it."

"Of course," I echoed. "Mary made Grant eat *marijuana* as an antidote." I paused again. "You can't imagine how that surprised me."

"I'm surprised anything still surprises you." Jack ran his fingers over the table—an idle, thoughtful, gesture. "The cannabis was native to their world. As was the poison, made from another plant. A delicate little thing with a red blossom. We learned those secrets from them, you know. They needed to protect *themselves* from the Lightbringers, in case any went rogue."

His fingers folded into a loose fist, and he rapped the table, lightly. "Some of us . . . seeded the antidote on as many worlds as we could manage. Call it a . . . protest, of sorts. For those who became disgusted with the direction of the war. We hoped that if any survivors found their way to those planets, they would have the comfort of knowing that . . . some protection was still theirs. That they weren't entirely alone."

A number of sarcastic comments filled me, but I didn't indulge. This was an old conversation, old and painful, and if I could forgive Zee and the boys for their interplanetary genocide, then I could forgive my grandfather and accept his attempts at redemption.

The only difference, of course, was that the boys never tried to make excuses or paint their activities in a different light. They never pointed out the good they'd done, if any . . . because they accepted that no good outweighed the terror. No good deed lessened the bad. Making the attempt was a sign of weakness. It showed no honor.

"I asked the Mahati to set aside the head of one of the creatures they sent. You'll need to look at it."

"Of course," Jack said, quietly.

"Do you know how they'll strike again?"

"Just that they will. Two of our kind have died in the last five years, both on this world. That's more than have perished in a *million* years, my dear. They sent a Messenger to question me, and she never returned, her connection to them severed. They'll know that *I* couldn't have done that." Jack rubbed his face, shaking his head. "A Lightbringer. The only being in the universe who can kill us. Besides you. And I suspect they don't realize what you're capable of, my dear. Let us hope they don't."

"They know our daughter is a threat."

"A worse threat than Grant. They can't allow her to live.

With the boys as her protectors, with your blood in her veins, they won't be able to control her."

"When they realize they failed . . ."

"They'll try again. Throw you back in the Wasteland if they can. Attempt to separate you from the boys, then carve her out of you. She's far more of a priority than Grant, trust me."

My knees almost buckled when he mentioned the Wasteland: a sliver on the edge of the Labyrinth. The endless oubliette where things were thrown to be forgotten. No light. Nothing at all. Almost as bad as the void. I still had nightmares from that place. I'd lost my mind there, lost my humanity. I'd only survived because the boys had nourished, even breathed for me. A baby would never last. The idea of it made me ill.

I looked him dead in the eyes. "How did they do it, Jack? How did they hurt my daughter? All it took was a look."

"Wasn't just a look," he said, sounding disgusted. "It took power. Perhaps, if it had been daylight, and the boys were protecting you, it would have been more difficult. I just don't know. But we made your bloodline, my dear. We might not be able to kill you—easily—but you are not entirely immune to us." He gave me a curious look. "You're lucky Grant was able to save your child. I would have thought your immunity to his power would have extended to her."

"Very lucky," I said, deciding not to tell him about the bargain I'd made. "Is there *any* place that's safe for us? If we leave this world?"

"No." Jack hesitated. "Run, if you like. But the Aetar *will* find you, and it will be war."

I stared at him, utterly deflated. "You should go take a bath. I'm getting cholera just from looking at you. And something's living in your beard."

"I got lonely." He glanced down at the metal box in his hands. "Is there a safe place to put this?"

"Jack," I began.

"You called me Grandfather, earlier," he reminded me,

and there was something about him that suddenly seemed very old and frail, and not even remotely immortal.

I tasted the word in my mouth. "Grandfather. Is there anything I should know?"

"Nothing. And nothing that would harm you . . . or her." His glaze flicked down to my stomach, then bounced away—to the television set, the window, anywhere but my eyes.

My entire body prickled: pins and needles. The boys and their rough dreams, struggling to wake. Not a good sensation. A warning.

But nothing happened. No explosions. No doorways opening to other worlds. My grandfather walked around me, and the putrid scent of him, that miasmic, fecal funk, made me swallow hard and lean against the table.

"A bath sounds delightful," he called out over his shoulder. "I saw a hose by the barn. I think I'll turn it on myself first, just to get the large chunks off. And the vermin."

I shook my head and turned off the kitchen television set. The front door opened and closed. I didn't move from the table. I didn't look at the bloodstain in the linoleum. Or out the window, where I'd probably glimpse one of the thousand demons hiding on this farmland.

I stared at my stomach instead, at my hands resting on my stomach. Specifically, my left hand. My wedding ring.

I'd never indulged in feelings of loneliness. Too dangerous. I'd learned that after my mother's murder. Loneliness could swallow you up, like a disease. Make you vulnerable to anything, even a smile.

But then I'd stopped being lonely. And what was more dangerous? Loneliness? Or having friends and family who could be taken from you?

"Grant," I murmured, reaching for him—which was as easy as opening myself to the love we shared. Always there, always burning. Heat speared through my chest, straight to my heart: golden light, hot as the sun, warming bone and blood. Our bond. In life, until death.

My cell phone rang.

I pulled it from my jeans, and smiled to myself when I saw the number. *Like magic.* I could cross vast distances in a heartbeat—travel through time—and at this very moment, five demons slept on my skin.

But a telephone felt like the biggest miracle of all.

"Hey," I answered, hearing a static buzz across the connection.

Grant said, "They're dying."

CHAPTER 11

———————◆

I never had a dog when I was growing up.

Once, when we passed through Miami, I made the mistake of warming up to a stray mutt that was rooting around the bench where my mother and I were having ice cream. She told me not to feed the dog my waffle cone—but, whatever. Dog was hungry. Dog had big eyes.

Dog needed a home. I was twelve and needed a dog. He wasn't very big, and he had a goofy grin and big, floppy ears. He stuck close to me like it was love. My heart wanted to put him inside me and never let go.

I didn't let go. I convinced my mother to let us take him. The dog was overjoyed. We put him in the station wagon and drove out of Miami.

Then, that night, the boys woke up.

And the dog, terrified by them, ran away.

I cried so hard. I looked for him like crazy. My heart broke over that dog. I worried about him for years. Sometimes I still worry, even though I know he must be dead. All I hope is that he found someone who loved him, that he didn't go hungry. I hope soft hands touched him and made him a home.

Peace. For the dog.

And very little peace for me.

IT was hot under the trees, and the flies that grazed my tattooed arms stuttered as though electrocuted and dropped dead into the grass.

There were a lot of flies. No discrimination when it came to dead bodies. Demons, humans, were all the same. Meat. Blood. Bone. I stood beside a dead Mahati—old, wrinkled, wrapped in the braids of his hair. Bloody vomit covered his lower chin and chest, and his one remaining hand was caked in a viscous red slime that still glistened in the afternoon light. The stench was vile.

Four feet away lay another Mahati, this one still alive. A child, with whole limbs and smooth silver skin pulled taut over jutting ribs. Vomiting had already begun, splashed over the grass: a color of red that was sharp as a prick in my eyes.

His mother crouched beside him. She didn't look well, either. Patches of skin around her throat and chest had darkened to the color of tarnished silver, and there was an unfocused roving quality to her gaze that couldn't settle on her child—or Grant, who stood over the young demon, singing: a low reverberating *om* sound that slithered over my tattooed skin like a million little snakes.

I'd found him like this. No attempt at conversation, not even on my part, but I'd placed a bottle of water in his hands, along with a bag of pretzels; and he'd stopped just long enough to eat a bite, drink the bottle, then carry on. All the while, watching me with those dark eyes. I wanted to reach inside his brain and give it a good shake.

"It is not working," said Lord Ha'an.

"Grant can manipulate energy on a cellular level to

induce healing. Broken bones, cancer, gunshot wounds. But this *is* different."

"Poison," he murmured with disgust.

I wasn't so sure we were still dealing with a poison; and that terrified me. Ha'an didn't seem to be picking up on the same clues—maybe, because his people had never fallen ill before. "You're sure none of them munched on those dead humans?"

"I am certain. They cannot lie to me."

"And you? You ate the hearts of the Mahati who consumed them. How do *you* feel?"

He hesitated. "No different."

I held his gaze. "Really."

"I am *not* deceiving you," he muttered. "But there *is* a . . . darkness . . . dimming the energy I share with my people. My strength comes from them. If this continues, it *will* affect me."

I looked back at Grant. Deep shadows surrounded his eyes, and his tight white knuckles had cracked, bleeding. Other parts of him were cracking, too: I saw a blister forming on his lip, and parts of his arms and face were mottled red, as if capillaries were bursting beneath his skin.

You are being cannibalized.

A child in the womb is the ultimate cannibal. As a mother, I was more than happy to be consumed. But the demons were not unborn children—and Grant was being deconstructed before my very eyes.

He needed help. More than I could give him. It hit me, suddenly, who I could ask. But the fact that it had taken me this long to realize that possibility said everything about my reluctance to engage her.

First things first. I backed away, gesturing for Lord Ha'an to follow. "We need to see what Jack can tell us."

"The murderer." The demon lord's voice dripped with disgust, and his long fingers made a violent, striking gesture that could have easily taken out my eyes if he'd been aiming his hands at me.

But it still seemed directed my way: all the frustration,

anger, and humiliation I'd seen in him at rare moments over
the last three months. Finally, now, reaching the tipping
point.

We found Jack in the same spot where the human bodies
had been discovered the previous night. The only difference
now was the silence. No Mahati had remained in the
vicinity—and that had everything to do with my grandfather.

Jack was crouched, scratching his beard—which was
rustling with far more vigor than his fingers should have
accounted for. He didn't seem particularly disturbed by the
rotting corpses surrounding him. Humans were just meat.
Clothing his kind slipped on and off.

Mary stood behind my grandfather, fingering her dagger
and staring at the back of his head. I half expected her to
stab him. She didn't seem particularly bothered, either, by
the dead.

She'd been waiting for us on the edge of the camp—an
old human woman standing unafraid amongst demons who
thought she smelled tasty. She didn't need a bodyguard—the
woman was the fastest decapitator this side of planet earth—
but she'd had a dozen small demon children buzzing around
her like she was their fairy godmother, and I couldn't see
any of the adults wanting to fuck with that.

Her secret, as far as I could tell, was that she'd been
sneaking those little demon kids into my farmhouse kitchen
for months, baking them cakes and cookies, and basically
buttering up their homicidal little hearts with the two most
potent human drugs ever: sugar and chocolate.

Sweets for sweets, she would say—totally nonplussed by
the claws and tails and inhuman eyes.

Jack, on the other hand, always generated a very different
response from her. No fucking treats for him. If he made it
through the next hour with his heart still beating inside his
chest, it would be a miracle.

"I do not like this," Lord Ha'an murmured. "I am allow-
ing one of the architects of our imprisonment to walk freely

amongst us. He is Aetar. His kind committed genocide against mine. Against all the clans who were imprisoned."

"Get in line," I muttered. "We've got bigger problems."

Lord Ha'an did not answer me, his long fingers continuing to twitch violently against his massive thighs. He stared at Jack, who had picked up one of the skulls, staring into its empty eyes as though a voice were speaking to him. He didn't seem to notice the blood smearing his hands.

Mary knelt just behind him, poking the dark cavity of an empty eye socket with the edge of her machete. Her brow furrowed, and she went down on her knees, sniffing the remains. Her upper lip pulled back, baring her teeth in a snarl.

"Old Wolf," she whispered. "Fool wolf."

Jack frowned at her, then snapped his gaze back to the skull. He drew in a deep, quick breath. "Maxine."

I started walking to him. He said, "Wait. Stay back."

I paused midstep, watching a terrible stillness fall over my grandfather—as though his foot were pressing on a land mine.

"Don't come any closer," he said, and lowered the skull: slow, careful, as if it might explode. Mary stood, gliding sideways, keeping her body between the remains and me. "These people were engineered."

"We know that," I said sharply. "Tell me how."

Jack didn't answer me. I'd never seen him so shaken, like the foundation of his soul were being hacked at with a hammer. I could almost see the tremor of each blow—as though every time he breathed, some intolerable torment afflicted his chest. His hand pressed there, rigid fingers digging into his dirty T-shirt like claws.

I tried going to him. Mary stopped me with her sinewy arm: a rock-hard bar of bone and muscle. "Danger," she whispered, her gaze flicking down to my stomach. That was enough to make me keep still.

Jack eased back from the remains and ran a trembling

hand down his dirty, equally trembling, beard. "These humans were infected with a virus."

I stared at him, a lifetime of terrible movies parading through my mind. I didn't need my grandfather to confirm what I already suspected, but hearing it from him made it all very real, very terrible.

"A virus," I repeated.

A small part of me still hoped my hot dread was misplaced, but Jack didn't fuck around. He looked past me at Lord Ha'an. "If it works as it was meant to, the entire demon army will be dead within two weeks."

⚜

ONCE upon a time, I would have been delighted.

A euphoric rapture, delirious and jubilant, would have showered me with righteous, ecstatic glee. Once upon a time, news like that would have been a miracle of riches.

But people change. Sometimes they change so much they become unrecognizable to themselves.

No delight. No euphoria. Not for me. There were some things I never wanted to hear. And there were things I never wanted to hear in front of a demon lord.

Lord Ha'an snarled and lunged at Jack.

I was standing between him and my grandfather. Mary stepped neatly out of the way. I didn't move.

I didn't even blink.

He slammed into me with all the force of a bomb, but instead of throwing me backward, I grabbed his smooth silver braids and held on like a rodeo rider, flying sideways with dizzying speed—only to find myself yanked around with neck-snapping force. He tried again to reach my grandfather, but I dragged him back, holding on with all my strength.

Ha'an growled in frustration, twisting hard to slash at my face. In that split second before contact, the weight of the boys flowed upward, covering my head. His fingertips scraped harmlessly against my cheek and throat, but the strength behind that strike was so powerful I knew that without the boys protecting me, he would have taken off half my skull.

It didn't make me angry, though—just barely annoyed, and not even entirely at Ha'an.

My fist struck his ribs. He didn't flinch, trying again to slam me away from him. He wasn't even looking at me—just past my shoulder, where my grandfather probably was. God only knew if Jack was making faces at him. I wouldn't have been surprised. I tried again to stop him, but my blows bounced like I was made of foam. Ha'an was just too power-ful, fueled by the strength of all his people—as well as his own rage.

My feet left the ground. He threw me into a tree, and I heard a crack that wasn't my back, but instead the entire trunk snapping in half. I didn't feel a thing, but the rever-beration made my teeth rattle.

Enough, I thought, and the boys responded. I was still holding Ha'an's thick braids in one hand, and his hair began smoking. I would have thought all my other blows would have hurt him more, but the moment his hair was singed, he let out a wounded cry that made me think it wasn't exactly hair knotted around my fingers.

I was ready to stop. That was all I needed—for him to relent just enough to listen to me.

But when I tried to let go, my hand wouldn't obey.

He must be taught, whispered a sinuous voice.

Not me, not my voice, nothing that belonged to my imagi-nation. My trespasser, that very real and separate entity—existing, perhaps, in that seam between flesh and spirit, where just beyond the border of skin and bone, the soul was vast.

Shut up, I told that presence. *Go back to sleep.*

You made a promise, it murmured, and pushed right the fuck back.

Took me by surprise. I didn't even have a heartbeat's

warning. I lost myself. I lost, and all I could do was stand there like a fool.

My vision flickered: static, a channel fading in and out. A smile touched my mouth, one that wasn't mine, a smile that was wide and fat, and hungry. I would have bashed my face against a rock if I could have, cracked my head like an egg to make it stop. I fought, I fought—and the smile on my face only got wider.

Lord Ha'an's growl of pain choked into silence. I was present enough in my own skin to see recognition flow into his eyes, and fear.

"See me," I said, but those were not my words, not my voice, born instead from the oozing crawl of some thick, serpentine body uncoiling from my chest into my mouth. Nothing there, nothing physical, but the presence had weight, a spirit flesh just as real, and it filled me, and I could not stop it. I could not stop the hunger.

No matter how much I raged, I could not resist the biting jolt of pleasure and power.

"Now see your Queen," I whispered.

Lord Ha'an shuddered, dropping his shoulders. I wanted to tell him to stop, to stand straight—he was too proud, too proud for this—but there were no words. I was as lost as he was.

"You are nothing," murmured that voice, heavy on my tongue. *"You will not even live in our dreams."*

The demon lord's knees buckled. Veins bulged in his head and throat, and his green eyes protruded in one massive, repugnant, disfiguring pulse. He sounded like he was choking on his own tongue.

"You forgot your God," I said, and the ground beneath me dropped away, and a great expanse yawned—soft with night, throbbing with stars—the darkness coiled and cool, and sweet. Above me, the sun, trees, a blue sky shining, vibrating with life. It all ran down my throat like water, and I tilted back my head, swallowing the light, feeling it pass through me into the dark.

"Maxine," said a quiet voice, and heat blazed: golden, like sunlight breaking.

Just like that, the ground was solid beneath my feet, and in my throat there was only saliva, and a bitter taste, like blood. The presence, the thing inside me, smiled against my mouth. Close to laughter.

Soon, it whispered. *Soon, we hunt.*

Fuck you, I told it, as ineffectual as a mouse shaking its fist at a lion. Warm satisfaction—not mine—gathered around my heart, but that was just part of the slow retreat, the even slower relinquishment of my mouth, which felt like a bubble contracting in my throat; until, suddenly, I could breathe again.

But breathing wasn't enough. My legs felt strangely unattached to my body, and my skin tingled, burned. My jaw ached like I'd been chewing rock.

It took all my strength not to shudder, and I turned—very carefully. It was that, or fall.

"Maxine," Grant said again. And finally, I saw what I'd done.

The earth had disappeared around me. No grass, barely even soil—nothing but black sand, smooth as the surface of still water. Trees were gone, erased from existence—not a branch or leaf, not a piece of bark. If there had been rocks, I couldn't see them. If there were insects, they were gone. For twenty feet in every direction, a perfect circle of destruction.

Only Lord Ha'an had been left untouched. Mostly. His forehead had been burned with a single mark, a small hollow circle the size of my thumb—as though someone had taken a cigarette lighter to him. Except no one had. He was trembling, sweating, his eyes shut in pain or fear, or prayer—I didn't know. I was afraid to know.

I heard movement: Grant.

"Don't," I choked out, afraid for him to touch that sand. But he didn't hesitate, and nothing burned him.

He closed the distance between us, sliding his hand

through mine. No trace of his earlier anger. Just that solid strength I knew so well.

"I felt you pull away from me," he whispered. "I felt the darkness."

I leaned against him, and it helped bring me back to myself. My body, my life, my soul. I did not belong to the thing inside me. I did not belong to anyone but me.

But that wasn't the bargain I'd made, was it?

"I'm okay," I said, trying to smile for him. I couldn't do it. It felt crooked, grotesque. Reminded me too much of the darkness that had possessed me. Physical echoes, making me sick with myself.

Grant touched my face, brushed his thumb over my lips. Such shadows in his eyes, more than I'd ever seen before. I squeezed his hand. "How's the baby?"

He glanced down at my stomach. "Unaffected. Her light's still strong."

I nodded, one of those automatic movements that meant nothing. I was too rattled to hold still, but pretending I was engaged made it easier to hide how upset I was.

Lord Ha'an was on his knees. I bent to help him, and he flinched from me. "My Queen."

"Don't. It's me again. It's me, Maxine."

"No," he murmured, with heartbreaking loss in his voice. "It was never so. But for a time, we could pretend."

I kept my hand extended, and finally, carefully, he brushed his palm against mine. He did not take my help, though. After that brief contact, he stood on his own, swaying ever so slightly, touching the mark on his forehead.

"I'm sorry," I whispered.

"Do not be," he replied. "Do not, young Queen. You were as helpless as I. A good lesson for us both, I think." And then he lifted his head, but it wasn't to look at me. He stared at Jack, and his eyes were rimmed in blood and hate, his face stone cold, stone hard.

"All we suffered," he said softly. "And yet, there will never be peace for us."

Jack didn't seem to hear him. He was staring at me with both horrified dismay—and unabashed, unconcealed, fascination. It made me afraid all over again.

I tried to find my voice. Grant squeezed my hand. "Jack."

My grandfather blinked, tearing his gaze from me just long enough to take in the black sand. "Yes."

Grant glanced at Lord Ha'an. "What about a cure for this disease?"

Jack crouched, running his hands over the sand. "There won't be one."

Mary gave him a disgusted look. I felt my own dismay—partially at his answer, but also with the distracted way he said it. This was life or death, and he didn't seem to care.

"Jack," I snapped, and finally he looked up, alert and fully present. "You're certain there's no cure?"

"We don't *make* cures. When we decide to take a life, we take it. And then we replace it with something else."

"Of course you do," Grant muttered. "But *you* must still be able to make a cure."

Jack gave him an incredulous look. "*You'd* have more luck, lad. Killing is easier than curing, I promise you that. And creating viruses is *not* the same as modifying flesh. That's not my strength."

I thought about the Mahati who had vomited herself to death and the others lying sick not far from here. "Then whose is it? We have to do something."

Jack said nothing. Lord Ha'an walked from the sand, but it was without his usual grace.

"He will not lift a hand," said the demon. "He would rather see us die."

Without another word, he strode away into the woods.

"Well," Jack murmured. "Temper, temper."

I briefly closed my eyes. "We don't have time for you to find a new body, or else I would have let him kill you."

Silence. I finally looked at him, and his expression was surprisingly serious. "I am sorry, my dear."

I'm not the one you should be apologizing to, I almost

told him, but there was no point. Damage was done. Now, at the very moment when we all needed to be strong.

Grant gave him a scathing look and squeezed my hand. "More are falling ill."

Jack exhaled slowly. "It's begun, then."

"Does it *only* affect demons?" My voice sounded flat, dead. I wanted to hear his voice tell me the truth.

"Yes.

"You're sure."

"I am *sure*," he replied. "Only demons will be hurt by this disease, poison . . . whatever you want to call it. Those six humans who died here were living bombs."

Boom, I thought. We were all going to hell.

CHAPTER 12

IN hindsight, we were more than stupid: We were pretty much a lethal combination of dumb and dumber. But that's what happens when you get used to thinking you're invincible. You become careless. You don't think about consequences. By the time you do, it's always too late.

Regret doesn't have the power of the resurrection, wrote my grandmother in her journal. *Someone dies because of you, they stay dead.*

And the part of you that killed them stays dead, too.

WE buried those human bodies.

It was Mary and I. Grant went back to tend the sick with his voice. I wanted him to take a nap and eat, but that was a lost battle before I even opened my mouth.

I got shovels from the barn, and we spent two hours digging a hole. Fire would have been better, but I didn't want to attract anyone with the smoke. Folks in this area took wildfires seriously. It would bring a cop or a neighbor out here faster than if I had a gun battle on the front porch of the old house.

It was quiet. No demons around. When I wasn't looking at corpses I could focus on other things—genocide, murder, baby names, what I wanted for dinner.

Visions of fire and death. Circles of ash. Not necessarily in that order.

Most of the time, though, I thought about these ravaged dead and the people they had been—who was mourning them, or sick out of their minds with fear because these loved ones couldn't be found. So much grief, so much terror. And for what? Because someone wanted to commit an act of genocide?

Turn it around. Innocents were murdered to feed the Mahati on their killing sprees. Dead is dead. Intent is just the window dressing.

But it still wasn't right. Life couldn't be that cheap.

Even if it was.

"I need to find the Aetar who made this virus," I said, after we'd nudged, pushed, and kicked the corpses into the makeshift grave.

My grandfather sat nearby with the decapitated head of the giant who had attacked us. It smelled. It looked absolutely hideous. I'd kept my back turned the entire time but glanced over just long enough to see Jack give me a sour look. "And then what, my dear? The chances are slim to none that its maker is even here on earth."

"Better than none," Mary chimed in, packing down the earth with a tennis-worthy grunt. "Aetar pride is bright. Maker will want to be close to see the cutters die."

That made total sense to me. "Jack. Why didn't the Aetar release a virus during the first war?"

He wiped sweat off his nose. "The bonds with the Reaper Kings made the demons immune to everything. But those bonds are gone. The army stands alone."

"And if they bonded to me?"

"Pfft," he muttered. "You *are* powerful, my dear. But don't make the same mistake Grant did. You're no demon."

You are a god, whispered that sinuous voice, deep within. I ignored it. But Mary gave me a queer, sidelong look—and even Jack stared at me.

"What?" I asked.

"Your eyes," said my grandfather, frowning. "They . . . changed color for a moment. Even the whites disappeared."

I blinked. Mary grabbed my chin, peering at my face. "Wasteland. Nothing but night."

I knocked her hand away. "You're both crazy. And don't change the subject. Who amongst your kind could have made this virus, Jack?"

"I don't know," he said with exasperation. "You forget, it's been a long time."

"You're millions of years old," I shot back. "A long time? Ten thousand years is a blink of the eye."

"And this moment is barely a molecule." Jack slammed his fist into his thigh. "Enough, Maxine. Let me think. I need time. This thing here"—he gestured at the head beside him—"might have some answers. We all leave a signature on our creations, you know. A mark of the maker."

"No time, Wolf." Mary took my shovel from me. "Death time."

It was late afternoon, cusp of evening. The boys would be waking soon. I looked down at my tattoos, taking in their silver veins flowing through muscular knots, winding through scales and flattened claws, and around glinting red eyes staring up at me from my palm and forearm. A tug, a tingle, a shimmer of heat between them and me, sinking into my bones like some radiant fire. My boys, always dreaming.

"Will Zee and the others be safe?"

Jack hesitated. "I don't know."

That wasn't good enough.

❦

I sent Jack and Mary back to the house. No need for them
to be here, especially my grandfather. The less contact he
had with the demons, the better.

I stayed behind to find my husband.

No walls between the four different demon camps. No
obvious divide in territory. It was just air, grass, sunlight,
and trees. And some unseen line that demons did not cross
without invitation unless they wanted to get beaten—or
eaten.

Other than that, I didn't know much. Even though it was
my land, it didn't feel like home anymore. *I* was the trespasser, uncomfortable in my own skin—not sure where I
fit in.

Then again, I'd *always* felt lost. Never allowed to be part
of the world, except for the world my mother and the boys
inhabited—and the loneliness of that life, the isolation I had
begun to shed with Grant, always surged back with overwhelming force when I was around the demons.

My childhood, catcalling from the shadows. With it, a
perverse need to defend everything that had once been
wrong. Death and violence—balanced with equal amounts
of love. Impossible to have one without the other. I didn't
want my daughter to have that same life.

Although, given that her father was currently half-lost
under a pile of sweaty maggots—all of whom *possibly*
looked like they were trying to mate with him, or each
other—I suspected she was going to have a totally *different*
set of problems than I.

Love in my family takes us to weird places.

"Bonding ritual," growled the demon lord crouched
beside me. "Shurik, tactile. Burrower in them."

Oanu, demon lord of the Osul: Battle Cat of all Battle
Cats. I glanced sideways, and up—skimming over his silver
pelt, tufted ears, and iridescent blue eyes. "Uh-huh. It's
gross."

"Shed my fur when I see them," he rumbled, which seemed very much like an agreement.

I almost smiled, glancing at him again. It was hard not to look. Six feet tall at the shoulder, more than sixteen feet long from nose to tail. Tiny hooked claws covered his legs, jutting from beneath steel gray fur. His tail had spikes growing from the tip, and massive pads of metallic armor clung to his muscular back. A helmet covered part of his face, revealing leonine features and ice blue eyes. Like Lord Ha'an, he was bigger than his own people, stronger, and more beautiful. Deadlier, too.

"Sorry about . . . the other night," I said.

"A King beating a scrapper?" Oanu's tail lashed the air. "Disrespectful cub. Would have done the same." He hesitated. "Well . . . might have killed him, eaten his brains."

"The boys get hungry for brains," I said. "Generally speaking, it's been a life of deprivation with me."

Oanu glanced at my tattoos and gave me a toothy grin. "Life isn't worth living without eating your enemies."

"Glad we're not enemies."

"But to fight a true Queen," he murmured, looking at me like I was delicious, "that would be *glorious*."

My smile warmed—but that lasted only as long as it took me to look past Oanu at the Yorana who had gathered beneath the trees.

They watched my husband with thinly veiled disgust. Tall, lean, humanoid, with skin the color of cherries: a dark, bleeding red. Long black hair swooped high off their scalps in tumbling Mohawks; and small jewels were embedded in their concave chests. Their demon lord had been seductive, magnetic. His people shared the same dark charm.

I glanced back at Grant, his body still teeming with Shurik—undulating over him with a distinctly ecstatic energy, like he was some kind of drug. I'd never seen them so worked up. I'd deliberately stayed away from most bonding sessions, but the few I'd witnessed—early on—had been as energetic as dirt. Things had changed since then.

A low hum rolled from Grant's throat, more vibration than melody. A shimmering wave of energy passed over my skin, making the boys tug on me, restless.

The Yorana flinched, as though hit. Oanu shivered.

"Lightbringer," he rumbled in his deep voice. "Never thought to see one again."

"You're familiar with his kind?"

"Collected history when I was not killing. Soothed me. But then, later, Aetar used enslaved Lightbringers as weapons." The demon lord slapped a huge paw against the ground. "Strong then, protected by the bonds of our Kings. We ate them." He gave me a sidelong look. "Not protected now."

No, none of them were protected. And this demon lord might be dead by the end of the week if Jack was to be believed.

Grant's voice trailed away into silence. The woods were so quiet, except for soft, Shurik hissing sounds and my own heartbeat. I wouldn't have known that Oanu was beside me if I hadn't been looking at him.

"Power," said Oanu, with admiration in his soft, rasping voice. "Stole the bonds that kept the Shurik and Yorana alive. Bound them to his heart. Did this with his voice, killed with a word."

"He's just a man," I said. "A man with a particular skill."

"Just as you are skilled?" Oanu's toothy grin seemed a little more challenging this time. "Power accepted means power controlled. Worry me more, you deny yourself. Makes you . . . unpredictable."

Given the bargain I'd made, I didn't think denial was going to be a problem for much longer. I gestured toward my husband. "He's getting sick because of what he did."

"Yorana," Osul murmured, glancing at them with disdain. "Selfish Yorana. Hate that he is human. Taking power, returning nothing."

Which echoed Jack's assessment of the problem. "Can they be forced to change?"

"Must fear him or love him. Shurik love him. Yorana do not fear him." Oanu tilted up his massive shoulder in a shrug. "I think there is more to fear than love, but the Yorana . . . maybe they are not wise."

I would have been happy if the problem rested with the ugly little slugs. But no, the big handsome red demons were the assholes. Of course.

"Grant," I called. My husband twisted to look at me, and his mouth softened into the faintest of smiles. He looked a little less tired, his skin not as pale.

He didn't manage to disentangle himself from the Shurik. Quite a few came along with him, clinging to his body and draped over his shoulders. Some had burrowed beneath his flannel shirt. I swallowed hard. Oanu made a small, grunting sound like he was gagging deep in his throat.

"You told the Shurik about the illness?" I asked Grant, trying to ignore one of the little demons wriggling happily on his shoulder. I couldn't imagine what he'd done to make it react that way, but it was making a hissing sound that could have been a good stand-in for a girlish giggle.

"Everything." Grant raked his gaze over the Yorana with a cold scrutiny that was another sign of changing times. He had been a priest, once—his kindness radiant. But now he was growing harder. Sometimes I thought I was getting softer. It wasn't, I thought, supposed to be that way.

"You look better," I said.

Grant hesitated. "It's the Shurik. They've been wanting to . . . give back to me for some time. I refused before. I thought it was better that I try to influence them first, revert them to their original natures. It's been a slow process."

"And today?"

"Today I let them in. Just a little." He spoke so quietly I barely heard him. "And yes, it helped."

I couldn't imagine what it cost him to say that. I turned to Oanu. "Thank you for coming to speak with us. You understand the situation?"

"Perfectly," he said, with a low growl. "The Aetar

attacked your consort, attempted to kill your child, then poisoned our army with disease. They are cowards, and we will murder them."

"That's right," I deadpanned. "Shit's gonna get *real*."

A smile ghosted over Grant's mouth. "We need to find a cure. And keep the rest of you healthy."

"I'm sure war and destruction will fall neatly into place along the way," I added.

Oanu's claws flexed with pleasure. Behind him, one of the Yorana called out, with disdain, "We have heard from the Mahati that there *is* no cure."

I shot the red-skinned demon a hard look. "Then you'll die. And if you don't start giving your lord what he needs, you'll die even sooner."

The Yorana stiffened. "He has promised us our freedom to choose."

Oanu's ears twitched with surprise. I didn't even blink. Grant leaned forward on his cane, fixing his hard gaze on the red-skinned demons. Shurik dripped from his shoulders; several opened their terrible mouths and hissed.

"I'll keep my word," he said, with unexpected menace. "But if I die, so will you. And as I weaken, so will you."

The Yorana held very still, all that seduction and glamour sliding off their faces like water. I blinked, and suddenly their perfect skin had lost its luster, pocked with nicks and scars; and their hair was dull, limp, their bodies no longer radiating strength, health. A startling transformation: I could see their bones poking through lean, starved muscle. The jewels in their chests turned black.

"We have nothing to give," one of them said. "We eat, but it does not feed us. We need the hunt. We need the seduction."

They needed the energy, I realized. But that was impossible.

"I can change that," Grant said. "Let me help you."

The Yorana male spat on him.

Oanu snarled, but I was faster. My fist slammed into the

demon's chest, cracking the embedded jewel. The demon dropped like a stone, limbs twitching, black foam at his lips. An instantaneous, violent reaction. I didn't expect it. I almost wasn't sorry, until I saw Grant's face—and I remembered what he'd said, earlier.

Shame flushed my cheeks, but regret warred with anger: at myself, at him—at the demon dying on the ground. Grant dropped his cane, awkwardly falling to his good knee, power already rising in his voice.

Nothing to be done, though. Too far gone for saving.

I held my ground. Oanu growled, low and deep in his throat. "Respect or death. You know better."

The surviving Yorana bowed their heads. Grant stopped singing, and closed his eyes. I didn't want to look at him but steeled myself and held out my hand. Inside me, our bond was quiet.

But he took my hand, and with that touch: light, between us.

You still have me, I heard inside my head; his deep, soft voice. *No matter what. And I have you.*

I drew in a deep, sharp breath—and pulled my husband to his feet. His gaze never left mine—those knowing eyes, that sadness that made me sad and aching with love for him.

Grant looked at the other Yorana. "Decide what you want."

The red-skinned demons bowed their heads even more deeply—both to him and me. Then, without a word, they stooped and picked up their fallen companion, easily negotiating his twitching limbs. Blood ran freely from the cracked jewel.

Oanu watched them go, tail lashing. "Needed that."

Grant said nothing. His silence, despite the light between us, made me tense. "I wish the lesson hadn't been needed," I said, and the demon lord glanced at me.

"You are too gentle," he rumbled; then, "Is it true there is no cure?"

Grant's expression became even grimmer. "That's what we were told. I don't believe it, though."

"Neither do I," I said. "There *will* be a cure, Oanu."

There had to be. Maybe Jack was right, maybe no cure existed, but I didn't believe that whoever had made this thing wouldn't know how to fix it. The problem was finding its creator—and then making him help us. All without losing our lives, our freedom, and maybe this entire world.

Rescuing demons is more difficult than murdering them, I thought.

And definitely not as rewarding.

⚜

SUNSET was on my heels. I told Grant that if he didn't come back to the house for dinner, I would let the boys cook for him.

He had some experience with that. The last time hadn't sent him to the hospital, but he'd lived in the bathroom for an entire day, making sounds that made me wonder if a bobcat was coming out both ends.

Grant sat beside me in the passenger seat. I didn't say a word when the giggling Shurik came along for the ride. Some perched on his shoulders, while others were tucked inside his shirt, stuck to his ribs. I pretended not to notice, but it wasn't easy. I remembered their former lord, who had taken near-sexual delight in inhabiting the bodies of humans, slowly eating them from the inside out until there was nothing left but loose skin, and viscous bone.

The six-wheeler bumped and rattled us across the grassy, rut-scarred pasture that separated the farmhouse from the wooded area of my land. Birds scattered before us, and several rabbits darted away, startled. I was surprised the smell of predators hadn't already motivated them to get clear of this place. Or that the Osul hadn't hunted them all dead.

A golden glow made the warm air shimmer; everywhere, a lush glint, a hush in the light itself as the day softened into that last evening gleam. My favorite time of day—though it was ruined by the feeling of something's watching me. I glanced sideways at the Shurik on Grant's shoulder. It didn't have eyes, but its sharp little mole mouth was pointed in my direction. I stared past it at my husband's strong, jagged profile.

"I'm sorry," he said, breaking the silence between us. "I shouldn't have said those things. Earlier, I mean."

My hands tightened around the wheel. "How long have you felt this way?"

"I don't," he said flatly. "I've never felt that way about you."

"That, I know." I suddenly felt nauseous, warm. "What I meant is . . . how long have *you* felt like a killer?"

Grant remained silent for the rest of the ride. It wasn't until I had parked in front of the porch and was ready to slide out that he grabbed my wrist. It was my right wrist, and when his hand touched the armor, I felt a spark flash through me, followed by an oozing heat. He didn't seem to feel it on his end—his hand remained where it was, and his fingers squeezed once, gently.

"I didn't notice it at first." A faint sheen of sweat touched his brow; and the bright flush was back, like a fever. "It started in my dreams. Nightmares that I was hurting people, nightmares that were so real that I was half-convinced I'd done those things."

"Memories. Not yours."

"I started feeling that same hunger while I was awake. Not to eat anyone," he added quickly. "But thinking about people as food isn't much different from looking at them as something disposable, that can be controlled, manipulated. The impulse is the same."

I sat on that for a moment, unsurprised. "I feel like there's more you're not telling me."

Grant pulled his cane from the seat behind us. "I don't know how to fix this, Maxine. Using my gift to hurt others has always been *my* nightmare. What happened with the demon in Taiwan . . . I didn't even think. It felt natural."

He was still hiding something from me, but I played along. "It felt righteous."

"Yes," he said quietly.

"Have you spoken to the demons?"

"The Shurik aren't the problem," he replied, as the fat little worm on his shoulder exhaled a rather pleased-sounding squeak and wriggled out of sight beneath his shirt. "They're very . . . receptive. It's the Yorana."

"They can go fuck themselves," I muttered, feeling the sun begin to set behind me. "Come on. I need pie."

Mary was already in the kitchen when we walked inside. Television on, playing a Hallmark movie, one of those Westerns starring an unconvincingly grim and battle-hardened Kevin Sorbo.

"Where's Jack?" I asked her. The boys were tugging hard on my skin, ready to wake. Soon, any minute now.

She made a face and dug into a little plastic bag of weed. Which had taken on a whole new meaning for me. When she offered some to Grant, he hesitated—and then took a pinch to chew. Made him grimace, but he didn't spit it out. I wondered if his physiology was just different enough to keep him from getting high on the stuff.

Mary also stuffed a pinch of that shit into her mouth. "Wolf is cutting off dirt."

So, he was finally taking a bath. Hallelujah.

Grant sank into a chair with a sigh. I ruffled his hair as I walked to the fridge—then stopped, frowning, and came back to him. I felt his forehead again.

"You have a fever," I said, feeling dumb. Yes, his face had been red. But I'd thought it was some symptom of the strain the demons were putting him under. Maybe it still was. But his skin was hot.

"I'm tired, that's all," he said, leaning his elbow on the table. Mary frowned, drawing close. She bent, peering at his face, and her hand darted out to grab his jaw. He tried to pull away, but she held him still, peering into his eyes.

The Shurik nosed free of his shirt, the tip of its sharp

mouth peeling back just slightly to reveal tiny, needlelike teeth covered in slime.

"None of those are inside you, right?" I asked warily.

Grant, still held in place by Mary, gave me an exasperated look. I shrugged at him, totally not sorry for asking.

"Not right," Mary muttered, and tore her gaze from him to give me the same hard stare.

"What?" I asked, always a bit unnerved when she looked at me like that. Mary's scrutiny was usually just a prelude to extreme amounts of violence.

She didn't get a chance to answer. My phone started ringing. Made me jump. Even Grant flinched.

I didn't recognize the number. Almost didn't answer. But my instincts tickled.

"Yes?" I said.

"Fucking Hunter," replied a woman on the other end. I didn't recognize the voice, but the anger was familiar. Definitely some human possessed by a demon.

I stayed silent, waiting. The woman let out a ragged sigh. "You tackled me last night. I'm the waitress from Houston."

"You have my number?"

She made a wet, hacking noise that sounded like she was gargling wet fur. "Forget that. I'm sick, you *bitch*."

"What?"

"Don't you understand?" Her voice broke. I heard another wretched cough, and I realized she was vomiting.

I didn't understand at first. I was in denial. All I could think was that she hadn't been anywhere near those dead bodies. It took me a long, confused moment before the truth hit: It wasn't her, it was me. The boys had been tramping all over those dead humans, touching them—then touching *me*. So had Zee.

Me, me, me. And I had touched *her*.

"Wait," I said, almost stuttering. "Which part of you is sick? Your host?"

"What the fuck do you think?" she snarled weakly. "Yes, my host. My host, who I feed from."

I looked at Grant, and his fever suddenly meant something totally different to me.

Jack had said this thing couldn't infect humans. But what if he was wrong? If I had infected the demon-possessed waitress in Houston, then perhaps she'd gone back into her restaurant and infected her customers. If they'd gone out and infected others . . .

I touched that possessed old woman in Taiwan.

"Damn," I said. "Oh, damn."

Grant had been watching me the entire time, his expression becoming ever more grave. But something else passed over his face—a tightening of his throat, his lips pressing so hard together they turned white.

That was the only warning we got. He stood so fast his chair fell over, and he lurched toward the kitchen sink. He was in such a rush, he didn't grab his cane. Mary caught him before he toppled over, but that happened anyway—he fell against the sink and started puking.

I stared, horrified. I heard the demon-possessed woman saying something to me, but I hung up on her and was next to Grant in moments. He had stopped vomiting, but was still spitting, coughing. I looked down into the sink and all I saw was normal puke—a swimmy goop of food fragments and bile. Relief sank through me.

"It's ok—" I began, just as a violent shudder rolled him up on his toes, and he bent over, again. The sound he made was terrible, like someone had shoved a barbed hook down his throat into his guts and was yanking up, yanking and tearing him inside out.

What rushed from his mouth was a blur, but I saw the glint of darkness, a splash of red in the sink—and parts of my vision blacked out.

The sun set, and the boys woke up.

CHAPTER 13

GROWING up, the plan was always this: I'd get pregnant one day, with a stranger. And then I'd die. Young.

As far as I knew, that was how it had worked for most of my ancestors. No one ever lived to see old age. No one ever got married. Maybe there was love, but no happily ever after. Just mothers and daughters, and demons. Wandering together, alone, down a road as old and dark as blood.

But I was married. I was in love. Which, when you think about it, is almost as rare as carrying five demons on your skin.

And much more precious.

FIFTEEN minutes later, the only light in the farmhouse living room came from the television, and it cast a flickering blue glow on razor-sharp spines of flexing hair and scaled, muscular chests. Raw and Aaz lounged on the floor in front of me, chewing on coils of barbed wire. The spikes jutting from their backs quivered with each breath.

Aaz reached over his shoulder, yanked one free with a wet crunch, and used it to pick between his jagged teeth. Bits of barbed wire hit the rug. Dek—coiled against his leg, gnawing a teddy bear—gave him a disapproving look and licked up the scraps with his long black tongue.

Grant lay on the couch, a cool wet rag on his forehead. A bucket was on the floor beside him. He hadn't puked again, but he had this sour, grim twist to his mouth that made me think he was fighting hard not to hurl. Zee crouched on the back of the couch, leaning down to sniff at him.

"You shouldn't be here," Grant muttered between clenched teeth.

"I feel fine," I said, even though I didn't, really. I'd never been sick a day in my life, but something in my body felt . . . off. The skin along my legs hurt, like the fibers of my jeans had suddenly contracted some spiky substance that was pricking me. My muscles ached. I felt warm.

Zee gave me a quick, concerned look when I told Grant I was fine—but he didn't blow my cover. Instead, he leapt over us to the floor, prowling around Jack and Mary. The old woman was pacing. My grandfather stood against the wall, arms folded over his chest. He was wearing Grant's clothes, and they looked odd on him. Grant dressed like one of the models from an Eddie Bauer catalogue: rough-hewn, an upscale lumberjack. Jack still looked like he'd be more comfortable in his old dirty sweatpants and T-shirt filled with holes.

He wasn't even looking at us. Instead, he seemed engrossed in a rerun of *Magnum P.I.* that Raw and Aaz were watching, sound on mute. The little demons had been skipping off to Hawaii some nights, bringing home tropical shirts and surfboards, and fragrant leis that they always dropped over my head.

My husband was dying while Tom Selleck flirted with a girl in a string bikini. Life could be horrible sometimes.

Zee pointed his long black claw at Mary. "Sick."

She didn't stop pacing. Zee looked at Jack. "You sick, too."

He didn't look away from the show. "I know. I felt the virus begin to work on me before I entered my bath."

"You sure were quiet about that," I snapped.

My grandfather finally tore his gaze from the television. "And what would I have accomplished with hysterics, or even a warning?" Fury blasted through his expression, a terrible desperate rage that made me feel, for a moment, afraid. I'd never seen him so angry, and it reminded me again that he was not human, no matter what he looked like—because no human, nothing mortal, was capable of the luminous, godlike savagery that lit his eyes.

"You said humans wouldn't be affected. You were *sure*."

"I was wrong." Jack closed his eyes. "The virus had been modified. I didn't see it."

"You see everything else."

"I made a mistake."

"You won't die from that mistake," I said simply. "But we will."

"Not you," Grant said, so quietly I barely heard him. But that had to be wishful thinking on his part. I hadn't said a word about not feeling well, but Grant had to know, just from looking at me. Jack, too. When he turned away from me, jaw tense, I had no doubt at all.

I'm sick, I thought, filled with dread. All I could think about was that Mahati who had died in the snow; and Grant, puking in the sink. *I'm sick, too.*

But for how long, really? Had the thing that lived inside me saved my daughter just to let me die, too? That wasn't part of the bargain.

I could make other bargains.

You have nothing left, whispered that sibilant voice, floating through me like a flake of drifting ash. *And a Queen does not beggar herself for nothing.*

I closed my eyes. Grant's hand found mine and squeezed.

"How long do I have?" he asked Jack.

My grandfather tugged hard on his beard; I heard a muffled squeak from inside that tangle of hair. "I don't know, lad. It works fast on demons, we've seen that. But you're still alive. Mary is still strong. Maybe it will burn itself out."

"I infected a demon-possessed waitress in Texas," I told them, glancing at my phone, which was on the couch beside me. "Another of her possessed friends texted me five minutes ago. Her host was just taken to the hospital. The parasite itself already fled."

I hadn't wanted to share that information. The room got very quiet. Grant said, "It doesn't benefit the Aetar to make something that destroys humans. You need their bodies, too."

Jack shook his head, all that rage leaving him, deflating his entire body until he sagged like a sock puppet against the wall. "We have billions of humans on other worlds. Worlds upon worlds upon worlds that we control. Earth is nothing to us but a historical footnote in an otherwise tedious existence. And it is easy to quarantine a world. They have no fear that this will spread."

"And if it did, they would be highly motivated to develop a cure," I said. "The Aetar don't want to lose their toys."

He gave me a sharp look. "My dear girl—"

"It was bad enough when it was the demons," I interrupted him. "But I can't take the risk that it'll wipe out humans, too. Even if it just kills a fraction of the population, that's too many."

Grant jerked and fumbled for the garbage bin. He barely reached it before he started vomiting. The little Shurik who had been hiding under his shirt—so quiet I had almost forgotten it was there—made a small, hissing sound. So did Dek and Mal, hugging my throat and quivering. Or maybe I was the one who was shaking.

Raw and Aaz scrambled to Grant and the garbage bin. I was already leaning over him. Not touching but close enough to give what comfort I could.

And that wasn't much at all. I felt so helpless. There was nothing to fight here. Nothing I could threaten or destroy. Disease had no voice, except for the voice of the man I loved. Disease was the ultimate possessor. A demon, all its own.

But I was good at fighting demons. Somehow, I'd fight this one. My daughter was going to have her father. I was going to have my husband. If I accomplished nothing else, it would be those two things.

I stood up. Grant tensed, trying to sit up with me. Raw and Aaz made annoyed, clicking sounds with their tongues, and pushed him back down. Dek bit into the remains of his teddy bear and slithered into my husband's lap with it.

"Can *you* make a cure?" I asked Grant.

He swallowed hard. Aaz dragged a bottle of Gatorade from beneath the couch and pushed it into his hand. "I wouldn't know where to start."

I tried to smile. "Then try to rest. I won't be far."

Grant gave me a wary look. "Whenever you say that . . . all hell breaks loose."

"I say a lot of things that precede bloodshed." I bent to kiss him gently on the mouth. "But I always come home to you."

He caught the back of my head and held me close, turning so that his face was buried in my neck. His skin was hot—but then, so was I. Standing wasn't as easy as it should have been.

"Love you," he whispered. "Sorry I haven't been myself."

I ran my fingers through his hair. "I'll beat you up when you're better."

He snorted and fell back against the couch, too exhausted to touch me for even another moment. I pulled back his shirt and looked at the pale little Shurik clinging to his chest.

"You," I said, in a cold voice. "If you and your kind value this man, then you will get those Yorana in fucking line, do you hear me? Because if he dies, you die. They *all* die."

The Shurik bared its sharp little mouth and gurgled at me. Zee muttered, "It understands."

"Good." I leaned close, battling a clammy surge of squeamish disgust. "Grant believes in you. I think he might even love you little turds. So you goddamn better deserve it. Protect him. Give him your strength. Give him what he needs. Or else *I'll* kill you."

This time the Shurik reared up and hissed at me. Zee snapped his teeth, and it shrank back just a little—but there was still something defiant in the twist of its flesh.

Zee snorted. "Tells you that honor and loyalty is Shurik heart."

I narrowed my eyes. "I don't think that's all it said."

"Also called you stupid."

"That's better." I looked at Grant, who laid a calming hand inside his shirt. The Shurik snuggled against his palm like a cat. Either I was getting brainwashed, or maybe I just didn't give a shit anymore, but seeing that didn't immediately make me want to vomit in my mouth. Probably a bad sign. "Did *you* understand what it was saying?"

"Not the specifics," said Grant, with the faintest of amused smiles. "But I could feel its intent. That was enough."

I kissed him again and backed away. "Jack, I need a word with you."

My grandfather looked at me like I was going to punch him in the nuts. But he followed me out of the farmhouse without a word, and the boys came with us, prowling the length of the porch and perching on the rail. Night hadn't completely fallen. The horizon held the faintest light of dusk, bleeding into the dark sky, washing out the stars just now gracing the night.

"What did you learn from that giant's head? Who made it?"

"The answer doesn't do us any good. The creature was designed by the Erl-King. You and I both know he's dead."

Dead years ago, by my hand—and Grant's. What a bastard. "How's that possible?"

"We've been engineering life for millions of years, my dear. The Erl-King had plenty of time to make those creatures before his imprisonment. No doubt they've been breeding on some Aetar-controlled planet and thought they were doing the work of their Gods by coming here to attack you and Grant."

I still didn't like the coincidence. "How many Aetar are there?"

"Now?" Jack thought a moment. "Before the war with the Lightbringers, we were a tribe that was one hundred and ninety-three strong. Now, our numbers have dwindled to a mere eighty-four."

It surprised me, hearing such an exact count. And how it seemed to be a number at odds with itself—large enough to feel dangerous to me, given what the Aetar were capable of—but small, too, when I thought that this was all that was left, forever. No ability to breed. No possibilities. Nothing but eternity.

No wonder Jack's kind clung so violently to mortal flesh—it kept them sane, gave them the illusion of life, death, evolution. They could have children—even if those children would never truly outlive them. They could pretend to have lives. Live the fantasy. Be the fantasy.

"Do you feel when they're close?" I asked him. "I know you feel their deaths."

Jack looked uncomfortable. "Yes. I can feel when my kind are near."

I stared at him. "And?"

"There is an Aetar on this world," he said, with some exasperation. "I can't tell you who or where."

"Can the others kill you?"

The question seemed to surprise him. "No."

"But they can imprison you. They've done it to others."

"Yes, and yes." Jack gripped the porch rail. "You want me to go to them?"

"Do you have any allies? Like Sarai?"

A rueful, bitter smile touched his mouth. "Of course. I suppose you're asking me to foment a rebellion? For what? Our greatest enemies?"

"For what's right," I told him. "And if that's not enough, then do it for me. And for your great-granddaughter."

"And Jeannie," he murmured, turning away from me— but not before his expression crumbled, ravaged by terrible grief. It made me think of Grant, the possibility of losing him, and I hurried off the porch before he could turn back around and see *my* face.

"Where are you going?" he called after me.

"For a walk." I managed to turn around and smile for him. "Don't look so scared."

Jack pushed away from the rail. "Maxine."

I started to run.

CHAPTER 14

I wasn't entirely human.

    My ancestors had been tampered with. Treated like animals in an experiment that resulted in a bloodline meant to serve only one purpose: to be a living prison for five of the most dangerous demons in existence. Five creatures responsible for the deaths of worlds. Five hearts filled with such hunger and rage that even those who considered themselves gods (the same gods who had massacred *billions* for their own entertainment) could not fathom their cruelty.

    What no one expected . . . what no one could have counted on . . . was that the prison made for those five demons would be the path to their redemption. That even *they* could have a change of heart.

    The heart is powerful.

    The heart is a weapon.

⊱⋅⊰

I didn't stop running until I reached the woods.

    It felt good. I needed the swing and rush of my body

flying across the land and the pulse of the boys thudding alongside me like wolves in the night. My footing was solid, my stride strong—I raced headlong into the darkness, nearly blind, and my thoughts scattered in a million different directions, trying to hold on to some idea, some truth, anything that would give me the answers I needed.

Dek and Mal sang, their voices twining as close and warm as their bodies around my neck. I looked up and saw the stars, like a scattering of diamonds, and a terrible longing pounded through my heart, a feeling of homesickness, and despair.

We have slept too long, whispered the darkness inside me. *The road sings, and we are hungry for dreams.*

Help me, I asked, ashamed and desperate. *I don't know what to do.*

You are the Hunter. I felt its cold smile press against my lips, and a terrible bottomless hunger crawled through me. *Even darkness cannot hide from you.*

I thought I was being teased, but instead of infuriating me, all I felt was resolve: an intoxicating, deadly conviction.

Yes, I could do this.

Yes, I believed. Even if it only lasted as long as this moment, that belief was everything, my entire world. It was power.

My left hand touched my stomach.

"It's okay," I muttered breathlessly, knowing some part of my daughter would hear and understand, even four months formed. "Mommy is good at impossible things."

Which was a lie. But for her, I could learn to be good at anything.

It was loud under the trees, but only because my heart was pounding so hard, it filled my ears with thunder. I saw flickers of movement, slender silver bodies slipping around the trees, but none came close. I thought again about the video playing on the news but couldn't muster even the same iota of concern I'd felt just yesterday. If humans knew about the demons—well, fuck it. I just wanted us to survive the week without vomiting our guts out.

Dizziness hit. I leaned against a tree, then clung to it. The moment I was still, I felt that fever gouge me—burning my skin. Pain crept up the back of my neck into my skull. Dek and Mal began kneading my shoulders with their little vestigial arms.

"I'm sick," I said to Zee.

"In us, too," he replied, dragging his claws through the dirt. "But, bodies strong. Bodies fight. Bodies burn it out."

"You can heal yourselves?"

"Already healing." Zee shrugged. "Aetar not stronger than *our* blood."

Relief filled me, but it was tainted with envy. Raw and Aaz pushed close, holding my hands. Zee tilted his head, studying me.

"I'm sorry," I said, ashamed I couldn't be more generous with my thoughts and emotions.

"No need," rasped the little demon, with terrible gentleness. "Not now, not ever. We already burn some from you, in sleep. We burn more, when we sleep again. Keep you, little light, safe."

I sagged against the tree. I didn't know how our physiologies were bound together, just that the boys were more than tattoos when they were on my body—they were part of me, as much a part of me as my own blood and bones. In times of starvation, they could nourish me. If I were thrust to the bottom of the sea, they could breathe for me. I should have known they could heal me, too.

But if I was still sick, even after their protection, Grant couldn't have much longer.

Just like that, exhaustion set in, tearing through me like a bomb. I'd never felt so drained, so fast. I sank down to the hard, uneven ground, and Raw and Aaz crawled into my lap. Zee hung back, looking into the trees, his expression thoughtful.

How do we survive this? I asked myself. *How do we all come out alive?*

I stared up through the trees, catching glimpses of the sky. I'd been alone for so long, sometimes it was difficult to remember I had friends, allies, people I could call on for help. Even now, desperate, I could still forget.

But I hadn't forgotten *him*.

Oturu.

I'd been trying to keep the demon from my thoughts. Been fighting, with all my might. Because he couldn't be here. Not now. It was too dangerous, too unpredictable. If he got sick, I'd never forgive myself.

All in vain, though. It was night, and my need had probably been broadcast across the stars—straight from my heart to his, or however we were connected.

Thunder first, but thunder without a sound. Just the rumble, a vibration in the air that purred through my bones and blood, settling in my chest, drifting down into my stomach. I looked up again and saw a shadow flash. Dek and Mal tensed with a chirp. Zee sighed.

Branches parted. I saw his feet first—a cluster of knives, shining and deadly—followed by the hungry folds of a flowing, drifting cloak. In the shadows, all the demon became was grace, a hush of space that his presence held, and swallowed.

"Oturu," I said, gazing at that hard, pale jaw, the slant of his mouth, the abyss that hid his eyes beneath the brim of his wide, sloping hat. "Stay back."

Tendrils of hair flowed through the air like crooked veins—twisting and floating down to my face. I staggered away from him, clawing at the trees to help me stay upright—but he made a sharp sound, and my body froze. No one else had that power over me. But Oturu was different. Oturu had the promise of my bloodline. That for him, we would be powerless, at his mercy, as a sign of the ultimate trust.

Our lives, as a pledge of friendship. A pledge that had created a bond that had transcended generations, all because of a single kindness my ancestor had shown him—one act of mercy that had created a link between our blood and his.

"Don't," I whispered, begging him with my voice. "I'm sick. You can't be here. You might get infected."

Oturu only drew closer, his floating tendrils of hair brushing my skin, lingering on my lips. He leaned in so close we could have kissed, and still I could not see his eyes. But I felt him, the weight of the abyss, the touch of his hair as it wound through my own. I should have been disgusted, disturbed, but I searched my heart and felt only fear for him—and a terrible, selfish, comfort.

"Our Lady," he whispered. "We have always known you will be the death of us."

I could move again. I began to fall, but Rex and Aaz were there, holding me up—and Zee braced himself against my legs. "Don't say that."

"Now, or in a thousand years." Oturu's cloak flowed around me like wings. "We are one. We will not live without you."

I touched my stomach. "You'll live for *her*."

His mouth softened, and those tendrils of hair grazed my shirt, sliding beneath the soft cotton to press against my skin.

"Another queen," he murmured. "But she will not be you. You are the last."

I swallowed hard. "Not the first time I've heard that. But I don't believe it. I am not the last of this bloodline."

The wide brim of his hat tilted forward. "It has already begun, Hunter."

Then, before I could ask him what the hell that meant, he said, "She is warm. What ails you surrounds her."

It was hard to find my voice. "Surrounds, or infects?"

"It wants to kill her." Oturu bowed his head, as though listening. "That is all I know."

I felt nauseated. Zee pointed at Oturu. "Too much fear you bring. We protect little light. We protect Maxine."

Oturu pulled away from me. "You cannot protect her from everything."

"I pick up my own slack," I muttered, trying to sound tough, strong, as if that would make me feel better. "But if you're going to take the risk of being near me, then I need your help. We've been attacked by the Aetar. I don't know how many of their constructs are on this world, or who else is coming for us."

"You wish us to hunt them."

"Hunt and kill," I said, and hesitated. "I'll need Tracker, too."

Oturu momentarily stilled, floating on the dagger tips of his feet—more than two feet, less than ten—some indeterminable number that was just as mysterious as his hidden face. He could have been a dancer—of the demonic variety—his grace utterly unmatched, even by the boys.

For a moment, deep within the drowning abyss of that living cloak, I saw a face press outward, contorted in agony. I almost stepped back, but then I recognized those features. My breath caught.

"Tracker," I said. "What are you *doing* to him?"

"He has not yet learned to kneel before our Lady," murmured Oturu. "Not in the deepest altar of his heart."

"No one has to kneel to anyone, for any reason," I said wearily. "Why do you still do this to him? Why won't you give him his freedom?"

"We promised not to," said Oturu. "We promised *you*."

I blinked, startled. I saw, from the corner of my eye, Zee—looking away from us, as though embarrassed.

But before I could ask them what the hell that meant, Oturu's cloak flared—wide as the hood of a cobra. I stumbled backward as Tracker fell from the abyss. Just behind him I glimpsed other faces pressing outward, as if trying to escape with him. Not all were human.

Raw and Aaz fell into the shadows around us, only their eyes visible: crimson, glowing. I heard their low growls. Dek and Mal coiled tighter around my throat. No purrs, no song—watching Tracker with all their deadly focus. Only Zee was relaxed, but that was deceptive. I wished I could be that smooth. My pulse was fast, and I felt nervous.

It had been six years, but Tracker still put me on edge, for reasons I could not explain. Maybe because he hated my guts. Maybe because he was part of a past that wasn't mine but that belonged to my bloodline, all the way back to the beginning. He knew things about the women in my family that I could never imagine, and I was envious of that. Protective of it, too.

Tracker knelt, shuddering and breathing hard. He looked the same as when I'd last seen him: skin the color of a cat's-eye, golden and tawny, his hair black and long, wild around his angular face. His nose was large, hooked, close to ugly—closer still to handsome.

He wore jeans, a black turtleneck; a belt buckle the size of my hand, silver and inlaid with lapis. A band of iron hid beneath his chin, peeking from the edge of his collar.

Looking at him inspired too much déjà vu—and not because we'd met before. This went deeper, part of some inherited genetic memory. Tracker was in the blood.

He tilted his head to look at me. Black eyes. Aggressive stare.

"Oh," he said. "It's you."

"In the flesh," I replied. "You need some water?"

"Water." He laughed bitterly.

I glanced at Raw, who gave Tracker a dirty look. Still, he pulled a bottle of cold water from the shadows and tossed it at me. I unscrewed the top, and the man grabbed it from my hand. He drank like he was dying, water spilling down the sides of his mouth.

A tendril of hair, delicate as a long finger, snaked beneath the man's collar. Oturu tugged, and Tracker choked, spitting water.

"Stop," I said.

"Stand," Oturu said in his soft, silky voice—ignoring me. "Your Lady needs you."

Hate flickered through Tracker's face, but he climbed awkwardly to his feet. "What now?"

"End-of-the-world shit," I said. "No big deal."

"Right," he said, wary. And then: "You're pregnant."

"Yes," I replied. "It happens."

I told him about the attack, which also required informing him of the broken prison—the demon army, residing on earth. Tracker's jaw tightened as he listened, his gaze growing dark, troubled. I kept expecting him to interrupt with disparaging comments, just out of principle—but whatever he saw in our faces, demon and human, must have told a story, because he rocked back on his heels and folded his arms over his chest.

"And who's died?" he asked. "The Lightbringer?"

A chill hit me. "Not yet. But I'm afraid that's coming next."

Tracker's gaze didn't waver. "And you? What part of you is dying, Hunter?"

"All the parts that matter," I told him.

CHAPTER 15

D ESPITE all evidence to the contrary, I have a very forgiving nature.

I've been stabbed, cursed, kidnapped, called some profoundly unfortunate names—and in a few of those cases, I've managed to go on with my life without indulging the need to kill anyone.

Tracker, for example, had once thrown me under a bus. His way of saying "hello." Fantastic start to what was, in hindsight, a very temporary alliance. I was totally over it.

"I should warn you," I said. "You're probably going to die."

A bitter smile tugged at his mouth. "I hope that's a promise."

Raw and Aaz dangled from a tree branch above his head. Zee prowled close, staring up at the man. Tracker scratched his nose, his smile becoming grim. "You have something to add, Reaper King?"

"Vows," rasped the little demon. "Remember them."

Tracker stilled. "Long time ago. Wardens are dead and

gone. Prison is open. All shot straight to hell. I don't think there's a point anymore to what we swore to do."

"Honor, then." Zee pressed forward, rising on his haunches. "The Hunter must live."

"Listen—" I began, but the demon held up his clawed hand, still staring at Tracker. Both of them, locked together in a silent battle that was so heavy, I could barely breathe the air.

"The Hunter must live," Zee said again, in a deadly soft voice. Hearing him say those words cut me to the core. I knew it wasn't just for his benefit. Without me, he and his brothers would survive, free.

No, this was about family. Love.

Tracker drew in a short, sharp breath. I wondered if he realized, if he could understand how much the boys had changed in all these years he'd known them. Could anyone really understand, except them and me?

I said, "I want my daughter to survive and grow up in a world that isn't populated by corpses. I want us all to have some fucking peace."

"No such thing." Tracker folded his arms over his chest, but he didn't seem as sure of himself as he had before. "Even if you'd never had this—your man, this life—if you gave it all up—nothing would change. You weren't made for peace, Hunter. None of you women were. And your daughter, whoever she is, will get used to the corpses. Just like you did."

I stared at him. "You're an asshole."

"But you still need me." Weariness flitted across his face, and resentment. "Nothing changes, even after ten thousand years."

I held his gaze, forcing myself to stay hard. "Then you should know exactly what to do."

Oturu drifted behind the man, those long, searching tendrils of hair caressing his back. Tracker stiffened, his face becoming a perfect, predatory mask. I half expected him to be punished for speaking his mind—Oturu had never before spared him—but instead, the demon glided around to me—reaching for me, surrounding me with his floating hair and the folds of his cloak, which unfurled and danced as though carried by a storm.

His hair traced a soft line against my shoulder. Dek and Mal purred beneath his touch. Raw and Aaz dropped from their tree branch, landing softly on either side of me.

"It is awake," he murmured.

I didn't look at him. "What is?"

"Your heart." Oturu glided away, floating on the tips of his toes. "Come, Tracker. We hunt the soldiers of the Aetar."

Wait, I wanted to say to him. *What did you mean?*

But the demon did not linger. His knifelike feet pushed off the ground, and he ascended through the tree branches like a ghost, making not a sound. Tracker forced a sardonic smile to his mouth, but not before I glimpsed a troubled look in his eye.

"Hunter," he said, simply, and vanished from sight.

I stared at the spot, heart beating a little too fast. Zee rasped, "Could have done without Tracker."

"No." I leaned against a tree, exhausted. "We need all the help we can get. One more pair of hands could make a difference."

Or get him killed, too.

Maybe. And there was still one more body I needed to recruit into this fight. Another set of eyes.

I pulled out my cell phone, could barely read the screen— vision blurry, head dizzy. It was hard to find the number I needed. My fingers felt fat, clumsy. My skin was hot.

Rex answered on the third ring. For once, I was happy to hear his voice.

He'd been the first of Grant's converts. A parasite who sided with my husband against his own Queen. Which didn't mean he was my friend. Just the opposite. But he was loyal to Grant, and that was all that mattered.

I heard laughter in the background, pots clanging—the distant melody of a show tune: something from *Phantom of the Opera*. Dinner was being made at the homeless shelter

Grant had founded—and that he and I had lived above, in his nice little loft. I felt homesick for the place.

"What now?" Rex asked.

"I need you to tap your parasite network," I told him. "Find out if anyone has seen Aetar on this world, and where. I'm going to assume Blood Mama already knows the answer to this question and is just holding out on us."

Rex was silent a moment. "What's going on?"

"Nothing," I lied. "Find me some fucking Aetar, Rex."

He grunted. "Bitch. I'll call you back when I have something."

"Thirty minutes. That's all I'm giving you."

He swore at me and ended the call. I tried to put the phone back in my pocket, but fumbled, clumsy. Zee caught it for me, but I didn't try taking it back. I sat down hard on the ground, lying back and feeling my body ache. My hands settled on my stomach. I held them there, sending good thoughts to my daughter. Pretending she was surrounded in light. Anything that would protect her from the disease inside me.

"I need to find who did this," I said to the boys. "Can you track? Is there a scent?"

They looked at each other. Raw had reached into the shadows for a figurine of Batman and was chewing on its head. Aaz also reached into the shadows, but he pulled out a footlong sandwich: thick crunchy bread spilling over with meatballs and melted cheese. He put it in my hands, and the bread was hot and the hunger that washed over me, hollow and immediate and dangerous. I hadn't eaten anything for almost a day.

I tore into the sandwich, while Dek and Mal hummed with satisfaction. Zee rasped, "Felt a pull, in dreams. Old history. But not enough poison to make a path. Not enough to see behind the mask."

I swallowed, wiping my mouth with the back of my hand. "So you needed to be *more* sick in order to track the source?"

Zee hesitated. "Like tracking a scent. Hunting memory.

Some strong, some weak. Could eat poison, make sick, but won't have same effect. Visions come from you. From healing *you*."

I thought for a moment. "So . . . burning the poison out of my body . . . that connection between us is where you could track the disease's origins?" I didn't know how that worked, but I wasn't going to argue with him. "What if I was . . . sicker?"

Dek and Mal squeaked. Raw's jaws froze over Batman's legs, which were sizzling and burning from the acid in his saliva. Aaz ripped a spike from his back and started stabbing himself in the eye with it.

"Okay, come on," I said to him. "Now you're just being dramatic."

Zee was also staring at me. "Dangerous, Maxine. Risk much."

I touched my stomach. If the Aetar won, what would the world look like? No demons, but no Grant, either. Maybe no humans, period. And Jack was right—they would never let our daughter live. Not with a Lightbringer's powers.

They had almost killed her, still in the womb. After she was born, it would be even easier for the Aetar to take her life. Or just take her, period. There was only so much the boys and I could do to protect her.

Unless I took my own life. Gave her over to the boys as soon as she was born.

It had been done before. Still might not save her, but it was a better chance. Still meant, though, that someone would have to be around to take care of her during the day while the boys slept. Tracker had filled that role for one of my ancestors.

But I wanted my daughter to have her father.

Then what? No matter what you do, the Aetar will keep coming. They'll send more soldiers, more sickness. Even if you save him now, Grant will never be safe. They're too powerful, too elusive.

So, just give up, then? That couldn't be the answer, either.

Not with my daughter's life on the line. Finding the one responsible for making the disease wouldn't stop the Aetar, but it *might* lead to a cure. I had to start somewhere.

My appetite was gone, but I finished eating the sandwich. As soon as I took the last bite, Aaz placed another in my hands—only this one was stuffed with grilled salmon and avocado. I forced it down and drank the water the little demon gave me. Food helped. But I still had a fever, and my muscles ached.

My cell phone buzzed. Zee handed it back to me. "Hey."

"Nothing," Rex said immediately. "We haven't seen anything."

"Do you need more time?"

"No." He sounded frustrated. "You're right about us . . . we're drawn to high-energy sources . . . and the Aetar are high-energy, even if we wouldn't ever bother getting close to them. None of my kind has observed any Aetar."

"That's impossible. One of them possessed a dead Mahati and tried to kill my daughter." Not to mention that Jack had told me he felt another on this world.

Rex went silent. I checked the phone to make sure he hadn't hung up, and said, "Hello?"

"It's started," he said, in a dull voice. "We all knew it was just a matter of time. If the demon army didn't kill this world, then it would be the Aetar."

"Stop it," I said. "Keep looking."

"There's *nothing*," Rex snapped. "Not in Asia, not in South America, not in this country. I know, the world is a big place, but we would *feel* it. How do you think Blood Mama has kept tabs on your bloodline all these thousands of years? How come she always knows when shit's about to hit the fan?"

I ignored that. "Have you tried Antarctica?"

"Fuck you," he said. "I'll call if anything changes."

He hung up on me. I sagged against the tree and looked at Zee and the boys. I felt their dread—or maybe that was me.

"We can't wait," I said to them.

I struggled to my feet and walked through the woods to where the Mahati were being quarantined. No music, no soft chatter—a few small fires glowed in the camp, but I felt the absence of movement, a quiet that was heavy and full of dread.

I smelled the dying long before I saw them: a wet swamp of caustic, fetid blood that spread through the air in a deadly haze. The area had grown to accommodate more of the ill—at least another thirty adults and children—all sitting or lying still, curled up in balls with shallow wood pans by their heads to catch their vomit. Their sadness and fear was horrifying, heartbreaking.

Lord Ha'an stood amongst them, holding water to the mouth of a child who lay limp in his arms.

"I'm finding a cure," I told him. "I don't care what it takes."

He didn't even blink. "What do you need?"

I looked around, found Zee crouched by an adult who looked pretty damn dead—if the slack, open-eyed, too-still expression of frozen horror was any indication. The little demon gave me a reluctant nod.

"That body," I said. "I need some of its blood."

"Then take it," he told me. "Now it is only flesh."

I crouched beside Zee. Raw and Aaz hopped close, clutching their teddy bears. Dek and Mal were absolutely silent around my neck. All of them unhappy, looking at me with concern.

"Maxine," Zee rasped. "Unwise act."

"Do you know a better way? Anything faster?"

He hesitated. "No."

"And you're sure you can draw the disease from me? That it won't kill my daughter?"

"Yes." No hesitation, that time.

I pointed to the Mahati's arm, and the little demon slashed it open with his claws. Dark blood oozed free. I took several deep breaths, trying to shut out the world and the other Mahati, who were suddenly watching. I tried not to look at the dead demon's slack face and staring eyes. I tried not to be sick.

Do it fast, I told myself. *Don't think.*

But I did. I looked down at my stomach, pressing out against my jeans. Little girl in there. My baby.

I was terrified of fucking her up. Our bloodline was like titanium when it came to having healthy babies, but the trauma of that almost miscarriage was still rich and alive in my mind. Probably it always would be. I could feel the tug in my gut, the heat of blood between my legs. The helplessness.

I still felt helpless. In a million different ways.

There was one option I hadn't tried. I pressed my right hand into the blood. The armor tingled, a shimmer of light racing over the metal—and with it, roses, ghosting to the surface, then fading. Each time I used the armor it covered more of my skin. In a few months, my entire right arm might be gone. Eventually, I'd have to stop. If I could.

Find the one who made this, I thought hard, closing my eyes. It might work. What the armor responded to had always been mysterious—and how it chose to fulfill my needs, even more so.

But when I tried to send us into the void, nothing happened. Seconds passed, a full minute, and we remained exactly in the same place, crouched by the same dead body, surrounded by the dying.

The only difference was that I heard screaming.

I began to stand—Zee caught my hand and shook his head. I turned, and found Lord Ha'an drawing near, still holding that sick demon child.

"The Shurik and Yorana are fighting," he said, just as the screams grew more agonized.

"Doesn't sound like the Yorana are winning."

"The Shurik have always been the most dangerous of our kind. The Mahati would not have survived against them." Lord Ha'an shrugged, looking totally unconcerned. "They are . . . friendlier . . . now. Even I can admit Lord Cooperon has been a good influence."

The screaming ratcheted into a higher, more frenzied pitch—absolutely desperate.

"Great influence," I muttered, thinking about what I'd said to that little Shurik on Grant's shoulder. I glanced at Zee and the boys. "Should I stop it?"

Raw looked at me like I was crazy. Aaz just smirked, and Zee nibbled on the tip of his claw, giving me the most uncommitted shrug I'd ever seen. On my shoulders, Dek and Mal began patting my ears in a fast rhythm and hummed an upbeat version of the BeeGees' "I've Got To Get A Message To You."

Fine. No aid. I glanced down at the armor and clenched my hand into a fist. The blood had absorbed, but I was getting *no* cooperation. I wasn't entirely surprised—just disappointed, frustrated. The armor had been constructed from a fragment of the Labyrinth, the stuff *possibilities* were made of. But that also meant it had a mind of its own, and sometimes—at the worst times—it liked to tell me, in its own silent way, to fuck off.

So, this was going to get dirty.

I took a deep breath, slid my left hand along that cut arm—and licked the blood off my fingers.

It was still warm. My first instinct was to gag, but I forced myself to lick again, and again, and something shifted inside me—that dark hunger, that caress of power rising from below my heart. But no pleasure came with that awakening. Only dissatisfaction.

We are not scavengers, whispered the darkness. *We do not eat death.*

We are death, I told it. *And this is a different kind of hunt.*

I sat back. I didn't feel any different—except sick to my stomach. I couldn't blame that on the immediacy of any disease, though. I was disgusted at myself. I wanted a toothbrush and a finger down my throat.

I wiped my mouth and looked at Zee. "Enough?"

His ears and hair lay flat against his skull; several of his claws pressed against his mouth like he was going to be sick. This, from the demon who had once eaten otherworldly intestines like spaghetti. "Maybe too much."

"I trust you." I reached out to grab Zee's wrist. Raw and Aaz hugged my waist. "Follow the trail."

"Need daylight," Zee said. "Need to be one with you."

"Got it," I said.

But we weren't going anywhere.

CHAPTER 16

N EVER take magic for granted. The minute you do, it will fuck you up.

❦

I have some pride. What good it does me. When I realized I wasn't going anywhere, I used my own two legs and walked the hell away from the quarantine zone. I avoided all Mahati. I trusted the boys to keep other demons away. I didn't think too hard about where I was going. Only one place on this land where I felt truly safe—and the dead were there, too.

The earth on the hill had been torn during the battle: everywhere, chunks of dirt and grass, and deep holes. Some darts were still in the ground, and broken pieces of spears. I smelled blood. Or maybe that was my breath.

I was relieved to see the old oak still standing, untouched. We'd been on our way to the farmhouse when the giants attacked, and the creatures seemed to have bypassed this spot. The grass around my mother and grandmother's grave didn't even look scuffed—and the boulder that covered them was still in place. I climbed on top of its broad, flat surface. Lay on my back, staring at the stars.

Whatever I'd done had worked. Twenty minutes after taking that blood into my body, I felt sick as hell. Walking up the hill took all my strength, and just resting on this rock was making me breathe in ways that felt like my lungs were about to implode. My skin prickled worse than ever; and it was the fever, the burn, that hot lick of death settling in. I couldn't believe how fast it was hitting me.

"I was stupid," I said to Zee, who sat beside me, very still and quiet. "I got lazy."

He said nothing. Raw and Aaz flopped down against my legs, dragging a six-pack of beer behind them, two tubs of fried chicken, and a small chain saw.

"M&M's," I said absently, and moments later, one of them put a large crunchy plastic bag in my hand, already open. I started popping chocolate. Dek and Mal slithered down my arms, and I fed them, too. Their purrs radiated heat.

"No Hunter has died of disease, right?" I asked the boys.

"Kill it in our sleep," Zee rasped. "Only one old mother poisoned. Refused to listen."

"Idiot."

He sighed. "Hated us. Hated daughter. Hated all her old mothers. Tried to forget life. Tried with blood and war. Tried with strong drink. Could not kill herself, so let another."

"How did her daughter respond?"

"Blamed us. Did not live long past own daughter. Better, after that."

I bet. "When was this?"

Dek hummed, then chirped. Zee nodded at him. "Four thousand years. More than. Came by boat and foot across ice-north in winter. Walked down along coast. Walked for years. Walked into jungle. Walked into blood."

Sick as I felt, that still made me smile. "So my ancestors

came to this continent four thousand years ago, then rambled on down to South America?"

Zee shrugged. "Had time. No fear. When no fear, go places."

Such true words. But I was envious of those women, envious that their world had been simpler.

"Nothing ever simple," rasped Zee, so quietly I barely heard him. "Not death, even."

I touched his head. "Do you ever wish you could die?"

Raw and Aaz stopped eating. Zee lay down beside me, curling close as the spikes of his hair flexed against my hand.

"Sometimes," he whispered.

I ached for him. "*Can* you die?"

"All are mortal." The little demon reached into the bag of M&M's. "All."

I swallowed hard, throat dry, skin blazing with fever. Tears burned my eyes. Shame, frustration, anger—all rolled through my heart, filling me up until I wanted to scream. I'd been so cocky. So sure of myself. Rushing headlong into danger because I assumed someone else would save me. Hadn't I learned my lesson by now?

And it wasn't just me I'd put at risk. That was the worst part.

"I'm afraid," I told them. "I'm afraid for my daughter. I screwed up."

Zee placed his claws on my chest, above my heart. "Last until morning. Fight."

Fight. Yes, I could do that.

Fuck it all. I'm not going to die.

Five minutes later, I started vomiting blood.

⊰❖⊱

DON'T take breathing for granted, my mother once said. *Never say for sure that you'll still be alive tomorrow.*

I wasn't sure I was going to be alive in an hour, and it wasn't even midnight.

Zee held a cold bottle of water, and a wet rag that he used to dab my face. Raw had shoved a pillow beneath my head and knees, and Aaz was on my other side, rocking back and forth with a teddy-bear paw stuck in his mouth. Dek and Mal coiled beside my head, under my head, across my chest—absolutely silent.

I needed that silence. Little jackhammers were assaulting my joints and muscles—my skin burned, I burned—and my head hurt so badly, I closed my eyes and breathed through my mouth, afraid to move. Even a purr would have been too loud. The more I hurt, the more I retreated inside myself, moving deeper, downward, part of me hoping to get so lost I didn't feel any of the pain.

The fear, I couldn't help. I was so afraid, afraid of everything, afraid for our child, afraid Grant would feel my distress through our bond and try to reach me—afraid that everyone I loved was going to be hurt, and lost.

Fight. Stay alive.

I vomited again, utterly helpless as that bitter burning wash of heat pushed up my throat. I tasted blood in my mouth and coughed, spitting out what I could—but it exhausted me so much, I had trouble rolling over to my back. I had to stay where I was for several long minutes, face pressed to cool stone, eyes wet with tears.

Fight. Stay alive.

I fell deeper into myself, awareness shrinking to breath, heartbeat, the stone against my back. I fell even deeper, aware of my mother's bones beneath me, and my grandmother to my left. Dead and alive, both at the same time. Dead here, alive in the past, and the walls were so thin between us. How often had I breached that wall, how often had I stepped through to another world? They were both so close: just on the other side of a thought, a wish, a dream.

I wanted them with me, so badly.

Zee ran his claws through my hair and pressed that wet rag on my brow. It was deliciously cool, but I wanted more.

I wanted to be buried in snow and ice, and I doubted even that would be enough to dim the heat. I thought of Grant, suffering through this, and my heart reached out to him. I couldn't help it.

Our bond. Our light. No Lightbringer could use his powers alone. If he tried, it would eventually kill him. A bond was needed, a person who could anchor and share the power of life.

I was that power. I was that life. And in so many ways, he was mine.

Golden light rushed through me, shining behind my closed eyes—brilliant and spirited, with its own clear tone that rang in my ears like some faraway song. I let it carry and caress me from the fever and pain; and with it memories, moments, shimmering in a haze through my mind—all of them, with Grant.

You're going to live, I told him, pouring my own heart and life into our bond. *You're going to live such a long time.*

Maxine, you're sick, I heard him say, but his voice in my mind sounded very distant, lost in the fog of infection burning once again through the light.

I love you, I told him, ready to push him away, close up our bond—lock it tight so he wouldn't feel any more of what I was going through.

Only, he wouldn't let me.

It was like slamming open a door in a hurricane. Light battered me, and no matter how hard I struggled, that storm held me in place. My chest tugged, a lure that hooked into my blood, pulling hard. Again and again, until it reminded me of a mouth on some open wound, drawing out poison. I could suddenly *feel* the disease inside me, feel it as if it were a rotting brown corpse, and inside my head, I saw it being broken apart and enticed down our bond.

Impossible. Grant couldn't heal me. The boys and I were immune to his voice.

But he wasn't using his voice, I realized. This was

something else, something deeper, the part that made us one person.

"No!" I said out loud, struggling to rise. Zee and Raw held me down. Aaz gave me a frightened look and sat on my legs.

No, I screamed at Grant. *No.*

He said nothing, but the light of our bond dimmed. Pain built inside my sternum, like a knife being pushed, inch by slow inch, into my chest. I writhed, crying out, looking for anything, anything I could do to make it stop.

But I couldn't, and a vision slashed through my mind—of Grant, on the couch, his fingers digging into his chest and his face deformed with pain. His breath, ragged and gasping, blood foaming around his mouth. Mary standing over him, calling his name. No one else there. Not Jack. Not me.

I was killing him. He was killing himself, trying to save me.

"Fuck!" I gasped, slamming my right hand into the stone. Sparks danced and the metal chimed. But nothing happened. I couldn't go to him.

Grant, I begged. *Grant.*

I fought harder, and the world beyond my body disappeared—all that existed, all that mattered, was the nightmare unfolding inside me. My human mind wasn't made for the abstract: Disease resembled a rotting corpse, my bond with Grant a shaft of golden light. The darkness inside me: a serpent wound deep around my heart. It didn't matter that appearances weren't real—what mattered was the reality behind the appearances and what it let me perceive.

And what I perceived was that my husband was going to die in the next minute if I didn't do something to save him.

No thought, just instinct. I threw myself down that bond into Grant's soul.

It was like diving headfirst into a hole the size of a rabbit, and the sensation was physical and mental, and overwhelmingly uncomfortable. It wasn't my body being compressed, just my mind—but the two felt so much the same that I was sure I was going to die, right there, from the attempt.

Instead, I dissolved. I broke apart.

And fell into my husband, just as his heart stopped beating.

CHAPTER 17

I felt his heart stop.
    It was just one of a million different sensations that assaulted me at that moment—a cascade of thoughts, memories, desire, and fear—ramming into my consciousness with all the pulverizing force of a bullet train. I flew, plummeted, crashed.

But I felt his heart stop.

I felt the absence all around me, the silence, the drift—and the light between us, the light that had brought me to him, began to dissipate. Everything else was a blur—threads and shimmers, voices crying out in pain—but it was the light I clung to, the fading light that I held, and I let it pull me into his heart, to the spirit of his heart.

There was nothing, then everything: a great floating mass in front of me, an island in a dark sky, but it was made of knots that were gnarled as roots, twisted and thick, and flush with veins, threads that shot in every direction, each one stretched to the point of snapping—just beginning to go dark.

Grant, I called, but there was no answer—perhaps, just the hint of a touch, the ghost of a man. His heart was in front of me: massive and quiet. No song. No drum. No beat.

And all over, slick and filthy, was that brown ooze of rot and disease. It was a wall between us, a wall between life and death—and a terrible fury filled me, an ache of revulsion so deep and profound, I felt the dying world around us tremble.

I reached out, hands tearing through the rot—

—and the world became fire.

It was a chthonic blast, straight out of hell: an inferno that ripped through me like I was rice paper fluttering instantly to ash. I had no defense against it. It pushed me out, and I found myself back where I started, on the edge of the rot, with lost time and a husband who was getting deader by the second.

For a moment, I remembered the vision in that crystal skull—my body, torn apart in fire.

Fuck that, I thought, throwing myself back into the rot: burning, again. I might as well have been flesh and bone—I could feel the crackling sizzle of my skin, the small internal explosions of my organs *pop pop popping*—the blistering of my life as it was scorched away.

I couldn't hold on. I slipped a second time and fell from the rot. Barred from my husband's still, quiet, heart. It stunned me. It was as if the disease were *alive,* something more than just a virus. Alive, with a purpose. Alive, with dreams.

I pushed my hands into the rot, threw myself into hell, again. I felt no fear. No space for it, past the fury, and the love. I focused on the love and pushed the rest aside. And when I stopped feeling love, I clung to Grant's face. And when his face burned away, I thought of our daughter, our daughter who needed a father. And when even that was not enough, I fell back on my mother, my mother and the boys, then just the boys, until there was nothing left but something deeper than even them, something that swam on the other side of the fire, already inside me, safe and cool in its untouched darkness.

But I didn't stop at the darkness, even though it reached for me, expectant. I moved past its grasp, past it to the other side, into another world.

I was weightless, without flesh, without anchor—less than a spirit, floating. Only this was not the void. Here, there was light: starlight, pricks of light, far away and scattered in a million billion gestures of burning life that I knew, I knew, would never sustain me. I could not eat light. It could not make me whole.

You are wrong, whispered a familiar masculine voice. *Light is filled with many wonders.*

A lean shimmer of silver flickered at the corner of my vision, but I could not turn to look at my father. "Right now I care about only one light. I want my husband," I said, voice breaking. "I want Grant."

A soft sigh rippled through me, filled with longing, sadness. The sound took away the pain from the burns and healed the fractures caused by those screams. It was cool and gentle, a balm to my soul. But it also made me afraid, in ways the fire had not.

I wanted your mother, came that whisper. *But even I could not keep her.*

I refused to hear that. I refused to think even a moment about what those words meant, but the meaning still sank into me, transforming into dread. I couldn't stand it, not even a little. I pushed it away. I pushed away from it all and fell back into the fire. Hell was safer than a broken heart. Hell was gentler.

Heat seared through my cells, and so did those screams—but it was different this time. Maybe because I welcomed the pain. I embraced it, falling deep, deeper, burning to ash, with nothing left inside me but heartbreak.

Until I heard a voice.

It wasn't a voice I knew—not Grant or the boys, not the darkness or that figure of light who had loved my mother, loved her so much she'd become pregnant with me. But it was a voice, and it was filled with power.

We are Gods, it whispered. *What is flesh, is ours.*

A shadow gathered in the fire, indistinct and immense. I pushed toward it, overwhelmed with the need to see its face. The fires parted. But instead of a man, all I saw was death.

Bodies, millions of them, as far as the eye could see—as if I stood on the edge of a great cliff, looking down. Except I wasn't far away—I was right there, nearly on top of them, and the rot covered their flesh, the rot was eating away at them: brown and filthy, and ripe with poison.

You have done well, murmured that deep, resonant voice. The quiet, assured malevolence of it was as dangerous, and threatening, as any rot or bullet, or knife. More so, because that was a voice that sounded as if it took pleasure in its power, and I knew that type too well. Pleasure and pain and death, part of the same delight.

The illness is efficient, replied another: a much lighter voice, with a certain affable tone that might have belonged to a cheerful Nazi. *But it must be altered. It must not be allowed to affect our flesh. Only the demons.*

Kill all the humans on that world, and you will starve the demons out, replied that other. *But, as you wish. Alter the disease. And I will fashion its cure. Just in case.*

You are the Devourer, came the almost-cheerful reply. *And ever wise.*

Fires crisped my back. I tried to hold on to the vision before me, but the bodies shrank and slid away, leaving me with nothing but my heart.

And my heart pulled me forward. The fires pushed. In front of me, where the bodies had been, I saw a mountain appear, except it was not rock, just flesh. Not a mountain, but a heart.

Grant's heart.

The rot was still all around us, but here—a patch. Here, a place where I could reach my husband. How long had I been lost? I still saw traces of light in those muscles, veins that held an echo of life.

Grant, I called, but there was no answer—perhaps, just the hint of a touch, the ghost of a man.

I touched one of those veins of fading light, and my hands sank deep inside. Everything in me that was alive, I poured into him. It wasn't mouth-to-mouth—just soul-to-soul, my soul searching desperately for his soul, my soul plunging deep and far away into my husband. The rot tried to surround me, but I burned it away, burned and clawed and beat it back.

Wake up, I begged his heart. *Wake up.*

Maxine, I heard, but that wasn't Grant's voice. It was Zee. I ignored him, falling deeper. Claws brushed my arms, scales soft as silk around my throat. Darkness engulfed me, but it only made the light shine brighter, hotter, until everything disappeared, everything. Except a pale hand that pushed free of the light.

I grabbed, pulled.

My husband's heart began to beat.

I almost didn't believe it, but I felt that solid, thumping rhythm, rich and deep as a drum made from a mountain thundering. I felt the boys with us, too, their spirits just as strong as their flesh. I pulled again on Grant's hand, hauling him toward me, tugging and yanking with every ounce of my strength. I didn't think I had anything left to give, but I found more—I found enough.

All around us, the rot began moving in. I reached out, laid my hand upon it—

—and the world shifted again.

⊰≡⊱

I opened my eyes and saw nothing but stars.

Stars, blurred, because there were tears in my eyes. I couldn't think—no memory, no sense of place—just a scrambling, wild pulse of anxiety that hit my chest, making it hard to breathe. Or maybe that was the demon sitting on me.

"Maxine," Zee rasped, sliding his cool claws down my cheek. I stared at him, struggling not to panic. Certain that something terrible had happened, right beyond my reach. I craned my neck, taking in my grandmother's grave, the old oak, and several pairs of red eyes blinking with uncertainty. All normal. All fine. But something was missing, something—

It all came back.

Panic exploded into outright terror. I shoved at Zee, trying to sit up. He scrambled off me, and I rolled off the rock—right onto my face. None of my limbs worked, and now that I was moving, I could barely see straight; dizziness made me cling to the grass. I took a deep breath, steeled myself—and stood just long enough to launch myself into a shambling run.

I was headed downhill, which gave me momentum. Nothing seemed to work right—my legs kept threatening to collapse, each step random, flinging, wild—and my spine seemed incapable of straightening beyond a hunched c shape. My right arm swung in the air, and the other clutched hard against my stomach. I might have been drooling, but I didn't give a shit. I was upright. I was moving. And I had the farmhouse fixed in my sights.

Raw and Aaz loped past me. I tried to tell them to go to Grant, but my voice wouldn't form the words—just a low, unintelligible growl that only confirmed I was drooling like a motherfucker. Zee, somewhere on my left, snapped out a sharp, guttural command—Aaz disappeared instantly into the shadows. I was only dimly aware of Dek and Mal on my shoulders; wrapped tight, warm and silent.

One foot in front of the other. One foot. One step. My life, reduced to nothing more basic. I didn't think. I couldn't. Only once did I try to find my husband's spirit through our link, but even *reaching* for the link almost knocked me out. It should have been easy as breathing, but that brief effort made me feel like I was at twenty thousand feet, out of oxygen, and still trying to climb a mountain.

I was mostly upright by the time I reached the farmhouse: breathing hard, dizzy, my skin flushed with fever. Zee caught me before I fell on the porch stairs, half-dragging me up to the door, which Raw opened with such force it broke right off the hinges. I was dimly aware of movement all around me: hundreds of Shurik, clinging to the porch boards and rails, curled up on the wicker chairs like amputated, hairless cats.

I staggered inside. Lights were on. Mary knelt by the couch, blocking my view of Grant. I wanted to knock her aside, and half a second later Aaz did just that. I barely noticed. I could finally see my husband. He was so still, a corpse shade of white that was almost gray: and the rest of him, hollow, covered in a blanket half-tossed aside.

I collapsed beside the couch, touching his face. Warm. Warm skin. His chest rose and fell, and my entire spirit rose and fell with that solid, living movement. I tried again to reach for our link, closing my eyes, trying to force myself to relax, breathe, sink deep. All that meditative shit I'd never needed to find my husband's soul.

Nothing. I found *nothing*. Just a gaping hole inside my heart, so real I could feel it—as if the void had settled part of itself inside me. And I realized that it wasn't my fault that I couldn't find the link.

The link was gone.

"Grant," I said, frightened.

I spoke his name again, louder, but he didn't open his eyes. He was breathing, alive, but not feeling him inside me—that golden, shining tether—made it seem like he was gone. The emptiness was devastating. I felt as though the light had gone out inside me, and all that was left was . . . the void.

I looked at Zee, so shaken I could barely speak. "What can you tell me? Is this a coma?"

The little demon gave me a helpless shrug. "Do not know. Scent sick. Yours, too. But less. Dying still . . . but less."

Which was a nice way of saying we were still fucked.

Grant's shirt moved; a small, pale nub poked free, glinting with jagged teeth that were barely tucked inside that wormlike mouth. Even that tiny movement seemed tired; the Shurik looked thinner than I remembered, pale flesh tinted gray.

I peered at the Shurik, more frustrated than relieved. If it was alive, then the link between Grant and his demons was still active; and if the link was active, then why the hell wasn't my husband reaping the benefits of being a demon lord? Even if the rest of his demons suffered the illness, that link alone should have protected him—long before he'd even *felt* sick. I didn't understand.

I didn't understand how he could still be connected to an army of demons—and not me.

Resentment wasn't a feeling I'd often indulged, but I let it bloom, briefly, as I stared at the Shurik, still half hiding beneath Grant's chest.

Doesn't matter, I told myself, as my husband, the couch—the whole room—swayed sideways. I sagged against the floor, violently dizzy. Terrible pressure gathered around my skull, like it was being crushed in a clamp, and shadows pushed into the edges of my vision—shadows that moved, and breathed, and seemed to bring with them the nagging sense that I had forgotten something.

Alter the disease. And I will fashion a cure.

That voice. That terrible, awful voice. I went very still. Had I glimpsed the origins of what was killing us? Had I listened to its creators? And if so . . . if so . . . what could I do with that information?

You are the Devourer. And ever wise.

"The Devourer," I murmured, trying to stand. "Zee, where's Jack?"

Silence. Stillness. As if I were suddenly alone. But I looked up, and Zee was right there, staring past me, as were Raw and Aaz. Mary's large, strong hands slid around my arm, keeping me upright. I glimpsed her face—furious and grief-stricken—and turned to look at what had captured Zee's attention.

It was my grandfather. Staring at me. For a long, agonizing moment, I didn't recognize him. It wasn't the shower or the change of clothes, or even the fact that I still wasn't used to this body he'd possessed for the last several months.

It was his eyes. The way he was looking at me. As if a million years of trauma had just coalesced into a living thing, and that living thing was represented by me.

I struggled to straighten up, to stand like I was strong—which I wasn't, not even a little. "Jack. Did you hear me? I said a name."

"Yes," he replied, quietly. "Yes, you did."

I took a breath. "Who is the Devourer?"

Jack stared at me, then turned and walked right out the front door. Mary swore, releasing me so suddenly I staggered. I didn't care. I watched her stride after my grandfather, one hand loosening the machete strapped to her massive belt.

"Zee," I whispered, trying to follow—but I was too slow, too pained—and too reluctant to leave Grant's side. The demon was already moving, though, intent on my grandfather. He slipped into the shadows, disappearing entirely. I forced myself to follow, almost falling against the front door, then staggering outside. Cool air flowed against my face; the night tasted sweet. All around me, faint hisses from the Shurik and the grinding sounds of their sharp teeth.

Mary stood in the middle of the front yard, holding her machete. I didn't see Zee. No sign of Jack, either.

He was gone. He'd run. All because of a name.

CHAPTER 18

THERE are plenty of things in this life that really piss me off, and that's fine. I'm a grumpy person. I don't like steaks that are too tough to chew, or the condensation that gathers on a cold glass in summer. Something about that wet feeling on my fingers. I hate dirty public restrooms. Passive-aggressive behavior makes me crazy. I don't like crowds, I can't stand guns, and I not so secretly want to bury anyone who remakes my favorite action movies of the eighties.

Also, demons. Demons piss me off.

And my grandfather.

The first time I ever met him, he was full of secrets and half-truths—riddles, mysteries. Annoying, but also cute. I trusted him more, then. But after all these years, I'd come to the reluctant conclusion that it wasn't *just* benevolence that made him so damn secretive. It was self-preservation. Not of his life, but his identity. A man unwilling to face his own demons was a man who could go on wearing a mask, able to justify, rationalize, moralize—all the bad decisions, the trauma, every bit of fucked-up-ness.

I sometimes also suspected that Jack still thought of himself as a god.

And gods don't have to answer for shit.

Not even to family.

⊰⊱

I dribbled water into Grant's mouth from a soaked, ice-chilled, washrag—and said to Zee, "Ask the Shurik what it feels through its link with him."

The Shurik started hissing as soon as I asked the question, and Zee leaned in close, eyes narrowed. Aaz and Raw were sprawled on the back of the couch above my husband, little legs dangling, teddy bears and bars of soap speared on their claws. The little demons were chewing on them with the sort of contagious mindless anxiety that made me want to rock into the fetal position alongside them.

Dek and Mal's soft-throated singing didn't help, either. It was an eerie, mournful version of "Against All Odds"— the one breakup song I *really* didn't need to hear right now. I patted their heads, but that only made them sing louder.

The Shurik snapped its teeth. Zee grunted, ears flattening against his skull. I said, "What?"

"Shurik trying to heal him," he rasped, dragging his claws around his feet, so hard and deep he almost cut the floorboard in half. "If cannot heal, then slow down sickness. But, resistance."

"Resistance," I muttered. "From what?"

Zee's gaze flicked to Grant. "Him."

I sat back, surprised—reaching instinctively for our link. Old habit. More of a habit than I had realized, before now. Of course, our connection was still missing, but I was taken off guard again by the hole left behind, the emptiness. Cut off my leg, arm, and it would have felt the same. Phantoms, echoes of memory, taking the place of what had been real, vibrant, and alive.

I laid my fingertips against Grant's feverish brow, wishing he would wake up. "That doesn't make sense. I thought he was moving past that. Why would he resist being healed now?"

The Shurik wriggled free of his shirt: a pasty, wrinkled worm with sharp teeth. It stretched across my husband's chest, writhing toward my hand. I forced myself not to pull away, holding my breath as it nudged my fingertips. Low hisses exploded from its mouth. I felt the heat of its breath.

Zee cocked his head. "Says he always resisted. Before this. Since first bonded. Resisted link. Created wall."

"But he feels the Shurik and Yorana in his head."

"Feels, but not accepts. Same as resistance. Part of him . . . is afraid. Yorana sense that fear, makes them disdain. Shurik sense . . . and understand."

The last creatures I would have expected to understand the fear of becoming one with demons would be the Shurik. Maybe that disbelief showed on my face, maybe it was in my scent or in my silence, because the little, wormlike creature flopped itself heavily across my husband's neck and let out a hissy little sigh.

Raw and Aaz stilled. Zee flinched. Even Dek and Mal finally fell silent.

Zee murmured, "Shurik remember old days, before we bonded to them. Old days, on old world, when nothing mattered but sun, nothing but water, nothing but peace. Ate plants. Explored sea. Got fat on light." He fell silent for a moment, staring at his claws. "Then we brought darkness."

We brought darkness. My boys, who were the last survivors of their world, who had prayed to their gods for help in fighting an enemy they still would not name but that had swept across planets, civilizations, and destroyed them.

Maybe there were no gods, but *something* had answered my boys. Answered, and invaded them, giving them power and the strength to gather together the last surviving clans of the last surviving worlds, to form an army that would push back the force that had come to destroy them.

But the price was that none of them could remain the same; forced to change into something else, something darker, harder, fiercer. Filled with hunger. Filled with rage.

Though my husband had never said so, maybe he felt the same fear of being swallowed up. Turned into the monster he'd always had nightmares of becoming because the power to alter and control others was too sweet, and so was the temptation. Even good intentions could lead straight to hell.

Mary walked from the kitchen holding a pan of water filled with ice. Her wrinkles had deepened, her hair even more wild—tangled and matted. Mouth set in a grim, hard line. I stood as she neared and let her take my place beside Grant. She was as much his family as I was—born from the same world, with memories of his family and history no one else would ever have.

Standing wasn't easy. Dizziness swept over me, and Mary caught my hand. But she didn't look at my face—just my belly.

"Grant's woman," she whispered. "You must stay alive. For her."

Tears bit my eyes; unexpected, hot. "I will."

Mary's gaze finally flicked to mine. "Use every weapon. No mercy. Must end now, or all begins again. War. Death." Her hand found mine, squeezing. "Grief."

I stood very still, staring at her, unable to pull away. Zee slipped between us, his claws hovering above Mary's grip. He gave her a long look, which I thought she didn't notice—until, slowly, her hand loosened, and she released me. She leaned back, looking at the little demon.

"Become Kings again," she whispered. "For your Hunter. For us all."

He stared at her, but I didn't wait to hear what he might say. My skin crawled. My heart was pounding too hard. I wanted to vomit or scream—scream at Grant to open his fucking eyes—scream at myself for living.

But I had no time to be that stupid.

I snapped my fingers. Aaz hopped down from the couch, reached into the shadows, and pulled out an ice-cold bottle of ginger ale. He gave it to me, I took a long swallow, and moments later he handed me a wooden geta tray covered in sushi. I didn't ask where it was from, and I was too tired to feel amused—the rice was light and filled with avocado, just right for my queasy stomach.

My grandfather had run. I could hunt him down, but there was no guarantee he would talk when I found him. There was someone else, though. Someone I could talk to, who was almost as intimately familiar with the ways of the Aetar—and their myths, and names.

I set aside the sushi and looked at my right hand, armored and glinting silver. Veins of engraved roses flowed across its surface, threading down my wrist between my fingers. I felt no heat from the quicksilver in my bones—but it was alive, and waiting. Listening. I'd learned the hard way that even fragments of the Labyrinth were alive.

Are you going to betray me again? I thought at the armor.

Not even a tingle in response. My gaze fell on Grant. My husband, dying. And me, dying alongside him.

Unless I found a cure.

I touched Mary's shoulder. "The Aetar might try to take him again."

The Shurik rose up and hissed. Just outside the open door, from the porch, more hisses: an undulating sound of fury that, for once, I found comforting. Anyone who tried to enter this house was going to get eaten from the inside out—slowly.

Mary touched the machete hanging from her belt and gave me a grim look. I nodded and stepped back. Aaz and Raw gathered close. Zee touched my left hand.

I closed my eyes, and stars bled into my mind: stars, and the glint of a silver figure haunting the edge of my memories.

But on its heels was the darkness, winding its coils around my heart, choking out the light. Filling me with a hunger that I knew no human meal would satisfy.

Do not make your mate's mistake, it whispered. *Release your resistance. Accept your transcendence.*

I gritted my teeth and curled my right hand into a fist. Held my breath. Dreamed my need, dreamed it hard.

We fell into the void.

It was almost a relief. In the void, I felt none of the ravages of the disease—no flesh, no bone, no blood hot with fever. Nothing at all, just the emptiness, the endless, chilling drift. But my reprieve lasted only a moment because I couldn't feel my daughter—not the weight, however subtle, of her body in mine—not the pressure and heat, and swell.

Not gone, I told myself, but the alarm had already risen. Panic and memory—of blood gushing, pain and loss—and it was a terrible thing to panic without a body, to feel fear and not be able to *do,* to just feel and feel without the relief of flesh as a distraction, an anchor, a foundation. Fear was finite within the flesh. I could die, and it would be done.

In the void, I'd go on forever.

But the void ended. I fell from it with a cry, my voice alien and small in my ears. Not like me at all.

I landed on my stomach, skidding several feet as if thrown headfirst from a moving car. I was too stunned to fight it—I just went limp, letting momentum carry me across hard-packed dirt. I didn't feel a thing—no pain, not even the impact. It was the sunlight that immobilized me. So bright, so unexpected, I had to close my eyes. Hot air blazed through my lungs, but I felt no heat on my skin. Through my lashes I glimpsed my arms, black with the boys. All muscle and claw, cut with veins of silver—and those red eyes, glinting at me, wide open in their dreams.

I rolled over, sat up. Had to catch myself, dizzy. Still sick. For a moment, I did feel hot—but it was internal, gathered in my chest and back, in my gut, and head. The heat faded, replaced by a chill—and then it swelled again, full force.

Made me nauseous, like a bomb was going off, contained within my skin.

I looked around without trying to stand. Had to shield my eyes. Found nothing but rocky desert filled with cactus and scrub. Blue skies shone without a cloud, and the mountains in the distance were cut with shadows. Felt like the American Southwest, but I'd just left Texas in the night.

So. Somewhere else, on the other side of the world.

I glimpsed movement on my left, so quick and fast it was as if the world shivered. I knew it wasn't my imagination—not with the boys tugging against my skin, raging to wake. Never a good sign. I looked again, harder, holding my breath.

I didn't see anything. But I heard a scream of rage.

I staggered to my feet, blinking hard, ramming the heel of my palm into the side of my head—like that would somehow keep me upright. Or at least stop the pain throbbing in my skull. I did manage to stay standing, but the headache was a total fucking beast.

I ignored the pain and started running. Kept my hand pressed to my skull, eyes little more than slits against the bright sun. The boys kept struggling, rippling across my skin in flat, obsidian waves that shimmered and sucked at the light.

Another sharp crack hit the desert air—the detonation of a woman's voice, still shouting in anger. I stopped at the crest of a shallow outcropping, staring down at a small oasis: a line of green grass, a few stubbly trees casting diminutive shadows—and a woman held on the ground by three robed figures, fighting like crazy as one of them muzzled her. A Mahati warrior lay near them, sprawled face-first in the dirt.

I knew who those robed figures were even though I'd never laid eyes on them before. Scouts. Soldiers. All with the same gift as my husband: able to control and kill, with just their voices.

But they were slaves. Genetically engineered and brainwashed to be obedient to those they considered gods: the

Aetar, who had captured their ancestors and raped their genes for millennia.

I had to stop them. Fast.

I ran down the hill. Almost tripped, stayed on my feet—then, moments later, felt a tremendous impact against my lower back. I went down so hard, the rocks cracked beneath my knees.

Going down that hard, that fast, made my head spin. But that wasn't enough of a distraction to keep me from noticing one very strange, impossible thing.

The impact hurt.

I rolled over. And got stabbed in the stomach.

I couldn't see my attacker—sunlight blinded me—but the tremendous force behind that blow pushed me so hard into the dirt, my body made a dent.

It should have been nothing. A feather should have made as much of an impact, pain-wise—I even heard the weapon break against my body. But none of that was important.

Because I felt it. I felt pain. In my back.

And in my stomach.

CHAPTER 19

VULNERABILITY does not run in my family.

That's the lie we tell ourselves. It's a good one. I think we've been clinging to it for ten thousand years. It's as much a tradition as nameless fathers, bad tempers, and black hair.

But again, it's a lie. Our skin is unbreakable, but not our hearts. And besides that, we do have one strategic weakness.

Our daughters.

Doesn't matter that Zee and the boys are the most paranoid and dangerous nursemaids in existence. Some things are just out of their power. Nature. Accident. Freak stuff.

A volcano erupted in 1610 B.C. on the island of Santorini. Mount Thera, it was called. An apocalyptic explosion, with the energy of several atomic bombs—followed by massive ash clouds, huge tsunamis, climate change. Totally fucked people up. Inspired myths. Changed history.

My ancestor was nearby when it happened, right in the middle of the Minoan settlement of Akrotiri. Actually, two of my ancestors were there: mother and young daughter. I don't know why—that's not part of the story that's been passed down—and the boys have never been good about sharing details. All we know, all we've been told, is that right before the eruption happened—in the seconds before—my ancestor *knew*.

Sun was shining. She would have been safe. But not her daughter.

So she killed herself. Right there, on the spot. A knife straight through her eye, out the back of her skull, by her own hand. The boys could have stopped it, even asleep—but they didn't. She died, so they could transfer their protection to the girl.

Because daughters must live.

Blood must live.

In the end, as my mother once said, *what else are we fighting for?*

⚬

JUST *feeling* someone strike me there—right where my daughter was growing—brought down a haze inside my head that had nothing to do with fever.

Something exploded in my heart, deeper than rage.

I lost time. Sprawled on the ground, then suddenly I wasn't—on my feet, sun blazing in my eyes—only, the light no longer blinded. Darkness surrounded my vision, a blur of shadows as I stared at the two pale figures standing tall, still, close. Details escaped me. Faces didn't matter. One of them, a woman, was holding pieces of a broken sword, and that was all I saw. All I cared about.

I didn't think. I didn't even feel my body move, but my hand was suddenly wrapped around her collared throat and I could see her eyes, her eyes and nothing else, bulging and staring in confusion. Her voice rattled. I heard another voice, a singing voice, filled with familiar power—but darkness rolled through me like a kiss, the sweetest kiss, pouring power into my muscles and bones, my bones and cells, through every inch of me like fire—and the woman's throat exploded into ash beneath my hand.

Silver flashed. A whip, lashing around my waist. I felt the burn of it through the boys, but the sensation was far away, trapped beneath the power flowing through me. I turned, saw a bald man yanking on that whip with all his strength, muscles straining beneath the metal collar strapped to his neck. I just stood there, staring at him: my feet rooted as a mountain—my heart just as uncaring.

Loose robes swung out from his body; a series of red lines had been painted on his brow. Young face, smooth skin, eyes that looked at me through a startled haze of confusion. His mouth moved—he was singing. I knew what he was, from that alone.

A weapon.

I was surprised that weapon hadn't already been sent after my husband.

I grabbed the whip, pulled hard with a strength not my own. The man staggered forward, eyes widening. He let go of the whip just before I would have been in arm's reach, but I lunged forward and caught his wrist. A cry escaped his lips, deep and melodic—and his skin smoked beneath my grip.

Mercy, part of me thought, but I felt an ache in my belly, and an image of my mother swept through me, eyes dark as death, face set in stone—beating a man to death for trying to hurt me. How many men had she killed for that reason alone? Had she ever regretted taking even one of their lives?

"No," I said out loud, and the man screamed, screamed and screamed as he watched his arm turn to ash, a wave of disintegration that flowed through his flesh: across his ribs and down his legs, through his chest and shoulders, claiming his throat and head. His eyes died last. His eyes, watching mine with horror. I never looked away, not once.

Something hit me from behind. I felt the point of impact

in the back of my neck—the edge of a blade. One blow, trying to cut my head off. I turned and found another man behind me, staring at the sword in his hands; the blade was dented.

"You," I whispered, and my voice was deeper, hollow— but it was *my* voice, and not the darkness, even though that power strained against my skin—strained and pushed, then melted—into my muscles and bones, simmering me in heat.

"Kneel," I said.

His large, pale hands tightened around the deformed sword, and his narrowed gaze flicked down to my stomach. His mouth tightened, twisted, with disgust, and disdain. "Abomination," he said, voice smooth and melodic. "Dark woman. Hunter. Your usefulness has ended. We, the Messengers, have come to carry out the beloved desires of our Divine Lords."

Ash flowed through my fingers, clinging to my jeans; what little touched my skin was immediately absorbed by the boys. I felt far away from them, far from my own body— drifting in warmth.

"Kneel," I said again in a soft voice.

His gaze flicked down to the ash, then the crumpled body of the woman who lay beside his feet. "Surrender to your creator. Surrender to those who gave your ancestors life."

I glanced down the hill and saw the woman I'd come to find, half–sitting up, hands bound behind her back, a leather gag covering the lower half of her face. Her eyes were furious, glancing from me to the robed men standing on either side of her—their expressions like stone: cold, remote, certain.

Nothing but masks. I'd seen how the others had died— astonished their entitlement to life had finally run out.

Stop playing games, part of me thought, though it was difficult, through a haze. My brain was fogging up. I had come here to find the woman. I needed to speak with her. Games of power, forcing others to acknowledge power—that was a waste. I had no time to waste though I couldn't remember why. I could barely remember the anger that had been so fresh only moments before.

I turned from the man and walked down the hill. I barely felt the ground beneath me—floating inside my own skin, floating on the edges of another world. A hand grabbed the back of my neck, fisting my hair—a touch I barely felt. A man's scream filled the air, abruptly lapsing into silence. Ash floated past me.

I was facing the robed men when it happened, witnessed the widening of their eyes, the splash of color in their cheeks. One of them reached down for the woman on the ground—who rolled swiftly away to her feet. Chains dragged from her ankles; her attackers had not finished binding her.

I started running. Faster than I'd ever run before, nearly flying with each step. The men froze, staring at me—careful masks finally breaking into fear.

Just before I reached them, they disappeared. Blinked out. I was so close I felt the air suck inward to fill the space where they'd been standing. I should have been surprised, but I felt nothing at losing them. I kept moving toward the woman I'd come for and tore away the leather gag.

She spat on the ground, eyes bloodshot. "Hunter."

Her name was on the tip of my tongue, but I couldn't reach for it through the haze. It didn't seem important, either.

"Hunter," said the woman again, but I ignored her. Something was still wrong.

I looked down at my arms, saw movement across my skin; obsidian muscles slithering in tight coils, veins of quicksilver pulsing, threading beneath shifting claws and glinting eyes.

My boys.

My head cleared a little, but that only made the uneasiness deepen. My boys rarely moved during the day, and only out of necessity. This was . . . pained. As if they were writhing in their sleep.

And as soon as I thought it, I felt it—that agonized pull against my body, the boys struggling against my skin. I stared at them, lost. My mind, still trapped in death, hunger, anger—part of me a million miles removed from my own body—as if I didn't really exist. All of this, just a dream.

It is a dream, whispered the darkness, so close inside my mind that for a moment I thought I'd spoken those words out loud.

Whose dream? I asked, trying to remember why I was so angry, what had happened to bring me here to this moment. It shouldn't have been difficult. I had to remember—
—my daughter.

Cold dread washed from my chest into my stomach, with such force my knees buckled. I didn't fall down, but I might as well have; giant bears could have been kickboxing each other in the nuts, and I wouldn't have noticed.

My daughter.

I yanked up my shirt, found my stomach covered in tattoos: a slow whirling churn of dark, gleaming bodies, spiraling around my navel like a demonic galaxy. I stared, running my hands over my stomach. My fingers lingered over my abdomen, a spot just to the left of my hip. I couldn't see an injury beneath the boys—but I felt the tenderness of that spot, a soft deliberate ache.

"Fuck," I muttered, and then again, louder. *"Fuck."*

My back was still sore—and now that I was paying attention to my body, so was my neck from the sword attack. My waist, as well, from that damn whip. I wasn't really injured, not that I was aware. But I could feel pain.

Impossible.

I wasn't as invulnerable as I should have been. Something was wrong with the boys. The disease, perhaps. Zee had said they could heal me once they were on my skin. But if it made them sick, too . . . if it hurt them . . .

I took a deep breath, but it didn't calm the torment. Worse, the darkness was awake. The darkness had been awake for some time, but this was different: Its presence hummed through me like a current of black lightning. It didn't hurt, but it made me feel . . . altered.

Alive, whispered the darkness. *You are coming alive, Hunter.*

I was alive before, I replied, troubled and afraid at how easily I had reached for that power, how little remorse I felt using it. Not the first time that had happened, but never had it felt so seamless . . . as if I didn't know where I began and the darkness ended. I couldn't see the line. I couldn't *feel* it.

And if I couldn't feel it, I couldn't tear it apart.

You would break yourself, came that soft hiss, coiling around my heart and squeezing, gently. *For nothing more than a mask. You cling to masks of who you think you should be. Who you believe is safe. But that is not being alive.*

What is beneath the mask? continued the darkness, softly. *Who is the Hunter and who is the Kiss? Who is the Queen and the mother, and the woman who bleeds?*

"Enough," I said out loud, to the darkness or myself, I wasn't certain.

Movement, in the corner of my eye. I flinched, but it was only the woman—and her name, our history, flooded back into my mind.

When she saw me looking at her, impatience slid across her face—mixing with anger, exhaustion—and she turned in silence, showing me her bound wrists. Chains dangled; silver manacles flashed in the sun. Her robes had been torn off one shoulder, with blood and dirt rubbed into her short hair and pale skin; and the scratches, bruises, were deep. She had been beaten for a long time.

"Messenger," I said in a hoarse voice. "I'm sorry I wasn't here sooner."

"You could not know," she replied, giving me a cold, repressive glare over her shoulder. "Free me."

I slid my left hand over the manacles, which were connected by a thin strip of metal, and started at that weakest point—digging in my blackened fingernails with a hard, sawing motion. My strength just wasn't there, though—and neither were the boys. I was distracted by their slow, pained movement over my arm, and their slight shift in color; from obsidian to a dark charcoal gray. My nails were weak, too—*weaker*, anyway—and I felt pressure in them bordering on pain.

I kept working, though, chipping and tearing away at the metal binding the manacles—until finally the Messenger jerked her arms apart with a grunt and separated her wrists. I flexed my hands, fatigue running deep into my muscles. My fingers throbbed. So did my head. I was suddenly so thirsty, I couldn't separate my tongue from the roof of my mouth.

I managed, though. "Are you okay?"

The Messenger flashed me a hard, uneasy look; her gaze swept down my body, no doubt reading my aura just as Grant always did: like a book that could spell out in one glance all the secrets of my soul.

"You are not the same," she said.

"No shit," I replied. "What just happened here?"

The Messenger walked toward the Mahati warrior sprawled face-first in the dirt. Chains dragged, from her feet and wrists. "You know what happened. I never returned to my masters—and now, after all this time, my old gods have decided to learn what happened to me. And why, as I am still alive, I failed to follow their commands."

Years ago, she'd come to us as the enemy, sent to investigate the deaths of two Aetar on earth. We'd fought, again and again, until my husband had snapped the conditioning that made her unquestioningly obedient to her gods. Sometimes, I suspected he'd done a little more than that. I couldn't really imagine anyone's switching sides so easily, not after a lifetime of brainwashing.

"They sent a small army after you."

"It takes a small army to capture my kind. Not that it is often required." The Messenger crouched beside the Mahati, and for the first time her expression fractured, and deep sadness flickered in her eyes. There, and gone, all in a moment. The hardness returned, the glint and cold.

"They killed him," I said, not seeing any movement, not even the faintest rise and fall of breath.

"He lives still," she replied, surprising me. "But they hurt him when they severed our bond." And then she fixed that narrow gaze on me, searching, focusing, seeing the invisible. "Did they do the same to you and the Lightbringer?"

A dull ache hit my chest. I reached for my bond with Grant, but the hole was still there, as gaping and horrible as ever. "No. Something else did that."

"And he has not reasserted the connection?" A frown touched her mouth. "Is he dead?"

"Not yet. But that's why I came to find you. He's been poisoned with a disease. All of us have, including the demons."

She did not look surprised. "Illness is a weapon that has been used before, on worlds that found disfavor with the Divine Lords. It is simple and efficient. A population dies until it is small enough to be controlled or exterminated entirely, then time erases the rest."

"You've seen this with your own eyes."

She looked down at the Mahati. "I have killed the survivors."

Of course she had. And I'd just turned men and women into ash by touching them. No fucking stones were going to be cast by me. "Do they ever change their minds? Give these people a cure?"

"It has happened," she said, running a slow hand through the air over the Mahati's back. The chain dangling from her manacle rolled against his side, and I saw his gray skin twitch. "Not often."

Flesh was cheap. Flesh was part of the game. It would, indeed, be more interesting—more *fun*—for an Aetar to create a new civilization, new life, from scratch. No matter the cost.

And to them, there was no cost at all.

It wouldn't cost them anything to kill this world, its humans and demons—even Grant.

Not true, part of me thought—a part that sounded too much like the darkness for comfort. *Because you are in this world, and you are the creation that cannot be undone.*

I looked back up the hill, at the piles of ash blowing toward us. I could barely recall taking those lives. Just the rage and righteousness, followed by the numb distance of the haze. What few memories remained felt cold, crisp: those pale, bald figures lost in their robes, lost to me and the power I had called on.

"They questioned me about your child," said the Messenger suddenly, fixing me with that cold, piercing gaze. "Almost as much as they questioned me about my own corruption."

"I'm sorry," I said, then opened my mouth again, about to begin my own interrogation. But the woman beat me to it, with a sharpness in her voice that made me uneasy.

"Do you know *how* my kind discovered she is a creation of the Lightbringer's seed?"

"I assumed they just . . . knew," I said, lamely. "That there were spies."

"Spies," she echoed, staring at me like I was a fool. "No spies, Hunter. Only betrayal. The Aetar were *informed* about your child."

Uneasiness became flat-out dread. "Who would do that?"

Bitterness touched her mouth. "They told me it was the Wolf."

The Wolf.

Jack.

My grandfather.

CHAPTER 20

I suppose some people would have called the Messenger a liar, but she'd never given two shits about deceiving me. Threatening to kill me, yes—acting like an asshole, certainly—but lies? I wasn't sure deception was even in her genes. Like, literally.

But I still didn't believe her. I couldn't. She had to be wrong; it was an Aetar trap, a setup. Plant some bad information, then let it leak. Watch me lose my shit and make stupid choices. It happened in the movies, right? Not that I needed a distraction to make stupid choices; I did that spectacularly well when I was fully focused and present.

"Jack wouldn't," I said, and inwardly cringed at the sound of my voice; like a plaintive five-year-old. My grandfather loved me. He could not have done this.

"He is one of them," replied the Messenger, with cold assurance. "The gods are bound together, Hunter, through time and spirit, and intent. How can mortal flesh compare to bonds that have lasted the age of stars?"

I shook my head, walking away from her—stopping after

just a few feet and bouncing on my toes. I wanted to run. "No."

"As you wish," she said, with only a hint of mockery, and crouched again over the Mahati. Her voice rose soft in song, barely audible, though I felt the chill touch of power shiver over me. It was all for the demon, though. I finally saw his back rise and fall. Still alive, just as she'd said.

The wind shifted. A sour, piercing scent filled my nose. I turned, looking deeper into the rocks and scrub, and saw a pale, naked foot. A couple steps closer revealed an entire person.

Several people, in fact, piled together and bleeding from their throats. Dressed in almost nothing, with hairless bodies and disconcertingly simple faces—as if a designer had been building androids that would only approximate human.

"Mules," said the Messenger behind me. "My demon killed them first. He was wise to do so."

Mules. Humans whose only function was to provide life energy. The engineered, enslaved Lightbringers would have brought them along as portable meals, necessary for their survival. Just as my energy, my life, had been necessary to keep Grant alive when he used his gift.

The Mahati demon stirred, shifting restlessly against the ground. He only had one arm; the other ended at the elbow. Scars from stripped, cannibalized flesh covered his back and thighs; long silver braids flowed around him in thick ropes. His head turned slightly, and his eyes began fluttering open; not quite conscious, but close. The Messenger sat back, voice dropping to a hum, gaze serious and dark. Her entire focus, on him. I didn't want to interrupt—but, whatever.

"The Devourer," I said. "Do you know that name?"

Her entire body twitched, a convulsive, electrocuted shudder; I might as well have jolted her with a cattle prod. Her voice broke into silence, and she tore her gaze from the demon to stare at me. I had never seen her appear so startled. It made her seem . . . young and human.

"Did the Wolf share that name with you?" she asked.

I shook my head, gaze never leaving hers. "Tell me about the Devourer."

She flinched, baring her teeth. "Do not say that name out loud. It is dangerous to speak of him."

"Really." I drew out the word, unhappy with her reaction. "Why?"

She hesitated. "The gods embrace creation and beauty, all the possibilities represented by the divine organic. It is life, for them, even when their motives are . . . off-putting. But *that* one . . . his art . . . is the opposite."

"Death, you mean."

"Suffering. Annihilation."

I gave up trying to be tough and sat down on the ground. The Messenger blinked and leaned back on her haunches, robes and chains hanging loose around her. Shadows winged. Vultures, already gliding high in the sky.

"He might know how to cure the disease that's killing us," I said, but saying those words out loud made the situation feel more impossible.

"He is a monster," she said, surprising me. "And there is no Divine Lord who would disagree, or punish me for saying so. It is known. It is truth. If there is a god whom other gods fear, it is he."

"So you're saying we're fucked."

Her brow lifted, delicately. "If there is a cure, you will find it elsewhere. Or, you will help the Lightbringer survive this illness through other means, and you will tell yourself that is enough."

"Enough," I repeated. "You mean, let the world die of this thing."

"There are wars that cannot be won," she said quietly. "But there is always a war, Hunter."

Fight to live another day. And then live to fight.

It was the same refrain I'd heard my entire life, and it was just as cold from the Messenger's lips as it had been from my mother's. It was no lie, either. No fool's advice.

This was the life we had been born into. The life our bodies had been crafted for—always, the fight. My daughter carried that blood. My daughter, built cell by cell from *my* cells, my soul, and the souls of those who had come before.

But violence was not the life I wanted to give her. Violence was not part of the dream I wanted inside her head.

Escape from that future seemed to be slipping away, though.

"Who would know where the Devourer is?" I asked.

The Messenger flinched again and gave me a cold look. "If you find him, you will receive no answers, there will be no cure. He will unmake you, Hunter."

"It'll tickle, I'm sure." I stood and had to close my eyes as dizziness kicked in, and black spots pushed into my vision. But my head throbbed a little less, and the burn of fever seemed to be fading. Was I healing? Were the boys suffering, so I could live?

"Who?" I asked again, opening my eyes.

The Messenger ignored me, reaching for the Mahati, who was trying to sit up. She never actually touched him, but her fingers seemed to strum the air, and another low hum left her throat. He tilted his head to look at her, and I didn't know what I saw in his eyes—anger or hate, or maybe something that could have been desire. Whatever it was, that look held power between them, and I felt like an intruder.

"The Divine Lords cannot hide from one another," said the Messenger in a soft voice, not taking her gaze from the Mahati. "Find the Wolf. He will know."

And then she finally looked at me, and her gaze was cool and still, not marred in the slightest by the swollen lip or cuts above her brow.

"I have ever been loyal to my gods," she said. "And you and the child you carry *are* abominations. Your power is dangerous. It will break too much that is sacred. The unknown," she went on, pointing to my stomach, "cannot be trusted.

"But," she added, softly, "you and the Lightbringer gave

me freedom, of a kind. I know to value it now. I understand
its worth. So for that I will tell you . . . be wary of the god
who is your grandfather."

"He wouldn't hurt us."

"Not even for your own good?" The Messenger finally
slid her hand under the Mahati's arm, and with her other
stroked the air above a deep gash in his biceps. "We also
tell stories about the Wolf."

"Yes?" I asked, wary.

Bitterness touched her mouth. "He is the hunter who
slaughters worlds."

<hr/>

I expected it to still be night when I returned to the farm,
with the Messenger and her Mahati in tow—but the sun was
just peeking over the horizon, a golden glint piercing the
farthest edge of a blue sky, and the boys seemed to sag
against my skin. Quieter now, sluggish. Exhausted, I
thought.

A small herd of cows was penned in by the barn, making distress calls and looking wild-eyed and uneasy. I
didn't know who had brought them there, but I had a strong
feeling they weren't long for the world. Meat, just like the
rest of us.

I charged up the porch steps, skipping around writhing
piles of Shurik, who ignored me but lifted their fat little
bodies off the old wood slates to hiss at the Messenger. Her
lip curled with disdain. Her Mahati flexed his one good
hand, the long tines of his fingers rubbing together with a
steel-scraping sound.

Heart was in my throat. Prepared for the worst. But Grant
was still stretched out on the couch, Mary seated beside
him—stuffing fresh marijuana leaves in her mouth with
one hand, dabbing his brow with the other. A machete was
in her lap. At her feet, the crystal skull that my grandfather
had been lugging around.

I looked at it and felt my stomach turn over. I didn't know what that feeling meant, but it came from a deep place, and the darkness—the darkness that was flowing through me, even though I was myself again, myself as much as I could be—curled around that sensation and tasted it.

A window, it whispered. *But light can distort sight . . . in ways that darkness cannot.*

I ignored that, looking for my grandfather. No sign of him, and that dread growing inside me only deepened. I didn't go searching the house, though. I sat beside Grant, taking his hand in mine. I felt the fever before I got close enough to touch him; his entire body radiated furious heat. His lips had cracked and peeled, and his face was sunken. The Shurik on his chest barely moved to greet me—all I got was a faint hiss. I almost patted its head but caught myself before anything embarrassing could happen.

"He dreams," Mary whispered, sagging in her chair. I gave her a second, harder look, and felt my gut clench.

"You're sick, too," I said.

"Disgusting," she muttered through gritted teeth, but she was staring at the Messenger when she said it. "Flesh, disgusting."

"Move, all of you," commanded the other woman, then glanced at the crystal skull and blinked. Disgust, dismay, touched her face.

"Barbarians," she announced. "Leaving an artifact of power on the *floor* like a footstool."

"Keep power close," Mary rasped with defiance—and winced, touching her head. "Power never sleeps."

The Messenger looked at the old woman like she wanted to argue. Or start a bare-knuckled boxing match that would end with someone's head popped off. My bets, if it happened, were on Mary—but someone had to be the adult, and I guessed that was me. Fuck us all.

I stepped between the two women, blocking them deliberately from each other's view. I had my own problems with the Messenger, but all Mary saw when she looked at her was the slave of a war fought and lost—the face of a child who should have been born free on a world that was now gone forever, except in her memories. And it always pissed her off.

I helped the old woman stand, which was harder than expected—mostly because she didn't know how to accept my help. When she began to stumble, she punched me in the arm instead of letting me support her. Strong old woman—I felt the blow through the boys. Dull, but there. The rest of my body was still sore, too. I expected to see bruises on my skin later on.

I tried not to think too hard about that. It made me afraid.

I slid my hand under Mary's elbow and led her to the kitchen. "Where's my grandfather?"

"Still gone," she muttered. "Shurik came to guard. Other demons staying away. Some sick. Rest are cowards."

Maybe, I thought. But this was survival for all of them— all of us—and I couldn't condemn a little cowardice when your entire species was on the line. I would give them all up to keep my daughter and husband safe, and they knew it.

When Mary collapsed into the chair, I knew she was sicker than she was letting on; she didn't even give me a dirty look. I drank two glasses of water—gulped them down so sloppily that a small river ran down my chin and throat— and then placed a third glass into Mary's hands.

Someone had turned on the television again but left the volume muted. I saw more images of the Mahati storming that cabin, but it didn't make a dent in me. Right now, with all this shit raining down, a ham sandwich would have caused me more anxiety.

I pulled my cell phone free of my back pocket and called Rex. He answered on the first ring.

"What?" He sounded wary. "I haven't found any more Aetar. And before you say another word, there are disturbing rumors coming out of that farm."

"We're all gonna die, we're all gonna die?" I replied, wryly. "Pfft. I mock your rumors."

Rex grunted at me. "You're a terrible liar."

"Whatever. I need you to tap that network of little parasites and find out where my grandfather is, and what he's doing."

He was silent a moment. "Are we officially spying on him?"

"Your kind spies on everyone, whether they want to or not. Give me a fucking break. Blood Mama probably has an army floating over my grandfather's head."

"You're nuts. I'll call you as soon as I find something."

Good, reliable, demon-possessed Rex. And to think, I'd once almost murdered him. I started to hang up, but he said, "Maxine."

He almost never used my real name. It was always, Hunter, or Hunter Kiss, or maybe just an expletive. So I hesitated, waiting, and he said in small voice, "I like this world. It's fucked up, but it's good. Please tell me that's not about to change."

"It already has," I said, and couldn't bear to say anything else. I very quietly ended the call.

I went to the bathroom. Sat on the toilet and tried not to cry. With my pants pushed down I could see the boys on my legs and they looked gray and pale, and dull. I ran my hands over them, held my palms over their slow-moving faces— and whispered, "Love you, love you, love you."

My reflection was shit. I had new wrinkles in my forehead that made my face look like a minitractor had been plowing right to left and between my eyes. My lips were cracked, bleeding, my cheeks sunken. Haunted, all of me. Haunted and sick, and exhausted.

I washed my face, patted my abdomen, and took a deep breath.

I could do this. I was not alone. I was beloved.

I went back out into the living room. Natural light pushed

through the windows, but the space was cool and dark, which only deepened the hush that fell around us.

The Mahati crouched in the corner, eyeing the Shurik through the open door. The Messenger had already taken Mary's seat and stared at Grant with unblinking, distant eyes. I wanted to pester her but kept my mouth shut and listened to my own body: dizziness fading, strength returning, headache almost gone. I wasn't as happy about that as I should have been.

The Messenger said, "I do not know if I can help him. He is torn inside."

I wanted to ask what that meant, but a low, smooth hum rolled from her throat. Power flowed over my skin, and the Mahati took a deep breath and strode from the house. Fled, really. He kicked some Shurik on the way out, and they hissed at him like he was their next Happy Meal. He didn't seem to care.

I hesitated, then moved in close and picked up the crystal skull. I didn't particularly want to touch it—the memory of that earlier vision was still too sharp. I was afraid of what I would see again.

Nothing at all, it seemed. I waited, holding my breath. Took me only a minute to start feeling ridiculous. I was going to jump at shadows soon.

The Messenger was right, though: It seemed wrong, having it there on the floor. I wasn't sure why Mary had removed the skull from Jack's hiding place.

I carried it outside to the porch. Five fat Shurik were tangled up in my chair, the one I always sat in with Grant when we wanted to feel like an old married couple.

"Move," I snapped, and all of them raised the tips of their wormlike heads to stare at me. I felt, quite distinctly, that I was looking at a bunch of petulant teens giving me the "fuck you, old person" stare, which would have been a lot more amusing if I hadn't already felt like an *actual* fucked-up old person. I waited a couple seconds to see if they were going to listen, but they didn't even twitch in the right direction.

I used my foot to sweep them off the chair. It was like trying to move cats. All hisses and Velcro grips and tumbling, curling bodies. One of them lost its mind and tried to bite me through my jeans. I felt its teeth connect, the immense strength of its jaw, but no pain. The Shurik, on the other hand, fell back with all its teeth falling from its mouth, covered in black blood and shrieking.

I sat down and pretended not to care. I also pretended not to watch as its companions dragged its writhing body off the porch into the dandelions, its little cries growing fainter and fainter as it was pulled farther from the house. The rest of the Shurik inched away from me. Not far—apparently, they had some pride—but just out of reach.

With my feet up on the rail, I balanced the crystal skull on my knees. Slid my gaze past those holes for eyes, down to the sharp piranha teeth. I felt light-headed.

"Jack," I said, thinking out loud.

Thirteen skulls. Created to amplify an Aetar's inherent power—enough to build a prison on a woman's body, a prison for five demons and the darkness inside them, a prison that would be inherited through blood: a reincarnation of mother and daughter and demon, for all time.

The boys had destroyed all those skulls, except this one. Jack's skull. Jack's weapon.

He wouldn't have betrayed us. He wouldn't have told the Aetar about Grant, or that I was carrying the child of a Lightbringer.

Doubt began to pick at me, though. Just a little. But a little was a lot.

"What did he see in you?" I muttered at the skull, picking it up and looking into its eyes. "What did he see, for all those months?"

And how could I use this thing to help us now? How could I use it to find the Devourer?

The Devourer.

At the exact moment I thought that name, a shock ran through the skull, straight into my hands. I almost dropped the damn thing, fumbling for it against my chest. Heat flowed from its core, followed by a sheen of light that arced through the crystal in a hot white flash.

My armor reacted as well—rippling like water, clashing against the edges of my skin like it was fighting to cover the rest of my arm and body.

The boys surged. Zee's face appeared in my arm, crimson eyes open and staring, his claws frozen, stretched over my skin in a grotesque image of battle. I heard a ringing sound, louder and louder, drilling through my ears, straight through to the center of my head.

The skull began to glow. My vision flickered to black. For a moment I was afraid I'd fallen into the void, except that I could still feel the chair beneath me and the breeze in my hair. I touched my eyes, but they were open. I was blind.

Heat flashed over my skin. So much heat, the air burned around me: popped, and crackled like bone. I tried to take a breath, but there was nothing: The air pulled right out of my lungs. In its place, smoke. A bitter cloud that coated the inside of my nostrils and mouth, plugging my throat like a hot fist pushing down my esophagus.

Fire. I was inside a fire.

I grabbed my right hand, desperate for the void—but all I felt was naked human skin. No metal. No armor.

Fear hit, mixed with the drowning poison of dread—so overwhelming I no longer felt the fire burning or the smoke choking me. No pain, just *feelings*, a toxic crash of emotion that slammed into me, and kept slamming, until I felt burned just from terror and not the fire. I fought for any escape— reached for the bond I shared with my husband—but that was still gone. Reached deeper, for the darkness.

It wasn't there, either. I couldn't even feel the boys on my skin. I was totally alone.

Open your eyes, whispered a voice in the fire, but I was so paralyzed and unnerved, I could barely hear it. I didn't want to open my eyes. I was afraid of the smoke and the sting. I was terrified, caught up in the unspeakable knowledge of dreams—that if I looked, if I looked—something terrible would happen.

Something terrible was already happening. I opened my eyes.

And blacked right the fuck out.

CHAPTER 21

WHEN I woke up, I didn't know where I was.

It took a moment of staring at the porch rail, the driveway, blue sky—my own propped-up feet—before my life came back to me. Even then, it was slow.

My body felt strange: too big and uncomfortable, like a giant had been stuffed inside my skin, stretching me out as if I were a balloon. My hands were full. When I saw the crystal skull, memories rushed back, so hard and fast I leaned over the arm of the chair and vomited.

Nothing came up, but some Shurik who had been edging closer stopped and inched away.

"Shit," I muttered, head pounding. I began to close my eyes against the pain but stopped as even more memories flooded through me. Worse memories. Memories that made my throat close and left me choking.

My breath wheezed, barely touching my lungs. I scrabbled at my chest, fingers digging in—but it wasn't the prospect of a slow, panicked asphyxiation that had me scared—it was one memory I couldn't shake that made me afraid to close my eyes. Like a kid afraid of the dark: The monsters wouldn't get me if I could see them coming.

And I'd seen a monster. I remembered that now.

Just for a split second: a terrible, obscene moment that stretched and stretched inside my mind, hanging in time, frozen and awful. An impression, more than anything else. Some . . . massive shape, lost in fire, radiating a feeling of immense, remorseless indifference that made me feel small as shit and just as worthless. It wasn't the implacability of a storm or earthquake—that, at least, felt natural. This was aberrance: alive and aware. And just one look had fucked me up.

I could breathe again, but my hands shook. All of me, trembling. I resisted the urge to toss the crystal skull over the rail into the grass, and instead I stood, very carefully, and walked back inside the farmhouse. I needed to see my husband. I needed some reminder of what was real. Maybe the monster was just around the corner, but not here— not now.

Nothing much seemed to have changed. The Messenger had left her chair and stood behind Grant's head, her fingers pressing into his temples. A low hum shivered through the air. I watched them both, still hungry for reassurance, then went to Mary.

She had left the kitchen to lie down in a nest of blankets in the middle of the living-room floor. Curled on her side, eyes wide open, staring at the couch. It was disturbing, seeing her so still. Her cheeks were red, feverish. I set the crystal skull beside her, and, in total silence, she pulled it close and hugged it to her stomach. My vision blurred. I was afraid I'd fall into another vision—but no, I told myself, I was just tired.

I made my way to the empty chair beside the couch and took Grant's hand. His skin was warm and dry, but not hot. Reassuringly alive—that was his temperature. The Shurik was still on his chest, but its color had improved—from death gray to death paste. That also had to be encouraging,

I told myself, and leaned in—staring at the damn thing like it was a measure of my husband's health.

Little teeth glistened at me. I bared my teeth in return.

But that was all I could do. I sat there, body aching, mind racing—gripping my husband's hand, squeezing his fingers, and lightly scratching his wrist.

I'd had everything I'd ever wanted, for a brief time. A man who loved me. A home. A family. I *still* had these things. But there was always an expiration date, wasn't there? Most people could ignore that, but the cold truth hung in front of me.

This won't last, it said. *Time is running out.*

"Rest," said the Messenger, breaking her song, looking at me with those cold, hard eyes. No use pretending that she couldn't see I was afraid and lost. "An hour will not break the world."

"An hour could save us."

"No," she said, still holding my gaze. "It will not."

I stared at her, ready to argue. But to what point? She was wrong about time being meaningless. Even a moment could make a difference. But she *was* right that I needed rest. I hadn't slept in . . . a while. It scared me to try. Especially now.

"Tell me about the disease," I said. "What do you see?"

She hesitated. "The Lightbringer could not heal the demons of it."

"No."

Again, she paused, her gaze becoming unfocused as she stared down at my husband. "It is a puzzle, Hunter. A poison that lives, that replicates itself with tremendous speed. It refuses to be killed or purged. All I can do is make him stronger and help his body fight. It will not save him, but it will buy him time."

And you? I asked the darkness. *What could you do?*

One life already saved, came the slow whisper, followed by a pulse that ran through my body like a second, massive heartbeat. *You have nothing else to bargain with.*

I'm asking. I'm begging.

You prayed, murmured the darkness. *You prayed with all the power of your soul for your daughter to be saved, and so your soul was given freely. Pray for this man, but it will never be with the same power as you prayed for your own blood.*

You're wrong, I said.

You do not love him as much as you love your child. You do not need him as much as you need her. You know she is protected beneath the shadow of your heart, and so you are reckless . . . but you would let this world die if she was not safe. Every life would crumble to ash to see her live. Including his.

My breath caught. The Messenger said, "Hunter," but I couldn't acknowledge her. A different, devastating dread was rising through me, and it made me want to puke.

I loved Grant. I loved him with all my heart. He was part of me in ways no one could ever be, and I would do anything to save him.

But in my heart of hearts, in that secret place where silence was power, the darkness held the truth. I wanted my husband to live. I wanted the demons to survive. I wanted to protect this world. And I would fight for it, with every breath.

But not my last breath. That was saved for my daughter.

I felt strange, unbalanced. Needing a distraction, I checked my phone—and straightened. Rex had tried to call, and there was a text from him, too.

Mongolia, I read. *Outside Ölgii. He's there right now.*

I stood, slowly. My lower stomach ached, but I told myself that was natural, just the baby growing and my body making room. "I know where my grandfather is. I have to go find him."

The Messenger's mouth tightened. "Remember what I told you."

"Thanks." I leaned in, brushing my lips over Grant's brow. "Keep him safe."

"I would not be trying to save his life if I intended to let him die by another's hands." The Messenger hesitated. "They should have already tried again to take him. And your daughter."

I touched my stomach. "What does it mean that they haven't?"

"I do not know. There seems to be little strategy involved. If they had truly been intent on capturing the Lightbringer, it would have been easy to accomplish by now. Sending giants to attack you was ill-advised. His slow death from this disease seems to have been an accident. Even the attack on your daughter appears opportunistic rather than planned. None of that is the Aetar way." She had never referred to the Aetar by their name; she said the word with difficulty, as if it cut the inside of her mouth.

"We've drawn their attention. You're evidence of that. We've been expecting them to come after us for years."

"But not like this. With such . . . sloppiness. Two Aetar died on this world. That is too important for anything but precision."

I couldn't argue with her. I'd had a nagging feeling that something wasn't right about this situation . . . and she'd just managed to give voice to what was bothering me. "What should they have done?"

"Captured me first," she said, without hesitation. "Interrogated me. And then sent an overwhelming force, more of my kind, to take the Lightbringer. During the day, when you are without the power of your demons. Or better, when the two of you are separated by distance. Drug him, remove him from this world. Poison the demon army, then. Wait for your child to be born, and—"

"I got it," I interrupted, disturbed. "The Aetar would not have come themselves."

"Never. They value their lives too much." The Messenger's eyes glittered. "Something is wrong, Hunter."

How could things be worse? I wanted to ask her. Instead, I rubbed my stomach and watched the slow rise and fall of my husband's chest. "If it's not the Aetar, then who?"

"There is no one else," she said. "That is what I do not understand."

"If we're being manipulated . . ." But I stopped, unable to finish that sentence. If we were being manipulated, it still didn't change the fact that my husband was dying and that we'd set loose a fatal disease on other humans. Something had to be done.

I backed away. "I'll return as soon as I can."

Uncertainty flickered across the Messenger's face. "I will do my best here."

"What is it?" I asked. "Is there something else?"

I wasn't certain she would answer me. But her shoulders stiffened, as did her jaw, and, in a low voice, she said, "Part of me still belongs to them. They made me, Hunter. It is . . . difficult for me to fight against the Divine Lords."

It was the closest to vulnerable I'd ever seen her. I didn't make any typical human overtures—no reaching out, no sympathetic noises. Not that I was very familiar with those, myself. Instead, I looked her dead in the eyes.

"No one gives two shits that they made you," I said. "All that matters is what you make of yourself."

She frowned at me. I felt like the worst Hallmark card ever.

"Just remember they'll kill you," I added. "How about that?"

Her mouth twitched. "They will torture me first. But yes, I see your point."

Great. I glanced down at my husband again, feeling useless as shit. Worse, I felt as if I had a monster breathing down my neck. Inside that crystal skull, I'd looked into the eye of Sauron like some little hobbit, and Sauron had looked right back.

I felt like he was still looking.

I tossed a blanket over the crystal skull. Mary didn't seem to notice, staring straight ahead, cheeks flushed, wild hair drooping. I stepped back, right hand clenching into a fist. Quicksilver glimmered across my skin, that mirrored metal etched with a slow-moving tide of tangled coils: roses spiraling, galaxies, or labyrinths. I fixed my mind on my grandfather and Mongolia, on my need for answers. I had to find him. I had to know what was true and the lie.

One last deep breath. No pain. No smoke in the air. I half expected not to be able to breathe at all—the memory of my burning throat was so strong.

That's not going to happen again, I thought.

You should stop lying to yourself, whispered the darkness, as I fell into the void.

⬦

IT was night where I landed, tumbling into grass beneath a sky filled with stars and a low-hanging crescent moon. The air was cold on my face, and I took a deep breath, bracing myself for the boys to wake up.

Only, they didn't.

Long seconds passed. A full minute. I counted the time in my head, waiting and waiting, growing sick with alarm. The boys tugged on my skin—an uncomfortable, intensifying pressure—but that was all.

I wanted to puke. I looked straight ahead, dimly taking in the flat grassland that stretched to the horizon. To my right, far away, I saw the prick and flicker of firelight. Just one small fire, not much bigger than a star.

Jack, I thought.

And still, Zee and the boys fought to wake. Except now, it hurt.

Rip off the Band-Aid fast, I'd always said. Slow was worse. Slow was horrific, like being chewed through a wood chipper, inch by inch. Each slice, every break, drawn out to its full potential for agony. I was, literally, being pulled in all directions at once—torn apart in the tiniest of fragments. I gritted my teeth, didn't make a sound. Screaming would have hurt, too. Screaming would have been worse.

You are not alone, whispered the darkness.

As if you care, I spat, with venom and fear and loneliness roaring through me. *I'm just the flesh, the flesh you want, and when you get me, I'll be nothing. So shut the fuck up with the pleasantries.*

I heard another whisper, but no words—I couldn't hear anything past my screaming skin—but what I felt, what cut through the agony, was a soft bloom inside my chest, like an explosion of ink released by a squid in the dark sea. A cloud filled with tendrils, tendrils filled with night, the night soft and sweet.

My relief was obscene. I floated, cocooned from the pain. I could feel it, but all that agony was outside myself, a heart-beat away—and that heartbeat was enough.

You are not just flesh, whispered the darkness, all around me. *You are not only the dream.*

Shit, I thought, weary. *What am I, then?*

The spell broke. I fell through darkness, back into my skin—just as the boys finally ripped free. It was a straining burst, a pop that exploded every nerve ending with such brilliant, devastating agony, I felt like I had swallowed a lightning bolt.

If this was what giving birth was like, I was totally fucked.

I lay on my side, limbs twitching—drooling into the grass. I heard my name, but that was shit. I could see the boys, little lumps in the shadows, but couldn't move to touch them. No strength. All pain. As if acid, bleach, and fire were being brushed tenderly across my skin.

Halfhearted hisses and snarls filled the night air. I rolled onto my back, staring at the stars. Even that exhausted me. My hands fell against my stomach and stayed there.

Baby, I thought. *Daughter. Girl. Woman. Me.*

Not me. Better than me. Better life, better heart. And even if that wasn't the case, then at the very least—a chance. A life of possibilities, all for her. Something more than terror and death, and betrayal.

I turned my head. Zee was sitting up, and so were Raw and Aaz. All three swaying, digging claws into their heads.

Dek and Mal barely had the strength to drape themselves over my neck; I fumbled for them, dragging their bodies close, tucking their bristly heads beneath my chin. Feeling their hot little bodies, hearing their purrs—however weak— was better than any drug. My boys were alive. We'd made it into the night.

But I still couldn't move. Too much trauma, and only some of it was physical. I realized, reluctantly, that part of me had been afraid the boys would peel off my body, right into their own coma—like Grant. That everyone I loved, my entire foundation, would be entirely silenced.

And even though I was relieved that wasn't the case, that small consolation was fraught with all the fear I'd refused to let myself feel. It rolled over me in a devastating wave, and I hugged Dek and Mal to my chest—so tightly their purrs broke. Zee and the others gathered against my back, solid and warm. We breathed together, held each other together, and if I could have folded them inside me, even deeper inside my heart, I would have. I was so frightened of losing them.

My pulse slowed from an eardrum-shattering pound to a slower, lighter thud inside my chest.

"Zee," I whispered. "You okay?"

"Sweet Maxine," he rasped. "Terrible dreams."

"You're sick," I mumbled. "Hurting."

"Yes." Zee shuddered, closing his eyes. "But that not the dream."

Dek made a sharp, keening sound. Raw and Aaz shook, burrowing their heads against me. Zee rocked, claws digging into his round tummy with such ferocity, I thought he might eviscerate himself. I smoothed his spiked hair, desperate to calm him. "What is it?"

"Fire." Zee spoke so softly I could barely hear him, but even silent I would have felt his dread. I tried so hard not to think of that presence in the flames, but it had already crawled into me, and the only safe place was the darkness, which caught me so softly in its coils.

"What was it we saw?" I murmured, afraid of taking comfort in the dark—but more afraid of the fire.

The little demon shook his head. But the darkness whispered: *A glimpse of what is to come, young Queen.*

I swallowed hard and rubbed Zee's spiny, sharp back. "Come on. We'll worry about this later."

He shot me a quick look—*yeah, keep telling yourself that*—but straightened up and rolled his little shoulders. "Alive. Staying alive."

Raw and Aaz lifted their fists, weakly, in solidarity, while Dek and Mal began humming the Bee Gees song of the same name. Which I guessed meant they weren't dying. Yet.

"Will get strong," Zee added, for extra emphasis though he didn't sound so sure. Guilt filled me. I couldn't keep taking for granted that they were invulnerable. Not now. We might all be mortal, for however long this recovery took. I had to be careful for their sakes, as much as mine. I had to be careful for my baby.

Careful, in preparation for whatever else was coming.

I tried to move, found myself anchored by demons. So I tilted my head, searching, and found that distant fire.

"Jack," I said. Zee lifted his head, nostrils flaring.

"Meddling Man," he agreed.

I was exhausted. I didn't want to walk, but I was more wary of the armor. Finally learning my lesson, after all. Using it might take me to the edge of Jack's fire—or perhaps I would land at the farm, or on a mountain in Norway. Might not do anything at all. My legs, at any rate, were something I could count on. If I could just figure out how to stand.

Zee pulled me to my feet. I grabbed Raw and Aaz, hauling them up behind me. Dek and Mal clung to my shoulders, their purrs breaking into pathetic little coughs. I patted their heads.

"We good?" I asked them, trying to sound strong.

"Good enough," Zee rasped, and bounded ahead of me. Not fast, not particularly strong . . . but good enough. That's all I needed.

I followed him. Raw and Aaz gathered their strength, dropping in and out of the shadows and using them to skip ahead of us. I trailed them by the glint of their red eyes and the darkness of their bodies, which swallowed what little light came from the stars.

I hunted the fire, too.

I saw Jack long before he saw me. Seated in the grass, shoulders slumped, several bottles of wine in front of him— and one in his hand. A big blanket covered his shoulders, tied in a knot at his chest. He was staring at the flames, eyes bloodshot, distant—and he was dirty again, his face even more lined than I remembered. If he'd slept at all since I'd last seen him, I'd be shocked.

I walked right up, so close I could smell him. He didn't look up at me, didn't move a muscle. Absolutely still, staring straight ahead, with a million miles in his eyes. Just like before, with the skull. I followed his gaze, looked at the fire—and memories flooded me. Burning alive, burning in the smoke and heat, opening my eyes and staring at—

"Jack," I said.

My grandfather twitched, but it was like a horse flicking off a fly. Zee prowled around the fire, watching him. He lacked his usual grace, and he swayed a little with each step—but his gaze was sharp, and the spikes of his hair flexed with agitation. Raw and Aaz also appeared, slumping in the grass with ragged sighs; almost panting with the effort of that run. Both of them reached into the shadows and pulled out: soft pretzels and hot dogs; a few bags of M&M's; and, finally, a teddy bear.

I crouched beside Jack and hit him in the face with the bear.

That worked. He flinched, blinking hard, and tore his gaze from the fire to stare at me with confused, startled eyes.

"Excuse me," he said, picking bits of fur out of his mouth. "Some respect for your elders is called for."

I almost hit him again. Except his eyes changed, and he leaned forward, staring at me. I waited, only pretending to

be patient. Dek and Mal rested their heads against the tips
of my shoulders; I could feel their weariness. I was just as
tired.

"Maxine," Jack said in a quiet voice. "My dear girl. You
are still very ill."

"You knew I was sick."

"I thought you would have healed by now. The boys—"

"You ran." I reached for a small bag of M&M's and tore
it open. Dek and Mal finally lifted their heads. "You heard
something you didn't like and got the hell out."

If part of me expected contrition, I didn't get it. Jack
narrowed his eyes. "There was something I needed to do."

I kicked a stone into the fire—sparks flew. "I can see
you're hard at work."

He was silent a moment, watching me. Dek and Mal
wanted down, and I set them on the grass. They slithered
directly into the fire, curling and twisting inside the heat.
Their sighs were loud beneath the crackle of burning dung—
a large pile of which was being snacked on by Aaz.

"You asked me to reach out to others of my kind, those
who are still my friends," Jack said finally, in a careful voice.
"So I did."

I held still. "And?"

"And," he said, very quietly, "they didn't know anything
about an attack on this world, or you and Grant."

"Bullshit."

"Maxine. My kind cannot lie to one another. An attack
is being planned, but the other Aetar cannot agree amongst
themselves on how it should proceed—if at all. You and
Grant represent too many unknowns."

I drew in a deep breath, held it. "Were you the one who
told them about us?"

Zee and the boys shifted around me, lifting themselves,
but staying close, staring at my grandfather like wolves.
Their red eyes glinted, and their skins swallowed what little
starlight touched us. I felt my own light swallowed.

"Did you tell the Aetar about us?" I asked him again, my voice little more than a broken whisper.

He didn't even twitch. I wasn't sure he heard me. His gaze had gone distant again.

"Jack," I said, and Zee leapt over me, snarling. He landed badly, his legs collapsing so that he banged his chin into the ground, but that didn't slow his momentum. In less than a heartbeat: eye to eye with my grandfather.

"Truth," rasped the little demon. "Truth is *owed*, Meddling Man."

Jack blinked, coming back to himself—to us. I would have thought he was going senile if that wasn't completely impossible. But if something else was the matter, if he'd sold us out, and there was a *reason* beyond his control, forced against his will . . .

"Of course I told them," he said, as if it was the most natural thing in the world.

I stared at him. "I don't understand. You *told* the Aetar."

"I didn't inform them about your child." Jack took a long drink from his wine bottle; his hand shook, ever so slightly.

Zee snarled and knocked the bottle away. I wanted to do the same thing, except with his head. Rage welled up, so tight and hard I could have hurled it like a stone. "You *betrayed* us."

He gave me a sharp glance, but there was a hint of guilt in his face. "No."

Zee pushed up hard against me, as did Raw and Aaz—watching him with predatory calm. I said, "You're the reason we're in this fucking mess."

"No," he said, again. "*You are*. You and Grant. Your very existence is the reason you are in this situation. That is no one's fault."

I closed my eyes, remembering my grandfather's passionate protectiveness. Always, he had pushed the need for secrecy—even when it had become clear that we'd crossed the line, that it was only a matter of time before the Aetar realized what Grant was—and what *I* had become.

He was right—our existence had created this situation. But that didn't excuse the rest. "I need an explanation. Or so help me, Jack, I will do something I regret."

"Like kill me?" A bitter smile touched his mouth. "Let's not get dramatic."

"Wolf," rasped Zee, in a quiet, warning voice.

A look passed between them—old and full, and secret. Neither Zee nor my grandfather had ever looked at me that way. For all that I was his granddaughter, Jack had a more profound connection to the boys, a shared history I could never understand. Too much murder between them, worlds full of blood, and regret. My ancestors were the afterthought, nothing but checkmate. What had come before us was the long game.

"I only meant to take a look," Jack said, still staring at Zee. "I've been away from my kind for a long time. I was lonely for them."

"Tough," I said, and he tore his gaze from the demon to meet mine.

"Yes," he replied, ignoring my sarcasm, "it was. For *eons* all we had were each other. And for eons after we found flesh, we still could not be far apart. Aetar share worlds because we find comfort in knowing we are not alone. Even if we despise each other, we *still* find comfort. Because no one else knows. No one else can *imagine* what it means to be us. And we are almost as afraid of losing *that* as we are of losing flesh."

Jack relaxed into the grass, his shoulders and knees popping. A decaying human body: fit skin for an immortal. "When we imprison our kind, it is torture. We know it is torture. We strip the flesh, we isolate. Imagine the void, my dear. Imagine being trapped there."

"You're not in prison."

"I haven't lost my flesh, but I *am* isolated. Ever since Sarai left . . ." He stopped, closing his eyes; for a moment,

I saw real loss on his face. "I needed a reminder of what I am. So I used the crystal skull as a conduit for my true form, so that I could reenter the Labyrinth and . . . see . . . how the other Aetar fared on their worlds. Just a look. It was for you, as well. I wanted to know if they were coming here."

"And they were."

"They were merely thinking of it," he said. "They already knew that two Aetar had died on this world and that their Messenger's bonds had been broken. Something was wrong. They would have found out what, regardless of me."

"You didn't have to say anything at all."

"I didn't expect to be caught watching them," he snapped. "Once I was seen, I had to give them something. I had to speak the truth. If I hadn't, if I'd run . . . I would have risked coming off as a traitor. They already suspected as much."

"You were afraid they would imprison you."

Jack said nothing. Zee held still, but I felt his tension; a mirror of my own. He rasped, "Not telling whole truth, Meddling Man."

Even I could see that. My grandfather was distracted again, as if what he was saying wasn't *that* important. He was telling me because he *had* to, not because it mattered.

Jack gave the demon a dirty look. I said, "All this time, you could have warned us. Why didn't you say anything, right when I found you?"

"I told you, I thought the Aetar were merely planning an attack. I was as surprised as you to learn they'd already come after your child and Grant. What else was there to warn you about, after that?" He looked away, and muttered, "There are more important concerns."

"More important than our lives?" I stood, and swayed, hit with dizziness. Zee pressed his claws against my leg, steadying me. My mouth was dry, my skin hot. A remnant of the fever, still in my bones. "Get up. I'm taking you home. We'll sort it out there."

I reached out to the old man, but Zee grazed his claws across my hand—a gesture of caution. I glanced down at

him, but he was staring at Jack. All the boys were, even Dek
and Mal, who slithered from the fire, smoke drifting off
their scales.

"Lies," he rasped again, so softly I could barely hear him;
but Jack stared at the demon, stared and stared, and his jaw
tightened.

"Lies are lives." Zee's eyes narrowed to slits. "Can smell
it now. Drank poison to taste the trail, and the trail is strong
inside us. Know where it leads. Know who hammered the
arrows."

A profound stillness fell over my grandfather. I studied
him, feeling the last of my hope crumble. All that flippancy,
that distance, had disappeared from his eyes. And it was
chilling.

I tore my gaze from him to look at Zee—at all the boys,
who had gathered around me. My wolves, watching the old-
est wolf of all.

He is the hunter who slaughters worlds, the Messenger
had said.

I couldn't bear to hear what else Zee had to say. I was
afraid I already knew what it would be. I grabbed my grandfather's shoulder, and with my other hand reached for the
demon. Raw and Aaz wrapped their arms around my knees.
Dek and Mal had already begun slithering up my legs. I felt
none of their usual strength—weak grips, no grace. But I
didn't give a shit. They were the family I could trust. That
mattered more than anything.

"Maxine," said Jack, but I closed my eyes against him.

Home, I thought, pouring my heart into the armor—
pulling myself toward Grant. *Home, before something terrible happens.*

The void opened: a massive jaw unhinging, taking us
into its mouth. I fell into the darkness, but it was the darkness inside me I felt, catching me softly.

Soon, everything will change, it whispered. *You, most
of all.*

I was alone. I could not feel the boys or my grandfather, not my own body, not the child inside me.

No, I said.

It is already done, murmured the darkness, and found myself released into light, right where I'd left: the farmhouse living room, with its air smelling faintly of chocolate and marijuana.

But it wasn't entirely the same. Because the floor was covered in blood.

And a man was being eaten alive.

CHAPTER 22

I heard the screams before I was fully free of the void. I was still listening to them when I snapped into the light, and the boys pressed hard against my skin—so hard my breath left in a gasp. It didn't feel right. But not much did, anymore.

I saw Grant first. His eyes were still closed, that long, lean body sunk deep into the old couch cushions. Shurik covered him: like legless, hairless, cats. All of them, hissing. Past him, the Messenger—standing beside Mary, who was sitting up from her nest of blankets, machete in hand. The Mahati warrior crouched nearby, very still and sharp, as if his entire body were a knife about to fall into flesh.

I followed their gazes. I'd already seen what was in front of them, but avoiding it for as long as possible seemed like a good idea. Pregnant woman, psychic trauma, all that shit.

One of the robed men from the desert was sprawled on his back, *mostly* dead. I knew he was mostly dead because he was surrounded by a teeming, writhing mass of Shurik, all fighting for the chance to burrow into his pale skin.

Invasion had already occurred; long bodies rippled beneath his flesh, sliding up his neck. His eyes were open, staring, leaking tears. His mouth still moved, but all I heard was a faint, hoarse gasp.

Beside him was the second man—but he was very much alive. Kneeling, covered in hissing Shurik that clung to his shoulders and wriggled over his waist. His pale, bony face was taut with barely controlled terror.

"They came for the Lightbringer," said the Messenger quietly, her gaze lingering on Jack. "But the Shurik were fast."

I felt a terrible burst of love for those little fuckers. "And they left this one alive?"

"For questioning, I presume."

Good call, I thought. A better one than I might have made. I glanced back at my grandfather, who was staring at the carnage: flat eyes, mouth set in a grim line. "You have anything to say about this?"

He said nothing. Just looked away, first at Grant—and then the crystal skull. I found it on the floor, but the blanket I'd tossed over it had been pulled off. Its surface gleamed; so did its eyes. I looked away, unnerved. Nauseous, too. But I blamed that on being pregnant and smelling so much blood.

"Cover the skull," I told the Messenger. "Make sure my grandfather doesn't go near it."

Jack gave me a sharp look, as did the Messenger. I didn't wait to see if she did as I asked—instead, I began to wade through the heaving, writhing mass of hissing Shurik that covered the living-room floor. It wasn't easy—but that had everything to do with me. My entire body balked, joints so stiff I had to use real muscle to unlock them. Tin woman, rusting to a full stop. No pain, though. No fever. This was something else.

The boys.

I knelt, with difficulty, staring at the trembling man who had come to kidnap my husband. We looked at each other too long. Anger and revulsion flicked into his face, replacing the fear. Which was what I wanted.

"Hello," I said. "My name is Maxine Kiss."

"Abomination," he spat.

"That, too." I smiled, and it felt so cold, cold as my heart when I thought about what these people would do to my husband and daughter if they had the chance.

I reached down—slow, unable to force my joints to relax—and picked up a Shurik. That hard, turgid body twisted in my hand: a seething worm, sharp teeth snapping, grinding, like a fistful of razor blades rubbing together. I gritted my own teeth, revolted, and held the little demon up to the man's eyes.

He shied away—or tried. Mary appeared behind him. Her face was flush with fever, but she held the man's shoulder in a sinewy grip that looked strong enough to break bone.

"You are going to talk to me," I said.

"No." He stared at the Shurik in my hand, twitching, as other demons began massing in his lap, wriggling beneath his robes. His gaze slid down to his companion: the dead man's body deflating like a balloon as his bones and muscles were liquefied and consumed. The Shurik were hungry.

"You *are* going to talk," I said again. "I want to know the name of the Aetar who sent you. I want to know what they have planned."

His gaze snapped to mine, defiance trickling past the fear. "You cannot stop us."

"I turned your friends into ash with just one touch." I leaned forward, holding his gaze. "I can do whatever the fuck I want."

I saw him remembering what I'd done, and his physical reaction made me queasy: His lips trembled, as did the delicate skin beneath his eyes—fluttering with his pulse.

"It does not matter," he said, hoarse. "If we cannot take the Lightbringer or kill your child, we will destroy this world. Even you cannot stop that."

Behind me, Jack spoke a ringing, melodic word. The

man took a sharp, startled breath—flinching so hard he almost toppled sideways. All that defiance vanished, replaced with almost-childlike timidity. The transformation was disturbing.

"Please forgive me," he whispered, so softly I could barely hear him above the hisses of the Shurik. "I am worthless for not feeling your presence."

"He is no God," said the Messenger, almost as quietly. The man didn't seem to hear her. His head was bowed, shoulders hunched. He might have prostrated himself if I hadn't been in the way.

"You *are* worthless," Jack said, in a dry, professorial voice. "Answer her questions."

The man shuddered. "The Divine Lord who sent for us had no name. We never were in his presence. We spoke only to his companion, who told us he had made arrangements with our master for our services."

It was careful wording. "Who was the companion?"

The man finally looked up—at me, then Jack. In his eyes, confusion, uncertainty—like this was some terrible trick, and he was being forced to play the fool.

"It was him," he said, looking at my grandfather. "It was the Wolf."

⇥⇤

DON'T believe everything you see or hear, my mother once told me. *And don't believe everything you feel, either. Our hearts are the best liars, baby. We know our weaknesses. We know what we want to hear. And those lies are the sweetest of all.*

But they'll kill you, in the end. All those deadly pretty lies.

But not everything could be a lie. I told myself that as I looked at my grandfather, cold on the inside, cold as death, studying his eyes as I'd never studied anyone before.

The expression on his face was dazed—filled with shock,

bewilderment. It was difficult for me to imagine it was fake. His eyes were so naked.

"No," he said, tearing his gaze from the man to look at me. "No, my dear. That is not possible."

I said nothing. I looked at the Messenger, who was also watching my grandfather. "He believes what he said," she told me, finally, which was no guarantee at all that any kind of truth had just been told.

"Did you tell this man to attack us?" I asked Jack directly.

"No," he replied, shaken. "I have never seen him before this moment."

I looked back at the man, who had bowed his head again. "You're sure it was the Wolf?"

"Yes," he whispered, trembling. "The souls of the Divine Lords cannot be confused. Their light is unique, even if their flesh changes."

"He *also* speaks the truth," said the Messenger, unease in her voice.

Someone is playing us, I thought. "After you captured the Lightbringer, what then? Where were you supposed to take him?"

His trembling worsened. "Back into the Labyrinth."

"Where?" Jack took a step toward him, his expression frightening. "Which gate?"

The man said something in a language I didn't understand. Jack paled, rocking back on his heels. I stared at him, but instead of seeing my grandfather, that vision of fire flashed through my mind—and with it, a terrible foreboding.

"What is it?" I asked my grandfather, but he wouldn't look at me. So I turned to the man, and said, "What is that place you would take my husband?"

"A world," he said, looking at Jack with confused alarm.

"You are young and stupid," added the Messenger in a tight voice. "That is not just any world. We are not permitted there. No one is. Not even other Aetar."

I recognized that look in her eye. I'd seen it once before,

not so long ago. My feeling of dread worsened. "Let me guess. This has something to do with the Devourer."

The man's reaction was almost comical in its violence. I could have stabbed him in the chest with gentler results—and the look he shot me was as if I'd become one part Satan, one part Satan's clown, with a couple extra horns growing out of my forehead. Like he couldn't imagine *anyone's* being so stupid to even *think* that name, let alone *say* it.

Behind me, the Messenger made a disgusted sound. But I also heard a quiet sigh, and it wasn't from Jack or Mary. I turned, slightly, and looked at my husband.

His eyes were open.

If a bomb had dropped, I wouldn't have been able to move. All the Shurik stilled, even those burrowing into the dead man. The demon in my hand went limp, exhaling a little hiss.

Grant's cheeks were hollow, his skin gray and flaking. But his posture was as relaxed as a crouched lion, and his eyes told no lies. His eyes were as cold as ice, so unlike him, so alien to his face, that for a moment I was afraid I was not looking at my husband at all.

But then his gaze met mine, and I saw the hint of a smile. And that smile warmed his eyes, and it was my man again. My man.

Grant's gaze lingered on me—and then the kneeling man, the Shurik, all that blood and death, a pile of robes on the ground, covering the wriggling mush that was all that remained of a man.

"Well," he said, hoarse, "this is interesting."

The man took a breath—sharp, purposeful.

I swung my fist and slammed him in the chest. It took all my strength to move that fast, and he still managed to gasp out a single note—a sharp cut in the air that sliced through every living thing in his presence. But it was a broken sound, distorted from my blow—and Grant snapped out a word so raw with power I swayed, and the Shurik flattened to the floor.

The man gasped, clawing at his throat, fingers digging

into the iron collar he wore—pulling until I thought he might break his own neck to get it off.

Grant lounged on the couch like he was watching some college football game. "I don't want to kill you, but I will if I have to. Calm down."

He didn't answer. His voice broke through, another attempt at making power. I didn't have to punch him down. Grant said another word, and the man shut his mouth, shuddering, staring at him with horror and revulsion. Even the Messenger gave him a sidelong, uneasy look. It wasn't just words he spoke—it was all power, power that rolled through the room, over my shivering skin—as if the boys were trembling with fever.

My grandfather had remarked, more than once, that Grant had the most raw, wild talent of any Lightbringer he'd ever encountered—and given all of them he'd killed, I guessed he might know.

The man beside me had no chance. It wasn't his fault. Any chance had been bred out of him.

"The Devourer," I said, forcing myself to focus, to look away from Grant at the Messenger and Jack. "Have you *both* known all along where he is?"

Of course they had. I could see it on their faces. But before I could press them, a loud crack filled the air, with such violence I felt the wave of that sound push against my back.

I twisted, ready to fight—but there was no enemy. The floorboards had split, was all. The floor, right below the crystal skull. The old dark boards had broken apart only a few inches, but it looked like someone had powered a fist through that spot. The skull was still there, sunken slightly—and once again, the blanket had slid off. Carved eyes, watching us.

"No," whispered Jack. "Maxine, what have you *done*?"

From the corner of my eye, I saw the man reach beneath his robes. His hand was a shining blur; the gleam of a bright edge flying toward my face as he threw himself at me.

Shurik burrowed into him, but he had momentum. Even

when Grant's voice rang out, it wasn't enough—the man's body was committed to the blow. I flung myself sideways, feeling the boys charge up my face. That sensation, their urgency, gave me new strength—I turned my head at the last second so that the knife skittered across my cheek instead of plunging into my forehead.

But I felt the blade. I felt the heat.

I was yanked away, so hard I flew across the floor. The Messenger crouched beside me, her hands still knotted in my clothing—staring with fury past my head. I turned, found Mary standing over the man. A machete jutted from his shoulder, buried so deep the entire right side of his body had nearly been severed. Shurik swarmed around the spurting blood, burrowing into his belly.

But the man was still alive, wheezing for breath; an agonized sound accompanied by blood, foaming and trickling down the sides of his mouth. His gaze, terrible and agonized, held mine.

I stared, waiting for him to move again, for his chest to rise and fall, but he went absolutely still. So did I.

"Maxine." Grant half fell to the floor, crawling to me. I looked at him, numb. He said my name again, but I barely heard him.

Grant pulled me into his lap, touching my cheek. I finally felt pain. I nudged his hand away to touch my face. I knew the boys were still there—I could feel their bodies heavy on my skin—but if I was hurt, they were hurt.

I felt something hot, wet. I looked at my fingers.

They were covered in blood.

CHAPTER 23

TRUST is a delicate beast.

Call it a shape-shifter for all the different forms it takes, all its identities and flaws and beauties, and its imperviousness to truth and lies. Trust someone, and that trust becomes a foundation. You can build a life based on trust. Might destroy lives, too. Your own, included.

But trust is the deal. Got trust, and you got *something*. So when people *do* give it to you, for real, don't fuck it up.

Because you can't put it back together.

SIMPLE truth: I could have died.

If that blade had plunged into my forehead, as it was meant to, the tip would have punched through the boys into my brain. Even that easy swipe across my cheek was a gusher—about an inch long, and deep. I'd never needed stitches, but this seemed like a good candidate for some. The boys soaked my blood into their bodies before it had a chance to roll down my face, but I could see that red burst welling up through the cut, I could *feel* it—and the entire left side of my face throbbed. The boys had to be in pain, too, but I couldn't tell who had gotten cut—too many scales and muscles, no glint of a red eye. It brought back bad memories.

I'd lost the boys, once. Lost them from my body, lost our bonds, almost lost our family. Cut from me, given their freedom. I'd been left vulnerable, night and day, forced to rely on myself—forced to learn that I could survive without them if I had to. A lesson for Zee and the boys, too. A lesson in how much they had changed in ten thousand years. A lesson in priorities and shifting hearts, and what mattered when power was no longer enough.

They'd been given a choice: their freedom or the prison of my bloodline.

My boys chose blood. Blood and family.

I couldn't lose them now. Five pieces of my heart, five fragments of my soul. Five little souls, born again in each of us women, for ten thousand years. Good, bad, weak, strong—but we'd carried them, and they'd carried us, and fuck me if it ended here, now. My daughter needed to know this, the pain and wonder. She needed to have her family with her. I sure as hell wouldn't last forever. And neither would Grant, no matter how much I wished otherwise.

It was late afternoon, close to sunset. Breeze had kicked up, swirling dirt from the drive around our legs. Hot sun, clear sky, birds swooping from barn eaves. The boys continued to cocoon my face, heavy and still, not even stirring in their dreams; a stiffness that continued to run deep, into my arms and legs. It was difficult to move, but I insisted on helping the Mahati warrior relocate the limp remains of the men to the barn. I couldn't leave the dead, even if there wasn't much left but skin and bone, to rot on my living-room floor.

Most of the Shurik stayed behind at the house, but a handful hitched a ride inside what was left of the bodies. In twenty-four hours, not even their bones would remain. Just a wet spot. It crossed my mind not to let the demons eat the dead men, but I remembered what Blood Mama had said, a day and a lifetime ago: This was a war, and there was an enemy. The demons needed a taste, just like hounds required a scent.

Never waste meat.

Grant waited for me on the porch, sitting in a rocking chair, with his cane leaning against the rail. Pale, underweight, but alive. His gaze lingered on the cut in my cheek, and he wordlessly held up a plate filled with sandwiches: ham, a little bit of lettuce, and cheese. Shurik surrounded him, nesting in the blanket thrown over his lap. Little guards.

"I'm still dealing with the whole machete-in-the-head incident," I said, climbing the stairs with deliberate, stiff steps. "Also, my hands feel like dead people. I'm not really hungry."

"So wash your hands." Grant leaned back, relaxing in his chair—his air of calm a little forced. "I'm not going anywhere."

I would have argued, except it was too nice clinging to the illusion of normality. Which totally went to hell when I entered the house and found a dozen industrious little demons rolling like dogs in shit through the blood on my living-room floor. An odd scent filled the air: vanilla, mixed with the metallic musk of death. Shurik body odor, maybe. A couple of them stopped to look at me and bared their teeth. I stared back and decided it wasn't worth saying anything. My poor mother's house.

Mary was on the couch, sleeping, with the crystal skull tucked in her arms, right next to her machete. A blanket covered the damn thing, but its shape still burned through me. Her bristling wild hair made her head look huge against her sinewy, skinny, body, and she stirred, opening her eyes to slits as I walked past.

I washed my hands, then filled two glasses of water and went back to the couch. I knelt, with difficulty, and helped her drink.

A faint, crooked smile touched her mouth, but she was

gulping water at the same time, and it dribbled down her chin. With one free hand, she grabbed my wrist. Her grip was weak, trembling. Even through the boys, I felt the heat of her fever. She pulled back the blanket and revealed the crystal skull. The armor covering my right hand tingled, tugged, as did the boys.

"It burns," she whispered. "It waits."

I backed away, forcing her to let go of me. The old woman's gaze turned knowing, and she settled deeper into the blankets.

"Hunt," she murmured at me, her eyes black and glittering.

Outside, the Messenger stood in the driveway, staring off into the distance, head tilted as if listening to some silent music. My grandfather sat on the porch stairs, slowly chewing a sandwich and watching her. I stared at the back of his head, but he said nothing to me, and I couldn't muster any words of my own.

Grant, giving Jack a wary look, patted the chair beside him. "Here. While we have a moment—"

"—don't waste it," I finished, leaning down to kiss his mouth. I lingered, deepening the kiss, my lips warm and hungry on his. Precious, beautiful. My man, still alive. My man, here, breathing. Both of us, together. Proof of miracles, right there.

He broke off the kiss with a violent coughing fit. The little Shurik poked its head from the collar of his shirt, staring up at him. I started to speak, but he held up his hand.

"Don't," he said. "At least we're still together."

"Damn straight," I whispered. "You better stay with us. Or else."

"Threatening a sick man. I get no love."

I kissed him. "All you get is love."

He pulled back, studying me. "Your cheek. The boys."

"They're sick. I'm not invulnerable anymore." I felt my grandfather turn slightly, to look at me. I still ignored him. "But I think they're flushing the disease from my system."

"Thank God."

"Not yet. Not until you're well. Not until they're okay, too." *And everyone else,* I didn't add. Which might be too much to hope for.

He squeezed my hand, then raised his other to touch the Shurik clinging to his neck, the same little demon who had refused to leave his side this entire time. It writhed happily under his touch.

"You saved me," he said in a quiet voice, holding my gaze. "I felt you pull me out of the darkness. But then I was stuck inside my head. I couldn't reach you. My eyes wouldn't open."

You terrified me, I wanted to tell him. *You cut me off. My heart feels empty without you in it. I'm scared and lonely and I don't know what to do, or even how to save you.*

"The Messenger did the real work." I pointed to the Shurik on his chest. "And we had help."

He grunted. "Answers yet?"

"More questions." I looked at Jack, and a deep ache boomed through my heart: a twist, like a knife was slowly turning. "Talk to us."

My grandfather didn't stir from the steps. He tossed the rest of his sandwich into the grass and wiped his mouth with two large fingers. Those hands, which were still unfamiliar to me. The body I'd first known him in, the body that had known my grandmother and made my mother, had been slender and tall, with the elegance of a retired dancer. This one, stolen from a dying homeless man, was bulky with fat and muscle, and hairy as a bear. Sometimes, though, I could still forget the differences—his eyes were the same.

"I'm afraid to talk," Jack replied, staring at the hill where my mother and grandmother were buried. "When I think about what I need to say to you, I'm reminded of all the ways I'm not human. I can't pretend that I'm just an old man with a granddaughter."

"I'm past caring." Through the porch rails, I watched the Messenger. She looked alien to me from this distance, as alien as the others of her kind—too tall, too angular, with skin that was flawless and inhumanly pale.

The Mahati emerged from the barn, his long fingers twitching in agitation. His braids gleamed in the fading light, silver chains chiming softly. He stood beside her with an ease that surprised me—such familiar intimacy, such strange sympathy; the way they looked at each other with grave eyes.

Grant took my hand. His skin was warm. Just warm. Not burning with fever. I reached for our bond—found only the hole—but I lingered in that empty space, holding myself there, pretending there was something to wrap myself around, the memory of light.

A memory of light is the same as light, whispered the darkness.

I suppose you would know, I replied, trying to stay focused on my husband. *You eat light.*

And the light eats the darkness. Heat spread behind my mouth, like a smile—exactly what that sensation was. *It is the eternal dance, Hunter.*

It was almost sunset: light stretching, glowing, cooling. Usually the boys would have been tugging at me, itching to be free. Not today. So still, quiet, as if they were conserving their strength. Or maybe they just didn't have any.

"Jack," I said. "Who could impersonate you?"

"No one. It's impossible."

"Then you *were* the one who orchestrated the attacks on us."

He gave me a sharp look. "Never."

"Then *how*?"

"I don't know," he snapped. "It doesn't make sense."

"No way he was lying?"

"He believed what he was saying." My grandfather scrubbed at his face. "Something else is happening."

I swallowed. "Could Zee and the boys have been deceived?"

Jack tensed. "In what way?"

I knew right then. No matter what he said next. It was the way his shoulders hunched, and the instant wariness in his eyes. "When Zee said he knew who had 'hammered the arrows' . . . to whom was he referring?"

He flexed his gnarled, brown hands. "You already know that answer, my dear."

I swallowed hard. "And the arrows? What are they?"

My grandfather finally looked at me, and if not for a split-second slip of pain in his eyes, I would have thought he was empty on the inside, absolutely hollow.

"You know that, too," he said.

I stared at him, stared and stared, and my heart died even more; just cracked and crumbled, and fell to ash. Finally, the boys stirred. But it was nothing more than their pain echoing mine.

"You made the disease," I said, barely able to speak above a whisper. "You designed the thing that's killing us."

"That is the one thing I cannot deny," Jack said.

I squeezed Grant's hand so hard, he stirred in his chair. *"The illness is efficient,"* I recited, recalling with perfect clarity the affable voice I'd heard as I'd fought for my husband's life, deep within the cells of that poison. *"But it must be altered. It must not be allowed to affect our flesh. Only the demons."*

Jack paled, teetering so far sideways he had to lean against the rail. "Where did you hear that?"

"It was you." I stood, feeling the boys tug on my skin, harder now, on the edge of sunset. "You, designing ways to kill, with the Devourer right there at your side."

"You don't know anything," he whispered.

"You lied to me. Your family."

"I had to."

"Bullshit! All this time, I've been searching for answers, and you stood there and said *nothing!*"

"I had to." Jack's gaze burned wild. "I don't care that you know I designed the poison. That was war, my dear. You watch world after world be ravaged and cannibalized, then tell me what you wouldn't do. You've had the *privilege*

of control and peace. You've had the blessings of not seeing babies *cooked*."

I leaned back from him, staring. Jack followed me, pressing his knuckles into the porch. I'd never seen him so angry. "You're a fool, Maxine. You're going to kill us all."

"Don't talk to her like that," Grant warned.

"My apologies, lad, but even you're not worth the price. Anything would be better than the arrival of him."

"You're sounding like an insane old man," I said.

"If you think I'm insane, wait until you meet *him*. Dearest child, I'm keeping you, and your Grant, and billions of other fools, alive. Normally, I'm all for extinction events, but one must draw the line somewhere. That is why I lied to you. There is more at stake here than our cozy little family. More at stake than, say, Grant."

"Jack," I warned. "It's not just Grant. Our daughter, too. Your great-granddaughter. What about *her* life?"

I had to give it to him—he actually looked ashamed. "I haven't forgotten her."

"Could have fooled me. You're the one who's going to kill us all—with that disease *you* designed."

"A drop in the bucket," he said, grim. "I don't know who has cloned my life, but even that means nothing compared to the larger danger."

The Devourer, I almost said, but the look on my grandfather's face made me swallow that name. He said, "Something unexpected happened when I used the skull to spy on my kind. I had a vision—of the future."

Fire flashed through my mind, the ominous heat and presence of that creature beyond the flames—staring at me, implacable and hungry. Full of menace, hate.

The darkness inside me was as hungry, and just as remorseless—but it felt different. Cleaner, somehow. Primal, a force of nature. Or maybe I was biased because the darkness was mine, on my side—my personal, inherited monster.

"We're waiting," I said.

Jack held my gaze, clear and unwavering. "I saw you

undoing the chains that will release someone who would be best left chained."

Grant stared at him. "I'm dying, Jack. We're all sick. We don't have time for this crap. Who is this you're so afraid of?"

Death, I wanted to say, still feeling the crackle of heat. Remembering, too, another vision: my body, dismembered by fire, torn apart like a doll.

Jack didn't look away from me, as if he were afraid I would disappear, or charge at him. He'd been so distant these past few days that having him present, focused on me, was unnerving.

He cleared his throat. "Let me set the scene: Imagine an eternity of the void. Imagine a million years, two million, three—spent in that terrible place. Imagine what that was like. And then, suddenly, imagine you are flesh again. Not just flesh, but any flesh you desire and can imagine for yourself—accompanied by every sensation. Endless water after an endless drought."

His gaze ticked left to my husband. "Some might hoard that water, despite its eternal qualities; some might drink themselves to death, over and over. Some might drink to excess for a while, until realizing that is no way to live; while others, a few small others, might abstain entirely, except for the smallest sips, to draw out the exquisite pleasure."

Jack smiled again, weakly. "But *that* one . . . his hungers were always a little too *outré* even for us. We reacted in different ways to having sensation. Some made the transition without suffering prolonged obsessions; some did not. Pleasure was one form of addiction; but for him, pain *was* the pleasure." My grandfather coughed, and it occurred to me that he looked a bit feverish himself. "I remember, over the course of a thousand years, watching him pick himself slowly apart in the most terrible ways imaginable. His self-torture was unappetizing, to say the least. In the end, there was nothing left of his body—he had stretched, beyond any expectation, his ability to live. And still, the pain was not enough."

"I suppose he tortured others."

"It goes without saying. His craft was the delicate deconstruction, molecule by molecule, of the living. It amused him. He would take what he learned on himself and apply it to others." Jack's jaw tightened. "Including us."

I couldn't even imagine that kind of depravity. "If he's so twisted, how come he's the one with the cure to this disease, and you aren't?"

"No one understood death better than he. Death, *and* its cures. It was his talent." Exasperation dimmed his voice, and regret. "None of us are the same. And he was still one of us, no matter how much he had begun to change. We relied on him. We needed his . . . expertise . . . during the war with the demons. He was fascinated by their immunity to us. It became another obsession—the power that protected them."

The power inside me, I thought. "But the Aetar imprisoned him."

"He began to experiment on us too freely. Flesh became boring to him. He wanted new sensations." Jack glanced at the Messenger, who had moved close to the porch, listening to him; her shaved head gleamed in the sunlight, her robes light in the breeze, and her eyes sharp. "We couldn't trust him."

"I need his knowledge," I said.

Jack shook his head. "He won't help. He'll kill you, my dear. He'll dissect you, your daughter—and the boys."

"We could make him," Grant said. "*I* could make him."

A chill swept through me. Jack stood, slowly, from the stairs. "You're a fool, lad. And you, my dear . . . for once, ignore your usual instincts. This time, be half as smart as I'd always wanted you to be. This time, listen to an old man and let it be."

I stood, too. "If I let this be, my husband will die. So will the demons. The disease has already spread to humans. You mean to tell me *that* is preferable to—"

"Yes," interrupted Jack. "That's exactly what I mean to tell you. And even if you are foolish enough to make the attempt . . . if you enter the Labyrinth, you will be lost."

"No," I said.

"Listen to me." Jack grabbed my arm "The Labyrinth is endless, and you do not know the way. You will wander, my dear. You will wander, without end. And this world . . . this world *needs* you."

I cleared my throat. "Maybe you didn't orchestrate this. Maybe you *have* been set up. But you still made the disease. You still lied. For whatever reason, you betrayed us." I placed my hand on my stomach. "How can I trust anything you say?"

"Maxine," he said, with that same cold frustration, "I could tell you how much I love you, or how profoundly I miss your mother and grandmother. I could make any number of melodramatic statements, defending myself. But in the end, all that matters is that you have no choice. You *need* me. Trust is irrelevant."

"Like hell it is," Grant said.

Jack gave him a withering look. But the Messenger, who had been standing just at the bottom of the stairs, said, "Hunter."

I looked at her, dreading the note of surprise in her voice. "What now?"

She stared back at me, frowning. "The sun has set."

I looked down at my arms, at the boys still sleeping on my skin—tugging now, but with no more strength than before.

"Shit," I said.

CHAPTER 24

"**S**HIT," my mother replied, the one and only time I asked her to tell me about God. Live with demons long enough, and the subject is bound to come up—even if we never talked much about religion. It might as well not have existed between my mother and me. We had rules, history— a mission—and *that* was our religion.

Still, God.

"Listen," said my mother, placing her gun on the kitchen table and strapping on a flour-dusted apron. "I don't know."

I was peeling apples—ten years old and handy with a switchblade. My mother began scooping flour into the mixing bowl, her forearms a tangle of scales and muscular tattoos. "God is the first mystery. There's no answer until we die."

"Um," I replied.

"But before *that* happens," she added, forking in the butter, "you can always count on all the *other* higher powers to really fuck you up."

❧

FIFTEEN minutes later, the boys were still imprisoned on my skin.

The pain should have been crippling—and it was—but I was pretending like nothing was wrong even though it felt like I was being gnawed on by a thousand starving rats. Each bite of pain, each tug on my skin as the boys fought to wake, made me dizzy. Much more, and my pride would have to go, along with the contents of my stomach.

My grandfather was inside the house, sitting with Mary. I shouldn't have let him out of my sight—I didn't trust him not to make a run for it—but I couldn't juggle him, the boys, and Grant, all together. I couldn't even take care of myself.

Grant said, "They're weak. As if their auras are being diluted."

"Don't tell me that," I replied. No matter Zee's assurances, I was afraid this was the start of something horrifying—such as the boys' dying—and me, forced to wear their corpses for the rest of my life. Not even the worst-case scenario.

Grant stood from the porch chair. Two steps with his cane, and he had to lean against the rail. Better color in his face, a deeper clarity in his eyes, but there was no confusing him for a healthy man. Not even a little. Even the Shurik seemed tired. They rested in little clumps across the porch, making soft, rhythmic, purring sounds—like snores. The light in the sky was still pale, but shadows were lengthening and before long it would be dark. Another day, our deaths postponed.

He and I shared a long look. I swallowed hard, heart so tight, barely able to form a sentence against the pain. "Time does run out, doesn't it?"

A bitter smile touched his mouth. "Sometimes I feel like we've stayed alive by luck and the tips of our fingers."

I was seated on the old porch floorboards, leaning against the house beside the front door. I turned a little, which only made the pain worse, and looked in. I glimpsed the Messenger standing in the corner of the living room, her face pale except for a faint red burn on her cheeks. She was watching my grandfather, who was seated beside Mary on the couch—pressing a wet cloth to her head and dribbling water into her mouth. I had been listening to the old woman puke, which was less and less often. Not because she was getting better, either.

"You could do *something*," I'd said to Jack, just before he escaped from me into the house. "What's the point of being able to manipulate genetic material if you can't make someone stronger against a disease?"

"It doesn't work like that, not with *this* disease," was his reply, which drove me crazy. One seemed inextricably linked to the other. Aetar knew how to craft immortality—I'd seen it, again and again.

I glanced at the blanket-wrapped lump across from me: the crystal skull, which I'd had the Messenger take from Mary as soon as Jack went inside. Grant looked at it as well.

"You saw something, too," he said. "The skull is different than it used to be. The energies surrounding it are more . . . alive."

"It doesn't matter," I told him because I couldn't bear to explain what I'd seen or how that might validate Jack's behavior. "We have something else to talk about."

He waited, and the way he looked at me was almost as much of a distraction as my enflamed skin: He was drinking me in, his gaze running so deep it made my heart ache.

I took in the gauntness of his body, the feverish hollowness; remembering how for months he had deteriorated before my eyes. I wanted to be angry for him—at him—but all I felt was tired, and still in love. God, I loved this man.

"The only reason you're still standing is because of the Messenger," I told him. "But it didn't have to be that way. I know you're keeping the demons out. You're refusing to let them help you stay strong."

"I'm trying," he said quietly. "But it's not easy. So let it go, Maxine. Please."

"How can I?" I gripped my right wrist, squeezing, fighting to keep my voice steady. I hurt so much I could barely see straight—gripping the armor, feeling its cool softness beneath my left hand, was like a balm. "You're not doing everything you can to stay alive."

Anger flicked through his eyes. "Maxine. If I'm going to die, I want to die as me. If the wall comes fully down between me and the demons, I'll be a different man. It won't be me and them. It'll be *us*. I'm afraid of who I'll become when that happens. The . . . hungers I might have." He looked away, jaw tight. "I can feel them chewing the bones of those dead men. I can taste the blood in my mouth. What will it be like if I let them all the way in?"

"If it's a matter of life or death, wouldn't you rather take the risk?"

"It can't be undone." Grant limped to my side and slid down against the wall to sit with me. He twined his fingers with mine—those big, strong, human hands, and my hands: covered in hurting, struggling tattoos and silver armor. "Will I be safe with you and our daughter? I could be a monster, Maxine."

"Someone, protect my virginity."

"I'm serious."

"So am I." I eased down to lie on my back, speaking now through gritted teeth. The pain was getting worse. "I'm completely terrified."

"You're in pain," he said quietly. "We'll talk about this later."

"You're dying, Grant. Maybe we all are. There's no more later." And then, after a moment's hesitation, I added: "You cut our bond."

If I expected remorse, I didn't get it. What I saw instead was a lack of anything resembling emotion: His gaze went flat, empty. Dead, even. I felt cold, looking at him—cold and lonely.

"Losing our bond was what almost killed me," he said.

"I've never felt so hollow. Like half of me died when you went away."

"I'm still here." I reached for him, which took more strength than it should have. "And so are you. Why haven't you linked us together again?"

He said nothing. I squeezed his hand, hard.

His jaw tightened, unhappiness and frustration flickering through his eyes. "If I die while we're still connected, you could be hurt—or worse. That's why I severed us before . . . and that's why I haven't put us back together again."

"Grant—"

"I don't need our bond anymore to stay alive. I have the demons. It's not the same, but I can make it work."

"Demons aren't me," I replied, hurt. "I'm your wife."

"You're my wife," he agreed softly. "I'm lonely for you, Maxine. I don't know what I am, without you inside me. But doing anything that might hurt you, just to have that feeling of you and me . . . I can't do that."

"Asshole."

Grant kissed me. "I'm your asshole."

I shook my head. "Just what I need."

He said nothing, taking my left hand and holding it— light, gentle. Melancholy bloomed inside me; a profound, devastating, wistfulness. We'd had so little time together, but all of it—all of it—transformative and good.

In a voice just as soft as his touch, I said: "Grant. I made a bargain with the darkness. When our daughter was dying. I promised it *me*. My life, my soul. So what happens when it finally makes its claim? What will *I* become?"

He said nothing. I gathered my courage and met his gaze. I couldn't read him, not at first—he was too still, his gaze too dark. I didn't know if that was anger or tenderness, and I held my breath, waiting.

"She was dying," he echoed, in a quiet voice. "I felt it. I saw her light slipping away, and I couldn't stop it. I couldn't touch her. And I knew . . . I knew we wouldn't have another chance to make another." A bitter smile touched his mouth. "I'm glad, Maxine. I'm glad you made that bargain. For her, for you. Whatever it brings. Whoever you become. I'll love you."

The hard knot broke. "You think I won't love *you*? No matter what you become? Who else could I ever love?"

"If one of those cartoon Thundercats ever sprang to life, you'd leave me in a red-hot second."

"Well," I said. *"Yeah."*

Grant laughed, leaning in to kiss me. But his smile faded, and a shudder raced through him. I said, "I'm scared, too. If I turn into Satan, I'm going to be a terrible mother."

"Huh," he replied. "She'll have a demon lord as a daddy, enslaving the entire world. Just for her."

"Why stop at one world? We need to think about her future."

"Queen of the universe." Grant kissed my brow just as the Messenger emerged from the house. She stared at me with a hint of disdain, but that was her normal bitch-face—what she really felt was impossible to tell.

"You should not be able to speak," she said, studying the air around me. "You are in tremendous pain."

"Yes," I replied. I could almost hear my flesh crackling as the boys fought to free themselves. "Grant knows I don't like to be fussed over."

She raised one cold brow. "You will hunt the beast?"

"I'll find him. I'll do what I can."

"I'm going with you," Grant said. "We don't know how strong the boys will be when they wake up. And you're too trusting of your grandfather. I don't have that problem."

I looked to the Messenger, but all she said was, "As ill as the Lightbringer might be, his power is still greater than mine. His strength has returned for a short time, Hunter. He should not waste it by staying here."

"I wasn't going to disagree," I said, closing my eyes again, turning inward as a shield against the pain—focusing on the boys, pouring my heart into them—as if that might help. "Someone . . . go and harass my grandfather."

"Rest, Maxine," Grant said. "I'll take care of it."

I believed him. I folded my hands over my hard, round stomach. Sleep would be impossible, I told myself. Just ten minutes of doing nothing would have to suffice. Ten minutes only. Maybe in that time, the boys would wake up. Maybe things would get back to normal, just a little, and I'd be able to begin the hunt.

Into the Labyrinth. Into the unknown, chasing fire, and eyes that wanted nothing more than to devour. I was terrified of those eyes. Frightened of what Jack might have seen, frightened that his own fear of the possibilities had led him so far astray from me. But what choice did I have? I couldn't just let everyone I loved waste away without *trying*, even if the attempt was crazy, even if it was a long shot and made no sense.

You will risk everything, whispered the darkness. *Do nothing, and you will at least save* something.

You can see the future now? I asked, uneasy.

But the darkness said nothing—merely curled even tighter around my heart, crushing it in its cool coils. My pulse skipped a beat, my breath caught, but then I found my rhythm again and relaxed.

The pain came in waves. The boys continued to pull against me. I rode with them, flowed into their fight, and that, too, was another kind of rhythm.

I dozed inside their agony. I fell asleep. I didn't mean to. It shouldn't have been possible. I didn't even realize what had happened until I opened my eyes and it was dark all around me. Night had fallen.

And I was completely alone.

CHAPTER 25

ABOUT a year after we first met, Grant and I went to an upscale restaurant in Seattle where a party at the table next to us was eating an entire roast suckling pig: crispy and dark, a gnarled, juicy parenthesis. I'm not squeamish, but there was something horrible about it. I blamed my mother—all her stories about humans cooked just like that, by the demons in the prison veil.

I never got the nice fairy tales.

Grant had a different reaction to the roast pig. He told me a story.

When he was fifteen, his mother moved the entire family to Hawaii. His father didn't care. He had a young, exotic wife, he was in love, and his business let him live anywhere he liked. Specifically, a little town named Hawi, on the northern tip of the Big Island where the volcanic rock gives way to lush.

It should have been paradise, but Grant had the *howli* experience: a white boy in a public school full of native

Hawaiians, Asians, and mixed-race Asians, where mainland English was a second language under the best of circumstances. He didn't have any real friends. Some of the kids were mean. One boy who sat behind him would ask every day: *When are you leaving, white boy?*

Grant was an outsider. And for a kid who was already different, more different than anyone else in the world, that was exactly what he *didn't* need.

He spent a lot of time by himself. It was safer that way. Safer for him, for other people around him. He didn't want to be tempted into doing something he shouldn't. Secrets, after all, could be dangerous. And unlike *my* mother, *his* never told him the truth about what, and who, he was. All he had to go on was instinct, and a good heart.

Thank God for good hearts.

Two months after moving to Hawi, four months before his mother would decide to return to the mainland—just in time to reveal she was dying of cancer—Grant heard some boys talking about a hidden beach, one of a hundred, or a thousand, that make up the coast of the Big Island. Only word of mouth will let you find them: on paths that cut across lava fields, state parks, front yards, descending along cliffs and through jungle.

He got it in his head to find that beach. Trail wasn't hard to locate. It started at a little compound that catered to white hippies from the mainland, who'd rent out cottages during the winter, and garden, and meditate, and practice weaving Zen mantras into their Rastafarian hairdos. Just beyond those gardens, on a dirt path that led to a wire fence with a broken gate, the trail zigzagged down a steep hill, into a valley, into a jungle.

It was beautiful. He was excited. The path was dark, narrow, walled in by thick-bladed grass as tall as a man. Hiding all kinds of things.

Such as the wild boar that trotted onto the path in front of him less than a minute into his hike.

A beast, he told me. Something out of the storybooks, as big as a Volkswagen. Stout, powerful chest, heaving sides: thick ropes of muscle sliding beneath its sleek black skin. Two long, sharp teeth jutting from its lower lip.

Howli or Hawaiian, anyone who lived in Hawi more than a month knew one thing: Boars kill people. They'll gore you to death. Slice open the arteries in your legs with six-inch tusks sharper than machetes, and your blood will drop out of you in seconds. And if that doesn't work, they'll just trample you right up.

Demons kill to eat you. Boar just kill because you're a threat, in their territory. I don't know which is better, but either way, you're dead.

"I was stunned, frozen," Grant told me, stretching out his bad leg, rubbing the part where the bone had never healed right. "And then all I felt was cold fear."

"Well, you survived the encounter," I said to him.

"I had power. I sang the boar away. Took me a long time to get the strength in my legs to walk back home. But on the way out of the bush, I ran into this kid from my class. The one who was always asking me when I was going to leave, and you know what he had on him? A machete. He saw my fear, and he just laughed. *Don't worry, white boy*, he said. *This is for a real pig.*"

"And then he asked me the one thing I'd been wanting someone to ask me the whole time I'd been in Hawaii. He asked me if I wanted to join him. *You want to help?* he said. I didn't say anything. I just kept walking."

Grant shook his head. "He was a nothing kid, skinny, but there he was with a little knife actually *looking* for a boar."

"You admired him."

"No, I *hated* him. But he had the courage. He had a need and determination, and nothing else. I had power inside me, but he was the one who went in. Me, I ran."

"Grant," I said.

"I'll never run again," he told me.

❧

THEY were all gone—Grant, Jack. Even the Shurik. Mary alone slept on the couch, and seeing her was such a relief I could have wept. I almost woke her, but I couldn't imagine she'd let Grant out of her sight without putting up a fight.

It was hard to walk. I had to bend over from the pain, and even the air against my skin was agony. The boys were pulling, pulling, struggling to wake, and if I didn't fly apart into a million pieces, it would be a miracle.

I searched the house. I called Grant's cell phone. *Calm,* I told myself. *It's nothing. He's close and safe. If there had been a struggle, you would have woken up.*

But I had a bad feeling. From the moment I'd opened my eyes.

The house was so quiet, and in that silence it no longer felt like a home. I felt like a stranger trespassing on emptiness, invading all the hollow spaces that should have comforted me, but now only looked alien and strange.

When I finally passed through the open front door, back out to the porch, I found life: the Messenger, and at her side, Lord Ha'an. He looked thinner, and his silver braids lacked some of their usual luster. His eyes held the story, though: grim and tired, and full of barely contained grief, and rage. Looking at him, looking into his eyes, frightened me almost as much as my missing husband.

"Where is he?" I asked, noting with dread that the crystal skull was gone as well.

"He left," she said. "With the Wolf."

"He *left*," I echoed, voice breaking from pain—and fear.

But as soon as I said those words, I *knew*. I could see it all, the crazy obscene logic. I wanted to kill my grandfather. And kick my husband in the nuts.

The Messenger hesitated. Lord Ha'an glanced at her. "It is my understanding that your consort forced the Aetar to lead him to what will cure our people."

I stared at them. "You're fucking *kidding* me."

"He took the Yorana and Shurik with him," added Lord Ha'an, with an edge to his voice. "The bonds were heavy upon them all."

"He took down the wall," I said.

"He is their true lord now." But he sounded uneasy. I should have been relieved that Grant had finally accepted their strength, but all I felt was a sick foreboding.

I looked at the Messenger. "You didn't wake me."

"The beast cannot be freed," she said, without a hint of remorse. "And though he is no god, I believe in the visions and power of the Divine Lords. If the Wolf saw that you would release the beast, then you cannot be allowed to venture near his cage. The Lightbringer is the more prudent alternative."

"He's dying," I almost pleaded.

"And so he will fight before he dies," replied the Messenger. "As should we all."

I forced myself to take a breath, then another, slow and careful. It was hard to think, hard to feel anything but desperately overwhelmed and lost. But I closed my eyes and let my mind go blank.

You have two options, I told myself. *Wait here.*

Or not.

I looked at my hands. Silver on the right, demons on the left. "I can't *not* go after them."

"You are vulnerable," replied the Messenger. "I will make you stay."

I stared her dead in the eyes—and kept staring. Sometimes if you hold a silence long enough and fill it with your rage, even genetically modified warrior women get a clue. The Messenger blinked and looked away.

I settled my gaze on Lord Ha'an. "How are your people?"

"Unwell," he said. "I can feel their weakness in me now. It will not be long before I fall victim to the poison. The Osul have fared little better."

"You're going to help them," I told the Messenger. "And

Mary. As much as you can, for as long as you can. Stall this thing."

Dismay flickered through her face. "I cannot."

"You'll try." I backed away from them, rubbing the armor with my left hand—which felt as though it might tear from my body. Lord Ha'an swayed toward me, long fingers twitching.

"My Queen," he said in a grave voice. "If you are hunting for what will save us, we should hunt alongside you."

It was so tempting. I was not at my strongest. One good blow would kill me now—if the pain didn't get me first.

But I had my own walls to bring down, on the inside. And it was time for me to start chipping at them.

My right hand squeezed into a fist. The Messenger took a step toward me, and, for the first time, I saw the fear and urgency in her eyes, and the doubt. "Time moves differently in the Labyrinth. If you return, this may not be the world you left. We may already be dead."

"Then you won't have to worry about the Devourer," I said, and fell into the void.

My body disappeared, and for those long seconds, the sudden absence of pain was so immediate and profound it was like having a second body—I could feel where my skin should be, the outlines of wild, miraculous relief—and I gloried in it.

⊰⊱

WHEN I fell back into the world, it was still night, and the full heat and agony surrounded me again. I choked down a gasp, sprawled in the grass, my mind a total scramble of need and memory, and doubt. From where I lay, I could see the boulder that covered my mother's grave. I hadn't gone far. I hadn't wanted to. I had something to do here that I'd been putting off since the beginning of this nightmare.

I rolled on my back, stared up at the stars, and prayed for help.

I didn't keep track of the time, just the pulse and throb

of the boys on my body, struggling harder now, with greater strength. The closer they came to freeing themselves, the more it hurt. I was nearly blind with it, crippled, when a tingle from the armor cut through the hurt—a cool interruption that I felt in the bones of my right hand.

"Father," I whispered. "Please hear me."

For a moment, I thought the stars began to move toward me, but that was just my vision blurring. So I listened instead, and heard the wind. And the wind deepened, and the wind grew strong, except the leaves of the oak were silent, and the grass was not moving around me.

Pray to the night instead, whispered the darkness. *Pray to what holds your heart and lives in your blood. Pray to yourself, young Queen, young Hunter, young Mother. You are the last of all these things. You, who are both flesh and god.*

I will never be a god, I said.

"Hunter," murmured a soft voice outside my mind: smooth and warm as fire. I opened my eyes and found Oturu looming over me.

I let out my breath, so relieved. I realized, in that moment, where my trust lived, and it was not with the Messenger or any demon lords—or even, anymore, old men who were my grandfather. It was with the boys, and Grant—and one other.

"Oturu," I whispered. "My friend. I need you."

"We are with you," he murmured. "We will always be with you."

I cracked open my eyes and glimpsed the shining daggers of his feet, spading into the grass. His cloak breathed against the direction of the wind, flaring like wings and swallowing light—and within its darkness, shades of movement: faces and hands, bodies roiling in the abyss.

Tears burned. I would have told anyone who asked that it was the pain—but it was the gentleness of his touch, the reassurance it symbolized: that I was not alone.

"Young Queen," whispered Oturu.

"It's time to hunt," I told him, hoarse.

And the boys finally woke up.

CHAPTER 26

I T'S easy to forget pain. We do it all the time. All the
discomforts of life fade away, and we forget—within minutes, hours, days, or weeks. Time heals.

Unless it doesn't. Because there is some suffering that
cuts to the soul—and that cleaves deep and does not fade.
It burns, almost eternal.

And you burn with it.

I was having trouble breathing, but only because I was so
exhausted. Raw and Aaz crouched on either side of me,
holding little electric fans that blew cool air on my face.
They didn't look too strong themselves, but they were alive
and had already eaten one chain saw between them, which
was a pretty good sign.

Dek and Mal coiled around my shoulders, lapping up a
pile of M&M's. Their purrs, hoarse. Zee crouched a short
distance away, on top of the boulder covering my mother's

grave. He was very quiet and watched the old farmhouse, far away at the bottom of the hill—occasionally glancing to his left at the small fires burning in the wood. Signs of demon life.

"Won't be back," he rasped. "Won't be the same."

A chill settled over me. "You sure about that?"

Zee looked at me, his silence worth more than words. For once, I felt as though I could see in his face the weight of his life—thousands upon thousands of years, thousands since my first ancestor, thousands before. He seemed tired. Tired and old.

"Death before resurrection," murmured Oturu, "but what is resurrected is never the same."

I stared at his pointed chin, the long, masculine line of a hard mouth. Black hair curled past his jaw, the very tips twining and writhing like snakes. He had no hands. And though his eyes were hidden beneath the brim of his hat, I felt him looking at me. His stare, like a brand upon my face, the heat of his gaze pushing through me with unfathomable strength.

I tried to sit up. Raw and Aaz pushed against my back, little claws piercing my clothes and scraping cool against my skin. Tendrils from Oturu's flowing, floating cloak wrapped around my wrists—also cool, cool as death—and helped pull me to my feet.

I sensed movement behind me. Tracker eased into my line of sight. His sweater was torn, and blood dotted his throat. But his eyes were sharp as ever, raking me up and down.

"You look terrible." He glanced at the boys, frowning. "So do they. That's . . . not possible."

"Will survive," Zee rasped, prowling close. "Others may not."

"Are you hurt?" I asked Tracker.

"It was nothing. A human matter, and not Aetar."

"He forgets himself," murmured Oturu, "and hunts for those who are not his Lady."

"You were a hero," I said.

A disdainful smile touched Tracker's mouth. "Someone has to be."

I didn't ask what he'd done, whom he had saved. I felt wistful, though. Had that been me, once upon a time? Had I ever really helped people? I liked to think I had, but I wondered sometimes. All those years, alone on the road, keeping to myself—the stranger, always passing through.

"No sign of the Aetar," he said. "Found none of their creatures. It didn't feel right, though. There was something in the air, everywhere we went. I haven't felt that weight in a long time."

"What did it mean before?"

His jaw tensed. "During the war. Before battle. We knew the demons were coming, and there was nothing we could do to stop them. We just had to be strong enough to stay alive."

"Great," I said. "It's not going to get easier. We're going into the Labyrinth. You've been there. You and Oturu, and the boys. I need all your help."

Aaz hugged my legs, while Raw handed me a cold ginger ale. I took a sip and extended it to Tracker. After a brief moment, he took it from me—or tried. I held on, for a second longer than necessary.

"I don't know how to do this," I said. "How to enter the Labyrinth. I can't afford to get lost. I don't have time."

Oturu loomed, his cloak writhing open, blotting out the stars as he surrounded us. Tracker shuddered and pulled away from me. I felt cold, but safe. It hadn't always been that way—once, I would have been terrified, skin crawling. But hearts change. Monsters become beautiful.

"We would hear your heart across the universe," Oturu said, in a voice as soft as death. "You will not be alone. But we might still lose our way."

"The Labyrinth has a mind of its own," Tracker added, rubbing his hand against his thigh. "We could wander for a thousand years and come back to this planet and find nothing the same. Or arrive just at the moment we left."

"My husband is there. I have to find him." The cure might be a fool's errand—but Grant was flesh and blood, and mine. My man. My heart.

Shadows moved through Tracker's eyes. I didn't understand that look, or his silence. But Oturu murmured, "As the Labyrinth wills it, so we shall be," then: "The hunt will be sweet."

It'll be terrible, I thought. *This won't end well.*

If I'd ever been certain of anything, it was that. My sense of foreboding had only gotten worse—a darkening dread that felt the same as memory, as if I'd already seen something terrible, and it was lodged inside me. I'd never felt that way before. Maybe it was just nerves, but I was afraid it was something else.

I was afraid Zee was right. We wouldn't be back here. Not like this. Not ever again.

I looked at my mother's grave, at my grandmother buried beside her. I stared and stared, wishing I could have stayed a child forever, that I could be a child again—a do-over, only this time I wouldn't take for granted what I had. I'd appreciate my mother and her sacrifices. I'd throw away all the resentment that had plagued me as a teen.

I'd be a better daughter.

"Just bones," Zee rasped, threading his claws through my fingers, holding my hand. Raw and Aaz leaned against me, dragging teddy bears from the shadows. Dek and Mal made a mournful sound, and began singing a very sad version of "On the Road Again."

"Just bones," I agreed quietly. "But you know it's more than that."

Zee rubbed his sharp little cheek against my hand. "Still have us."

I swallowed hard. "Always."

Tracker made a rude sound. "I have no idea what we're supposed to be killing, but if I have to watch one more second of this shit, I'll murder *myself.*"

Oturu yanked so hard on the man's collar, he fell to his

knees. For once, I didn't protest. "Besides Grant, we're also hunting an Aetar. A powerful one. Goes by the name of the Devourer."

Tracker started. "Are you out of your mind?"

I ignored him. "Please," I said to Oturu, holding up my right hand, with its armor gleaming.

Tendrils of his hair slid around my forearm, caressing that rippling, silver artifact. "You are a daughter of the Labyrinth," he replied, softly, as the bottom half of his face began to glow, as though bathed in moonlight. "You have your birthrights."

I stared at him. "I don't know what that means."

Tracker grunted, grim and mocking amusement in his eyes. Zee rasped, "Means you *want* it, and door will open."

What I wanted was Grant, safe. I closed my eyes, focusing on him, on my need. It wasn't like opening the void to hop from place to place—another mystery, as yet unexplainable. This, instead, felt bigger. A wider leap. I could feel a wall just beyond my thoughts, a barrier that I pushed against, and kept pushing.

I thought of my mother—then Grant—and imagined a door.

A door that opened.

❦

WHEN I could see again, I found myself in a forest.

I was sprawled on my stomach. Moss cradled my body, and a snail oozed past my nose, less than an inch away. I glimpsed a massive fallen log, bursting with ferns and twisted saplings, and when I turned my head, just slightly, I was confronted with the base of a tree trunk so immense I could not see the end of it from where I lay. I was lost in roots the size of minivans, and the canopy was a distant cloud of green, far above my head.

There are mysteries, and there are *mysteries*, and it's all a bit like porn—you know it when you see it, and your mileage may vary.

For me, there was no confusion about the Labyrinth. I didn't know what the hell it was. I'd been in it before but never by intent—and then, only for such brief moments, I still wasn't sure what I'd seen or done. If, even, it had all been just a dream.

This felt like a dream.

It was not dark—not exactly—but there was no bright sun to be glimpsed, either. An odd twilight, caught in shades of silver and heather. The boys were scattered around me, despite the light. I kissed Dek's little cheek, then Mal, hugging them close. Their purrs were quiet, a bit broken and uncertain. Zee perched on a root, staring into the distance—while Raw and Aaz climbed the tree beside me. Teddy-bear backpacks, the kind small children wore, were strapped to their backs.

I tried to stand. Took several attempts—my legs were weak—but I managed to grab hold of a massive root structure and haul myself up. I glimpsed more trees—scattered and impossibly massive—an endless number of them disappearing into the shadows. I craned my neck and still couldn't see the top.

I tried to find Tracker. Glimpsed movement, but when I looked up again, all I saw were dark birds, winging silently above my head. Ravens, perhaps. A soft breeze lifted my hair.

"The Labyrinth has no wind," said Tracker, just behind me.

I managed not to flinch. "Then what did I just feel?"

"Wind from another world." He scrabbled on top of the root and perched there like a hawk. "Stolen through open doors. Same with the birds, or any life you find here. None of it is native."

"And the forest?"

Tracker hesitated, rubbing his chest like it hurt. "I don't know. I've never . . . been here before."

"So who taught you those other things?"

A faint furrow gathered in his brow—rare sign of confusion—but he did not answer me. Just slid down the other side of the root and disappeared. I searched for Oturu and felt a tingle at the back of my neck. I looked up again, just in time to glimpse a shadow floating amongst the trees.

I scrabbled down from my mossy nest, using the fat, coiled roots around me as a highway system, a forest sidewalk. I felt small as an ant compared to the trees, each of which seemed fat as an entire city block. Skyscrapers had never made me feel so insignificant—nor any man-made structure, mountain, or canyon. But this was different.

This was breathless wonder. First twilight, first hush, a silence so expectant and pure that to make a sound, to even breathe, felt as though I was intruding upon the gestation of miracles. *Ancient* did not belong in this place, *ancient* was too young a word, but for every step I traveled, I felt more certain that I walked amongst immense and dreaming souls and that I was nothing but a dream, a fragment, an echo lost in the heart of eternity. I wondered if mankind had been born from trees, or if trees walked amongst men as their own dreams, born and born again.

We are home, whispered a small voice inside my head. *We are home in the heart of the endless wood.*

And the darkness, which had been silent all this time, murmured:

It is in the blood.

I found Tracker moving toward me through a clutch of large ferns, each frond nearly as large as his body. He rubbed his chest like it hurt—which was odd enough to make me stare. Tracker did not show pain. I had stabbed him in the foot once, and he'd practically asked for more.

"What is it?" I asked him.

Tracker faltered. "Nothing."

"I'll take that as a *something.*"

He balled his hand into a fist. I picked up my pace, passing a mossy knoll covered in small purple flowers, like bluebells, only tinier. "This isn't what I expected."

"I'm surprised you had any expectations."

I hesitated. "I was in the Wasteland, remember?"

A place where souls were thrown to be forgotten. I had

walked the dark side of the Labyrinth, buried alive. Nothing but a heartbeat in the endless dark.

I was the only person to ever escape the Wasteland. And though I knew that the Labyrinth was much more than that dark, endless hole, I could not help but associate one with the other. The Wasteland was the nightmare that never died.

Tracker was silent a moment. "I'm sorry for that."

I shrugged, watching Zee prowl ahead of us, slinking over roots and through the ferns with a hushed, preternatural grace. Raw and Aaz were still in the trees, leaping from trunk to trunk, absolutely silent. I could only see them because of the little teddy bears dangling from their backs.

"You've been here before?" I asked him.

"No." Pain flickered through his eyes as he looked through the trees, but when he turned his gaze on me it was flat, empty. "Oturu didn't free me, then. But I felt this place around us."

"What is it like when you're not free?" I asked him, impulsively. "When he has you . . . inside him?"

"What do you think?"

"I think it's hell," I told him. "I'm sorry."

Tracker pulled ahead. "You brought me here to help you, not be friends."

"Wait—"

"I track," he interrupted. "That's what I am. When the Aetar made me, I got a skill. I can find anything."

"Yes," I said, wishing I could take back my question.

His jaw tightened. "Your husband is somewhere ahead of us, but I can't tell you anything else except that he's far away and alive."

I said nothing. Tracker ran ahead, little more than a lean shadow darting along wide root structures that tumbled and twisted between the massive trees. He looked as small as I felt, but far more graceful. I hurried to catch up, falling into a careless run that made me feel as though I were flying; helped by the boys, who fell down from the trees and raced alongside me—my wolves.

A tingling sensation arced across my back, raising goose pimples. I thought I was just cold. But the sensation intensified until it felt like a live wire was being threaded from the base of my neck, down between my shoulders. Dek and Mal made an alarmed trilling noise, tightening their hold on my neck.

Zee skidded to a stop, looking back at me with his eyes wide, alarmed. From above, Oturu called out. I could barely hear him. I was still running, but my body felt strange, like it was being sucked sideways into a massive vacuum cleaner.

Oh, shit, I thought, right before I went completely blind.

I tumbled, upside down—jerked to the side—shaken like I was in some giant's fist. I couldn't see. My teeth rattled. Hot air washed over me with such violence and intensity, my skin felt singed. I reached for my first source of relief—the darkness inside me—but all it whispered was, *Open your eyes.*

But I'd already started coughing. The air was bitter, searing my nostrils and eyes. Tears streamed down my cheeks. I glimpsed a dry, cracked plain in every direction, straight to the horizon. Nothing else. No life. Del and Mal clutched my ears with their little claws. Looming above us, blocking out a dark purple sky, were two huge moons. Pale and white as ice, and creased with gas clouds.

I tried to take a breath, but the air couldn't seem to reach my lungs; and it burned, it burned.

But I almost forgot that because when I looked down, covering my mouth, I glimpsed a splash of red at the corner of my eyes.

Bodies. Ten feet away on my left, skin crimson and peeling.

Yorana. Demons.

CHAPTER 27

I tried calling out Grant's name, but the air was killing me. I grabbed my right hand, feeling the armor flow beneath my grip. Dek and Mal were keening in my ear.

Help, I thought, choking. It must have been night on this planet. No tattoos on my skin, no boys—who could have breathed for me.

A dark blur slammed into the dirt, cracking the earth. I stumbled backward from the shock wave of the impact, which sounded like a tree breaking. Glimpsed bladed feet, long and straight, just before a sheet of darkness billowed and heaved in the still air, whipping about with such violence it could have been hit with the winds of a hurricane. Shadows filled those folds, bottomless, endless. Reaching for me.

I fell forward into that embrace, and was swallowed.

It wasn't the void, and it wasn't a dream, but what surrounded me for those brief moments was alive, crawling over me, into me, through my mouth and ears, pressing against my eyes. Hands grabbed my wrists, then let go, only to be replaced by grasping fingers tugging my hair, and the scrape of something sharp, like teeth, against my leg. I couldn't see what was touching me. I couldn't fight.

Below my heart, the darkness tightened its coils, rising to look through my eyes.

You dare, came its slow whisper, and the crawling sensation stopped: Those hands and teeth fled from my skin. Strength flooded my limbs, washing through me like a cleansing, dark fire.

And then I was free, on my knees, vomiting into a fern. Cool air surrounded me, but the slow burn remained beneath my skin—power, skimming through me, making the hairs on my arms stand straight up. I closed my eyes, listening to that night fire, listening to its absence of light, which felt like another kind of star—falling, falling, inside me.

This is what waits, whispered the darkness. *It is freedom. And the hunger?* I asked. *Your hunger destroys.*

Hunter. That is beautiful, too.

Dek and Mal chirped. I opened my eyes, vision blurred with tears. Zee knelt in front of me, so close his nose rubbed mine. Raw and Aaz were pressed on either side of him.

"Maxine," he rasped.

"What happened?" I croaked.

"Fell through a door." Tracker knelt, tilting back my head and peering into my eyes. "You hit another world."

"Dead world." I pushed his hands away but started coughing. "Dead Yorana were there."

"But not your man. He's not there."

Zee rammed his claws through a fern, agitated. "But came this way."

Yes, and some of his demons had fallen through that door, just like I had. And died there. I didn't want to think about the same thing happening to Grant. But maybe his ability to see fields of energy would save him. I'd felt a tingle, right before the fall—that had to be something that would alert him as well.

Oturu loomed. I turned, peering up at him. His mouth

was set in a hard line, and the shadows beneath the brim of his hat were especially dark.

"Thank you," I said.

Tendrils of his hair reached for my hands. But before Oturu could touch me, Tracker placed himself between us—grabbing my waist and helping me rise.

"Be more careful," he said in a gruff voice, steering me away from the tall demon. "You might not survive the next drop."

I stared at him, remembering the assault of hands and teeth inside Oturu's cloak, wondering if that was what Tracker had to endure—and if so, how he could survive that impossible prison.

I looked back at Oturu, who stood perfectly still in the twilight shadows of the Labyrinth forest, watching us. Even his cloak did not move.

Raw tugged on my hand and pulled a bottle of water from his teddy-bear backpack—along with a small packet of M&M's. I took both, grateful. My throat still hurt from breathing the air on that planet. Aaz was hugging his own teddy bear, giving me a mournful look. I stopped, dropped into a crouch, and hugged him as tight as I could. I needed to, more badly than I could admit.

"It's okay," I said, feeling those mountain-crushing arms hug me back, very gently. Raw pushed close, as well. Zee leaned against us, ears pressed flat against his head, eyes squeezed shut. Dek and Mal licked his brow.

I glanced up, found Tracker watching with all the sharp scrutiny of a hawk.

"Excuse me," I said. "But we're having a moment."

The corner of his mouth twitched. He stepped onto a gnarled, massive tree root, balancing there on the balls of his feet, and looked back down at us.

"It's good to have moments," he said, with what could have been menace—or wistfulness. "Life is nothing without them."

━◆━

I don't know how long we walked, but the light never changed, and neither did the forest. And even though I was here, with the ground solid beneath my feet—even though I had fallen through another door—it was still difficult to imagine that this was the maze. A forest as the crossroad between here and there: a place of possibilities that was a world unto itself.

"The Labyrinth reflects the heart of its god," said Oturu, floating past me, tendrils of his hair stroking the deep, cavernous creases of tree bark, so large my hand could fit inside. I heard the high trill of a bird, but nothing answered that lonely call. "The god who is your father, Hunter."

I felt uneasy hearing him say that. My father was something I still hadn't dealt with. I didn't know how. But that hadn't stopped me from sending out a silent call to him from the first second I'd fallen into the Labyrinth. He hadn't answered. But then, I almost didn't expect him to. It was easier on me that way. Less disappointing.

"Did you ever meet him?" I asked.

Oturu tilted his chin toward me. His silence was long.

"We do not know," he said; and then, very softly, "Our embrace made you afraid."

I was wondering when he'd bring that up. "Who are they, inside you?"

His mouth tightened into a hard line. "We told you once, Hunter. We are the last of our kind."

"Yes," I said, gently. "I'm sorry. But what does that have to do with those creatures?"

"We are the last," he repeated, and I realized he wasn't just talking about himself. I stared, trying to make sense of it—but all I could think about were those hands and teeth on my skin. Lives, lost in darkness. Lives, hidden away. Who were they, and what? And how long had they been trapped inside the demon who floated beside me?

"But why are you . . . containing them?" I asked, confused—but also a little horrified.

"So they might live." Oturu's cloak flared, and I saw those faces and hands surging against the wall of darkness; fleeting glimpses, pressing out and receding. A gruesome dance. "Their worlds are gone. No others will sustain them. And so we are together, and together we hunt, and we are not alone."

Not alone. My heart broke for him. For all of us. *Not alone.*

How fundamental that was beginning to seem. From Aetar to demon, to human—all of us suffered from being alone. Solitude was different. Meditative, even. But loneliness . . . that was the curse and killer.

Zee made a low, growling sound. He was perched on the side of a tree, claws digging in like hooks. Moments later, Tracker appeared.

"Come on," he said. "There are dead demons up ahead."

More Yorana, but this time they hadn't died on another world. Their bodies had been tucked within the roots of a tree, half-covered in ferns. A quick burial, it seemed.

"Don't go near them," I told Tracker and Oturu. "They were sick."

"Clearly." Tracker kept a wide berth. "It's been years since I've seen their kind. I'd almost forgotten what they looked like."

"You fought them?"

"Briefly. The Wardens were created prior to the Reaper Kings being imprisoned on your ancestor. The Yorana were difficult because they could charm, make you feel relaxed, sluggish, with just a look. It was easier to kill them from a distance."

"Does this mean Grant is close?" I asked Zee.

Raw crept near the bodies, and his lips peeled back with disgust. Aaz prowled on the other side, head tilted, ears slick against his head. He made a chittering sound. Zee glanced at him and shook his head. "Old dead, not new. We came fast, but time already stretched. Week, maybe two, for Grant."

"A week ahead of us? Or *two*?" What a horrifying thought. I stared out at the forest, which was not a forest—hoping by some miracle I'd catch a glimpse of him.

And I did. Only it wasn't him. I saw movement far from us, between the trees. Only for a split second, but it was human-shaped, and that was alarming. Especially because it wasn't shaped like my husband. I'd know his shoulders anywhere.

"Zee," I said, noticing him looking at the same spot. For a moment I wasn't sure he would acknowledge me.

"Safe," he rasped, finally meeting my gaze. Oturu drifted in that direction, then went perfectly still.

"Yes," he said, then, "We should continue, Hunter."

Tracker barely glanced in that direction. "Like I said, life comes through those doors, sometimes by design, mostly by accident. But just in case it's an Aetar, I also don't think we should investigate."

I was sure it wasn't an Aetar. Not with the way Zee and Oturu had reacted. But I didn't have time to indulge my curiosity. I already attracted enough trouble without looking for more.

We kept on. Avoiding doors, listening to the sounds of the Labyrinth and its lost life. Lost ourselves, in the twilight. I entered a strange mental state—one part of my brain acutely aware of our surroundings—while the other half drifted. I thought about my mother so often that sometimes I felt as though she were at my side—and I'd look, half-expecting to see her, only to find a tree, or one of the boys giving me a curious look.

More dead Yorana appeared. Bodies, like breadcrumbs. No Shurik corpses, which puzzled me. But again, it began to feel like a routine. The monotony never changed. I felt no hunger, no real thirst. I forced myself to eat what Raw would put into my hands: little bits of trail bar and fruit, stored in his bulging backpack. But I ate because I thought I should, not because I felt any hollowness. I didn't see Tracker eat, either, even though I'd offer him food. He'd shake his head and glide into the shadows between the trees.

Grant occupied my thoughts, but after a time, I felt the distance grow too vast, and I had to pull away from thinking of him. I missed our bond, and it was easy to feel resentful that it was gone. That link between us, in this place, would have made all the difference.

I thought mostly, though, about being a mother. A mother like my mother. Or a mother that was wholly me, with all my terrible mistakes. Like deliberately bringing my unborn child into a dangerous place, risking her life and mine on a dream, a possibility—on love.

I finally understood why relationships couldn't last in my family—why no one married, no one stayed tied down— why strangers were better, cold and quick, and anonymous.

Love was too great a risk. Love was the destroyer. Love might kill us faster than any demon.

Or save us.

Zee held up his clawed hand—a sharp, urgent gesture— and muttered: "Listen."

I didn't hear anything, but I trusted Zee. I stood there, head tilted, relaxing into the silence. Sometimes it's easier to see a star when you're not looking directly at it. Stare just to the left, and the light will shine brighter.

It was the same here. I didn't focus, just stayed relaxed . . . and after a long minute of hushed waiting, I heard a high, sweet sound. A flute.

A very familiar flute. I knew that tone.

"Grant," I said, and took off running.

CHAPTER 28

I remember my mother once asking, *Is there anything in the world dumber than men?*

I hadn't answered. I was only a kid. But if she had said that today, I would have agreed with her.

Grant, you fool.

That's what's strange about loving men. Really loving them. You love them even when their stupidity is so profound it could put out the world.

Which is not to say you don't have second thoughts.

I mean, *seriously*.

IT wasn't my husband. I found Jack instead.

He was nestled in the hollow of a massive root system, playing a golden flute. He sounded just like Grant, except the melody had the weight of age on it, a melancholy spirit. A song, I suspected, that had not been heard by anyone for a very long time.

He had company. But it wasn't my husband who stood with him.

A unicorn rested at his feet.

It was smaller than a horse but no less shocking: pure white, the white of virgin snow, with a delicate back and trim muscles, and a long neck that supported an impossibly lovely, fine-boned head. A touch could have shattered that skull; it looked so delicate, even the weight of the horn spiraling from the center of its brow, gleaming like mother-of-pearl, seemed too much for it to bear.

Black eyes flicked from Jack to me. They were filled with so much naked intelligence, I immediately forgot the fantasy—and felt cold all over again.

"Sarai," I said, taking a guess. Only one Aetar I knew of had ever assumed the identity of the creature in front of me—though the last time I'd seen her, she'd been a woman: the owner of an art gallery in Seattle, elegant and assured, who had spent just as many years as Jack on earth, being born again in different bodies. I'd liked her, then. Watched her human body die in my arms before I knew she was immortal. I was still troubled by that death, sometimes.

The unicorn inclined her head. *Hunter.*

Her voice was soft inside my thoughts. I stared a moment longer, then pulled my gaze to Jack.

My grandfather hadn't stopped playing when I ran into the clearing. His eyes met mine, briefly—before he closed them and turned his head. I bit my tongue. I bit it so hard I tasted blood and waited for the song to end. Around me, the boys gathered, crouched in the shadows, red eyes glittering.

The last note trailed away. In the silence, I said, "That's Grant's flute."

"Yes." Jack hefted the instrument in his hands, a bitter smile playing against his mouth. "He left it."

"Bullshit," I said. "For him, it's a weapon."

"He needs few weapons now," replied my grandfather, unmoving from his perch. "I knew you would come, Maxine. But I wish you hadn't."

"No one gets what they want." I stepped forward and felt a tingle run down my spine. I was better now at spotting the entrances to other worlds, and there was one in front of me—a haze that was stronger, heavier, than other doors I'd encountered, and one that carried a sparkle—dusting motes of light. It didn't look or feel threatening—there was no warning sign. Just a tingle of cold dread, a strange and awful premonition.

Reconsider your actions, said Sarai, and there was no longer anything soft about that voice pushing through my mind. *Jack has apprised me of what has happened on your world. This is not the answer.*

"Then what is? Let everyone die?" I moved closer but stayed out of reach of her horn. "Why are you here, Sarai?"

A snort flared those delicate nostrils. Jack said, "She's the only one brave enough to meet you in the flesh. Most of the other Aetar are convinced you'll try to kill them."

"You told them I was coming."

We felt you inside the Labyrinth. Sarai tilted her head, staring at me with those bottomless eyes. *We felt the Lightbringer and the demons. The Labyrinth is a tuning fork of energy, Hunter. One ripple, and it affects all who reside in the forest.*

"I'm surprised you didn't try to kill Grant."

Jack looked down. "That is still the question, my dear. Your presence here just might trigger our own civil war. Long-brewing, I might add. Those who are done with the killing, who regret our brutality all those eons ago—"

—against those who would do it all again, and happily. Sarai stood, an impossibly graceful unfolding that seemed to happen in the blink of an eye. *We cannot afford such a battle. We are too few. Too many innocents would be killed.*

"Same tired argument," Jack said in a sour voice. "It saves us the trouble of having to confront who we have become. Of course, once the others realize where you've come—what you intend to do—it will be a moot point. Even those who would let you and your family live would kill to stop this."

I held up my hand. "Where is my husband?"

"Where do you think?" Jack rubbed his face, looking weary. "I couldn't bring myself to go in after him. Which shows you the limits of my courage."

"You hoped I would arrive to be brave for you?"

"I hoped you would never come at all. Sometimes bravery is doing nothing. Giving up the man you love for the greater good would have been such an act."

Old Wolf, Sarai admonished. But his words rolled right off me.

"The Devourer is in there, isn't he?" I said. "On the other side of that door, in the world where you trapped him."

"It's not a world. More of a foyer, per se," Jack replied. "But yes. And Grant went through with his demons. *And* his demons."

I gave him a cold look. "Watch it, Grandpa."

Jack grunted, glancing from me to Tracker—who appeared around a hairy, giant fern that could have sheltered a small family from the rain if there'd been any. Oturu, curiously, did not make an appearance. Now that I thought about it, he'd never shown himself to anyone but the boys and me. And Tracker.

"You," said Jack.

"Apparently," replied Tracker.

"You know what awaits her?"

"I do. Any last words before we all die horribly?"

"Shut up," I said, and made toward the door.

I didn't think Jack could move that fast. One moment he was seated on that root—and in the next he stood in front of me, grabbing my arm and trying to pull me away. Zee hissed. Dek and Mal puffed flame at his face, but that didn't slow him down.

I tried to twist free without hurting him, but it was impossible; his grip was like steel. Tracker drew close, expression inscrutable, but the old man was not so composed; the strong lines of his face showed the ravages of terrible distress, and his cheeks were flushed.

"I must strongly advise against this course of action."

"You think I'll let this freak go. Is your prison really that shabbily constructed? I mean, it must be if Grant was able to waltz in."

We made it impossible to leave, Sarai said, voice cool and dry. *We were not worried about the fools who would fall in.*

"You're not a normal woman," Jack said. "So no, I don't know how you might break his shackles, just that I've seen the possibility."

I'd seen the fire. Witnessed myself torn apart within it. And he was right, maybe being brave meant I should walk away and let my husband rot in that place. But I couldn't even contemplate that. I couldn't even face that option.

I stared him dead in the eye. "Tell me the truth, old Wolf. Can a Lightbringer of Grant's strength control that Aetar?"

Jack hesitated. "I don't know. Grant is not like any one of his kind who ever existed. But neither is the Devourer."

"You still managed to imprison him."

"Barely. Because we used the crystal skulls. It was our last act with them, after we broke the power of the Reaper Kings." Jack glanced at Zee and the boys. "You destroyed the other skulls. If he goes free, we will have nothing to use. Nothing that is strong enough."

Sarai had also positioned herself in front of the gate, her head lowered ever so slightly—just enough to make that horn seem like a weapon instead of a decorative piece of fantasy. Raw and Aaz gathered close to my sides, watching her with glittering crimson eyes. Claws flexed.

Tracker studied her, then my grandfather, his gaze inscrutable.

"The Wolf is right," he said. "This is too incredibly dangerous."

"Of course it is," I said. "It may be suicidal. But what would you have given, Tracker, to have someone risk herself to keep you safe? What sacrifice would have been too much to keep that iron collar off your neck?"

"This one," he said.

"Liar. Even the *attempt* . . . someone *trying* for you . . . would have changed *everything*."

I stepped away from the men—and the unicorn—clenching my right hand into a fist. Zee and the boys gathered close. "Get out of my way."

Jack shook his head. Zee rasped, "Nothing lasts, Meddling Man."

"Except foolishness," he whispered. "You're a mother now, Maxine. What do you owe your child?"

"Stay here," I told Tracker, ignoring that dirty play. "Watch them."

I didn't wait for a response. I ran to that shimmering haze, demons at my side. Raw and Aaz slammed Sarai out of the way when she tried to charge me. I heard Jack's choked, startled shout—but that was all. I hit that shimmering haze, passed through.

And got a surprise.

I found myself inside a white marble foyer. Wide and curved as two cupped hands—and gleaming, shining, with an unnatural brightness that permitted no blemishes. In fact, it was as though the stone and walls had been airbrushed to absolute perfection. No color, anywhere. Just a pure, alabaster white.

It was the visual equivalent of hearing a prim old woman speak in a man's booming lumberjack voice. Unexpected, given certain expectations. I was anticipating hell, after all.

"Tell me," I said to Zee, who prowled across the floor, looking like some obscene blemish against that pure, luminous marble. "This is kind of fucked up, right?"

Dek and Mal began humming the melody to "Strangeness," while Raw and Aaz pressed against the walls, scratching them—leaving claw marks that oozed black tar, like blood.

"Excuse me," said a quiet male voice.

I flinched, surprised. Zee also twitched—all the boys, jumping a little—their surprise even more visceral than mine. No one ever sneaked up on them.

I turned and found that an elderly man stood just behind me: stout, with spectacles hanging down his nose. He was dressed like a butler, all in black, his skin very pale and his eyes a watery blue. He held slippers in his left hand.

"Please announce yourself," he said.

I stared, heart still pounding so hard I wanted to vomit. "Who are you?"

One stubby brow arched up. "I am the butler. And you are?"

He was polite, proper, the very epitome of *nonthreatening*—but the skin-crawling menace I felt at those simple, quiet words made me want to run screaming.

"My name is Maxine Kiss," I said.

"Ah, very good." He extended some slippers. "Please put these on. The master abhors noise."

Zee sniffed at them. The slippers seemed to be slippers. Still, I felt very strange about it. I stared from them to the butler, who straightened and fixed me with a cold look.

"You *cannot* see him, otherwise," he said in a crisp voice.

I frowned, slipped off my boots. Slippers went on. The butler took my shoes from me, holding them away from his body and between his fingers, as if they carried some disease.

"This way," he said, and led me up the stairs.

I caught glimpses of halls, rooms, none furnished—doors that were closed that I wanted to open. But I kept my hands to myself and followed the old man to a set of double doors, also white marble, which he tugged open with the lightest of touches.

"Maxine Kiss to see you, sir."

I heard no greeting, but the butler gestured for me to enter.

I did, and found my grandfather.

CHAPTER 29

A couple years back, I got a letter in the mail.
    It was from the New York law firm that had handled
the affairs of several generations of Kiss women, and which
was doing the same for me, though I rarely checked in—
except when I needed information on some random property
I'd vaguely recall my mother saying we owned.

There was a note, brief: "For delivery on this date, at the
request of Jolene Kiss." It was clipped to another envelope,
this one sealed, and slightly battered with age. I recognized
my mother's handwriting on the flap—no one else wrote
my name with quite that flourish.

A single sheet of paper was tucked inside. More of my
mother's elegant writing. I was startled, a bit breathless with
the discovery. I remember sitting down on Grant's couch,
bathed in sunlight, my tattooed hands shaking just a little.
I had the armor by then—I'd traveled in time. But this was
another kind of breach from the past.

I should just die and be done with it, I read. *That's the
proper way, to let a daughter move on with her life, instead*

*of coming back from the grave. But you've always been a
bit different, and experience has taught me that you don't
mind conversing with the dead. And I find that I don't mind
sending letters to a daughter who in my life is still in diapers
but who will one day bear all the burdens of being a woman.*

*You won't have an easy life. You've had a taste of that
by now, and more. You'll discover things, if you haven't
already, that will make you question me and this life you've
been born into. Feel free to be angry. I'm dead, after all. It
won't bother me.*

*But you did come to me once, by accident. You, as an
adult, with that particular ability to cut through time. You
were afraid, you were sick, and I couldn't help you then. I
hope I've judged the delivery of this letter so that I can help
you now—which won't be much help at all.*

*There are miracles, Maxine. Even in death, and betrayal,
and grief—there are still miracles. Cling to that, cling to
hope. No matter how terrible things get, or how helpless
you feel. Hope is what will save you, again and again.*

So get up. Get up off that floor where I found you.

Fight, Maxine. Fight for your life.

Fight for other lives that haven't been born.

Fight for your hope. Fight for your heart.

You'll find a miracle if you do.

I promise.

MY grandfather.

My grandfather, as he had appeared when I first met
him, years past. Trim, long legged, elegant. Dressed in sleek
tan slacks and a cream-colored cable-knit sweater. Quite
polished. Clean-shaven, his gray hair swept back. He was
pale and sat in a soft chair with a brown blanket thrown over
his legs.

Yes, the epitome of torture and evil.

Until I saw his eyes, then it was no joke. I knew those

eyes. I knew the hunger behind that glittering black stare, and it was old and bottomless, and utterly implacable.

"Greetings, my dear," said the old man, with a faint smile. "So delightful finally meeting you. Imagine my surprise when I learned that I had *family*."

"You're not my grandfather," I said, feeling the boys spreading out around me. "You're just wearing his old face."

That faint smile widened, and it was so much like Jack—so much, yet not—I felt off-balance, dizzy. I'd passed through the mirror into another universe, and here was my grandfather, as he might have been. Cool and bland, and polished like a stone. He scared me, and it wasn't just because of his eyes. He terrified me, even—and I was grateful for Dek and Mal, coiled tight around my throat.

"He *has* kept you quite in the dark, hasn't he?" His hands smoothed out the blanket in his lap, and he turned his gaze on Zee and the boys. "Reaper Kings. We meet again. You're weakened this time, which fills me with no small amount of pleasure."

"Don't remember you," Zee rasped.

Delight touched his mouth but not his eyes. "I was there the entire time, hiding in plain sight. Reduced, ignored, betrayed . . . but ever present. You knew me, little Reaper King. Yes, you did. I was the architect of your prison."

"You're *not* Jack," I said, unnerved. Even more so, when he looked at me, and I saw a flash of anger so profound it verged on insanity.

"Actually," he said softly, "I am."

I stepped back as the old man rose gracefully from his chair, his blanket slipping away to the floor. The butler moved in, stooping to pick up the blanket, but froze when the other man touched his back, ever so slightly. The butler's face went carefully blank, but that was enough. He was, I suspected, one of those fools who had fallen through the gate into this prison. And fuck only knew what he'd been put through for however long he'd attended this old Aetar, who my grandfather said was in love with pain.

I glanced at Zee, who watched him with careful, narrowed eyes. "He's lying."

But the demon gave me a brief look that chilled me to the bone. "He is not. He believes."

The old man laughed, ever so softly—standing behind the butler, who had finished picking up the blanket and stood there, holding it to his chest.

"Of course I believe," he said, holding my gaze, all while he ran a thick, strong hand down the back of the butler's neck. "I was Jack, I am Jack, I am what he threw away, all those years ago."

I swallowed hard. Raw and Aaz were prowling around the room, sniffing at the walls. No sign of Grant or the Shurik, which frightened me. I fought to keep my mask on, though, to be strong, unbreakable. "I don't understand. You're the Devourer. You're not him. You can't be."

The old man's smile deepened—God, he looked like my grandfather, even his eyes—and I watched in horror as he reached around the butler and sank his hand into the man's chest. I couldn't believe what I was seeing at first, it didn't make sense, but I stared at his hand, slipping through flesh like it was water, pushing in deep until even his forearm was embedded. The butler turned ice white, bottom lip trembling, but he did not make a sound.

I lurched forward, intent only to make it stop—but the old man yanked his arm out with a flourish, and blood sprayed across my face. The butler collapsed, blood pooling around him. In the old man's hand was a human heart. Which he offered to me.

When I just stared at him, unmoving, he shrugged and took a deep, wrenching bite from it. Blood ran down his chin. Blood dripped on the white floor. Blood stank up the air and made me sick.

"My kind go crazy sometimes," he said, after a hard, slow swallow. "We're made of little more than light and energy, so to say we lose our minds is a bit inaccurate. And yet, more accurate than anything else. We lose our minds, young Hunter. Or we become more of ourselves in ways we never dreamed."

"My husband came here," I said.

"Your husband is still here," he said, crouching over the butler, "and you can kill me, but you won't. Not until you're sure I can't help you. Such a sorry predicament you've put yourself in."

The butler's limbs twitched, as if waking from a nightmare. I wasn't surprised he was still alive. I said, "You orchestrated this."

"I was awakened," replied the Aetar, looking up from the butler to study Raw and Aaz with the calculated eye of a butcher measuring meat. "When my lesser half used our crystal skull to spy . . . he found me instead. That brief moment of shared essence not only allowed me to see inside his life, but it established a link that I used to slip outside my bonds. It was not easy, I admit. I could not often take advantage of it. But it was rather useful, for a time. Long enough to set things in motion."

He met my gaze. "You, for instance."

"You're not Jack," I whispered.

"I am," he whispered back. "Just not the part he wanted."

The old man lunged at me. I was expecting an attack, but nothing so fast. I couldn't see him move, just a blur, then impact. He was faster than the boys, even.

I slammed into the floor, breath knocked out. Dek and Mal reared, breathing fire, snapping at the old man. Raw and Aaz clung to him, tearing at his limbs, ripping him to pieces like he was made of tissue paper while Zee stood over me, spiky hair bristling, snarling with rage. And all I heard was laughter, his cold, delighted laughter, filling the air. The more they hurt him, the more amused he seemed—and I realized that all the boys were doing was giving him pleasure.

My right hand glimmered, power surging through the armor. But before it could transform into a weapon that I could use, the world around us broke. Those white walls, that perfect marble—all of it cracked. No earthquake, no shaking—just a fracture that grew with each heartbeat, splitting apart the room. Heat burst against my skin, crackling over me like I'd just been shoved into an oven. Smoke filled the air.

Zee snapped out a single sharp word. Raw and Aaz leapt away from the old man, skidding across the floor to me. I saw the butler climbing to his feet, but he looked different than I remembered—thinner, taller. Younger.

And he favored his right leg.

"Fuck," I said, just as fury passed through his face, and he opened his mouth to sing. It was a sound made from thunder, raw and glorious—and the Aetar, in his shredded, old-man body, choked a little.

Just as we fell into hell.

It was a true fall, a descent that scrambled everything inside me. I couldn't see or move—I just had to trust that I wouldn't die when I landed.

But there was no landing. When I could see again, I realized we hadn't moved at all. It was the world that had changed.

Fire, everywhere, dotting a swift-moving lava field that churned in a blast furnace of awesome, terrible heat. But beyond that, towering over us, was a pillar of flame—a warped, raging mass that writhed and twisted like a snake. I couldn't see the top of it. I could barely encompass its width with my gaze. I was an ant in comparison, and all I could remember was that terrible vision: the implacable hunger, and those eyes, those eyes that I felt even now, focusing on me.

Zee and the boys huddled at my side, shielding me against the sparks that lit upward and might have caught on my clothes. It was hard to breathe the air. I felt like Frodo sitting on a rocky outcropping at the edge of Mount Doom, trapped and waiting to be cooked alive. All I needed was my Samwise.

And I found him, twenty feet away, on another outcropping that rose above the fire.

Grant, kneeling, surrounded by Shurik—who clung to him with stubborn ferocity. I didn't know where they'd been before, but I could barely see my husband beneath their squirming white bodies. I thought, *Thank God.*

My husband was singing, but it wasn't music—just a powerful, throbbing *om* that filled the air with such weight and heft and presence that I felt as though I were breathing his voice, wearing it on my skin. I clenched my right hand in a fist. I had killed Aetar with the armor I wore. Grant had killed them with his voice. But we needed something from this creature.

Fuck it. I slammed my right hand against my thigh, and we fell backward into the void. Just for a moment. Blissful disembodiment, safe from the inferno.

We were spit out just behind Grant's back, clinging to stone. I dug my hands between Shurik, wrapping my arms around my husband. Holding him close, letting him know I was there. His voice altered its tone, growing deeper. His hands found mine. Up close, I could see the sweat pouring down his face, and the glow of the flames couldn't mask the gray poison in his skin. He was tired, sick, not at his full strength.

"Reaper Kings," whispered a voice from the fire. It came from all around us, and was surprisingly quiet—though it still managed to cut through Grant's song. *"Kings and their maiden. Kings, a maiden, and a dying Lightbringer who is bonded to demons from the old army."* Soft laughter, chilling in its menace. *"So many surprises and delights."*

Arms of fire reached out. Zee and the boys clung to us. I felt them all around me. I felt the hardness of my pregnant belly. Grant was shaking with effort, but those arms still moved toward us—as if all his powers had no effect. I didn't understand how that was possible, but I stood—demons clinging to me—and stepped around my husband. I stood, facing the Aetar, and my right hand shimmered, warped, transformed—into a shield, light as a feather, round as the moon.

Behind me, Grant placed his hand against the small of my back. Gentle, so gentle, but heat bloomed inside my chest—a wild burst of golden light filled with so much power I could see the glow from behind my eyes. I felt that light burn my tongue, tingle against my lips. All of me, burning.

And it felt so good. Like home.

Maxine, I heard inside my mind. It wasn't just Grant's voice, but all of him—inside me, shining and warm, filling that hole that had drowned my heart. Our bond, resurrected.

Don't be stupid again, I thought at him. *It's us or nothing.*

That's a lie, too, he replied, but there was only love in his voice—because he was right about that, too. There was another life that mattered, and if push came to shove, we both knew whom I would choose.

But in the meantime, I wasn't going to give up without a fight.

Except, I was surprised again. Fire moves fast. Fire controlled by an Aetar, even faster. Those arms turned into whips, lashing out to hit the shield. They sizzled on impact, dissolving, but the fire kept coming—again and again. I'd killed Aetar with nothing less than a touch of the armor. I couldn't understand how it was surviving this contact.

My confusion distracted me. One tendril snaked around my shield. It happened so fast, I didn't see until it was too late. Even the boys were too slow though Raw was the closest and tried to block the blow.

The blade sheared through my right arm as though my flesh were made of silk.

I didn't feel anything at first, but I watched my arm fall away with distant, numb surprise. *My arm,* I thought. *My arm is gone. How strange that looks. My arm, all the way down there.*

I staggered, watching the Aetar's flaming hand cover the armor that still clung to my dismembered arm. A terrible hiss filled the air when it made contact—the creature flinched—but it did not pull away. It sank my entire limb down its massive throat, and as my flesh disappeared I glimpsed the armor shrinking, shrinking, and I remembered how I'd first found it—as nothing but a ring.

"Maxine." Grant dragged me away. I didn't resist, but I barely felt him. I couldn't stop staring at the fire, searching it for that piece of myself—or even a glitter of quicksilver.

And then the pain really hit. I tried to fight through it, but dark spots filled my vision, swallowing up the fire, the heat—even the agony eating up my right side. Grant cried out, but not in pain. It was a command, and in his voice, a click. Like a door opening.

I slipped in and out of consciousness, aware of a shadow that loomed over my body, tendrils of hair that touched my face. I was carried and dragged, past the fire to twilight, as cool air washed over me—which did nothing to dull the bombs exploding inside my body.

"You morons," I heard Jack shout, shoving everyone aside and falling to his knees beside me. He pressed a cool hand to my brow, and his voice was thick with fear. I didn't want him touching me, but couldn't make my throat work. "The wound's been cauterized," he said. "You, pick her up."

Strong arms slipped beneath me. Tracker. I screamed when he lifted me. Dek and Mal, who were coiled around my neck, howled in shared agony. Raw and Aaz gripped their own right arms, and Zee raked his claws through the dirt, eyes narrowed with pain and rage.

"He has a fragment of the labyrinth," Jack said, somewhere to my right. "We must leave here, now. He'll free himself, for sure."

More voices, but they were fuzzy. I tried so hard not to cry out. I told myself it wasn't worse than the boys waking up, but that wasn't true.

My arm was gone. *My arm.* Swallowed up, burned to ash—except I could still feel it there, as if it were attached. My brain, playing tricks. Had any of that been real? The white room, the fire—that old man's familiar face, and what he'd said about my grandfather?

I lost track of time. Once, I heard Jack say, "I don't know how, lad. He was the best at building bodies that were stronger than anything the rest of us could imagine. They had to be strong, to last longer for his torture."

Your torture? I wanted to ask him. *Are you the Devourer?*

I didn't hear Grant's response. I was already gone.

CHAPTER 30

THERE was no pain inside that darkness, just the drift. And I kept drifting, right into a field of stars.

I wasn't alone. I saw a man made of silver, radiating a cool, clean light. He stood on my left, but no matter how hard I stared, I couldn't see his face.

I didn't need to. I knew what my father looked like.

On my right was a creature made of obsidian—not a dragon, but close enough—a wyrm, sleek and lean, and coiled with power. It writhed and twisted, and ate the light of the other man. But it was a fair trade. His silver skin absorbed the shadows that flowed from the wyrm. Both of them, consuming the other.

You are safe, whispered my father, his skin shining with starlight. *Let go of the fear. Let go.*

Let go, murmured the darkness. *Embrace the hunt and the hunger. Be the vessel that is needed.*

Why? I asked them both, so weary. *Why does there need to be a vessel? Why did you go to so much trouble to engineer this?*

I woke up before I could get an answer. Not that I expected one.

But that didn't matter, either. Because we were no longer in the Labyrinth. I saw stars above, and in the distance, city lights. I wasn't sure what city, but it looked familiar, and very much of earth. A dream, though. It was just a dream. I couldn't feel my body. I floated like a ghost.

My relief, though, was short-lived. Because the sky opened up, and fire burned away the stars.

Fire, in every direction, rippling outward. I kept expecting to see the edges, but the flames never stopped, spreading over my head, raining down an inferno.

I looked back at the city, but it was already burning. Millions of voices, crying out, and none of them would have a quick death. An entire world would die slowly, just for the pleasure of the beast—who would devour their pain.

And it was my fault.

No, I said, and—

—opened my eyes, again.

I stared, breathing hard. Nothing but the forest around me: gnarled roots and trees as big as skyscrapers, and a soft twilight that clung to the air and seemed part of its scent; sweet, light, with a hint of rose. I was surrounded by demons: scales and spikes, sharp elbows, and even sharper claws. Red eyes gleamed. Purrs rattled.

Still, just a dream. Or a vision of the future. I couldn't take the risk, though.

For a moment, I dared to imagine that losing my arm was part of that bad dream—but no, I turned my head, and all I saw was shoulder and air.

Grant whispered, "Maxine."

I was in so much pain I could barely see his face. I looked harder, and found him pressed against my left side, surrounded by a teeming pile of Shurik, who had spread out over the small clearing, rolling in the ferns.

His cheeks were gaunt, eyes reserved and weary—but

still alive. He even managed a small smile, but it was filled with pain and regret.

I tried to reach for him, but it hurt too much to move. Grant placed his hand over mine. Between us, light flared: heart to heart. I closed my eyes, savoring the glow that spread within me.

"He tortured you," I whispered, unable to speak louder past the pain. "You were the butler, and I never realized. Neither did the boys."

"*I* didn't know who I was anymore," Grant said, hoarse. "It was as if he expected me. I never had a chance to even open my mouth. He . . . altered me . . . immediately. Even when I saw you . . . when I saw you in that place . . . I didn't know you. I still remember how I didn't know you." He swallowed hard, closing his eyes. "I can recall . . . all the things he did to me. When he was finished, when I should have been dead, he would bring me back to life. Heal my wounds until he could start again."

"I'm so sorry," I whispered.

"It was my fault. I was cocky." He kissed my brow, then my mouth, lingering there. "I don't know what comes next, but we're going home."

Fire burned inside my mind. "We can't. We have to stop this thing here, or else it'll destroy earth. I'm sure of it."

I heard a small sound of discontent. "I wish you had thought of that before, my dear."

Jack paced into view, arms folded over his stomach as though he was holding himself. For a moment, I was frightened—I couldn't separate my memories from the present moment, and all I could see was that doppelganger with his smile and those deadly eyes. Behind him, I glimpsed Sarai. But she was lingering in the shadows, and there was a hesitance in the way she stood—even in that nonhuman body—that struck me as odd.

Grant squeezed my hand. "Jack. There's something else you didn't tell us." His voice shook a little; he was as rattled as me, which was a small comfort.

"The Devourer," I said. "He says that he's you."

Jack stared. "What are you talking about?"

Zee leaned forward on his claws. "You, Meddling Man. Monster is part of you. Broken away. Locked up. But you."

My grandfather looked at us like we were crazy—and I *felt* crazy for even considering it. But the truth had always been strange. And there was something about this, what had happened in that place, that made me wonder who was living the real lie. I couldn't afford to discount *anything*.

"He said he was you," I told Jack. "The part you didn't want."

He appeared genuinely affronted. "That's ridiculous. What's even more ridiculous is that you would believe him."

"Jack," said my husband, in a deceptively calm voice, "your light is identical to his."

That surprised me. And terrified me at the same time. It was the confirmation I didn't want to hear.

My grandfather froze. "No."

"The energy patterns, the essence . . . it's the same." Grant leaned forward, Shurik tumbling from his chest into his lap. "I don't know how, but you *are* part of each other."

I'd never seen Jack look so lost and confused—so utterly bewildered. It hurt; my first instinct was grief—for him, for me—except I didn't know if I could trust what I felt.

"You can," Grant murmured to me, rubbing my hand. "He *is* confused. I don't think he knew."

"Of course I didn't!" Jack's voice was hoarse, strangled. "How . . . how is this . . ." He turned, seeking out Sarai. "This can't be possible."

If anything, she seemed to sink deeper into the shadows. Inhuman body, but so *human* in her posture, in the way she carried herself—as if secrets were a burden that had been freshly pressed on her shoulders.

"Sarai," Jack said again. "You have always been my friend."

And I am still your friend, she whispered, across all our minds. *But you have not always been as you are now, Old*

*Wolf. And I am sorry . . . I am so very sorry . . . that this is
how you must learn the truth.*

My grandfather staggered. I saw movement behind
him—Tracker. I hadn't noticed him nestled in a knot of
roots, but he glided free, jumping down to press his shoulder
against Jack's so that he wouldn't fall. His eyes were hooded,
dark, his mouth set in an impossibly grim line.

Jack sank to his knees. "No."

You do not remember. Sarai moved closer, bowing her
head. *We all changed after we found flesh. You changed
most of all, my friend. As if two different beings inhabited
your skin. It happened slowly, over time. You were always
good. But the shadow in you lengthened. And it became a
force that was just as strong, and terrible.*

He could not have looked more lost, or devastated. "But
I remember what *he* did. I remember what he did to *me*. We
couldn't have inhabited the same body."

*Same body, different mind. The tortures he inflicted on
you were very real.* He *was very real. Someone wholly different from you. Of course it felt as if another entity was
torturing you. Because that was the truth. One truth, anyway.*

"He had a split personality," I said, haunted by the memory of my grandfather's face, my grandfather himself, eating
what I now knew was Grant's heart. "That's what you're
telling us."

We made the split permanent, whispered Sarai, pressing
her delicate white snout against Jack's brow. *We loved you,
brother. We could not abandon you to the sins of your
shadow. So we pulled you both apart and cast him away.
And you did not remember. No one remembered, save us.
We have many secrets, but that is our greatest. We wanted
to protect you from it.*

Jack shuddered, bowing his head into his hands. I struggled to rise, which hurt so badly I almost went unconscious.
Raw and Aaz pressed me down, and instead it was Zee who
went to my grandfather. The little demon crouched and
pressed a gentle claw against his cheek.

"Meddling Man," he whispered. "All have shadows."

"The things he did," Jack breathed. "What I did."

"No," I croaked, wishing I could cry, wishing I could stand and go to him, whole. "It wasn't you."

But that only made him curl harder into himself. Zee sighed, letting his little hand drop.

Grant turned his head to cough. Blood flecked his mouth. I'd almost forgotten he was sick, and I watched that, and forgot my own ravaged flesh. I would heal. He would not.

Somehow, I found the strength to touch his back. Inside my mind, he whispered, *I should have accepted my own death. I should have known this would never work. But I wanted to see our daughter, and so I got selfish. And I dragged you into it.*

I was already selfish enough for both of us. If you hadn't gone first, it would have been me. And I'm the one who's pregnant.

So we're both idiots, he said. *Great.*

All I wanted to do was cry. *I love you.*

I love you more, he replied, and glanced down at my stomach. *I wrote her letters, before all this happened. Just in case. I stored them in your mother's chest, in Seattle.*

I was dying on the inside. I couldn't imagine life without him. I couldn't even think past this moment we were in— which was already so full of grief.

But you will, he said. *For her.*

I hadn't seen Oturu this entire time, but from the shadows, deep beyond the trees, I heard him whisper, "Hunter."

All the little demons sat up, alert. Even the Shurik went still. I listened, breathless, but there was nothing to hear. Except, after a brief moment, I saw a faint glow against the trees: a blush of fire.

"Hurry," Jack choked out, but it was too late.

I heard a low, moaning wail, and a tendril of fire snaked around one of the massive Labyrinth trees. Heat rolled over me. I wanted to gag on the terror I felt, a sudden dread of losing even more than an arm.

Grant stood, fierce, but I rallied all my strength and pushed him out of the way as the tentacle snapped down. It caught us both, and we were snatched up like pieces of straw, hauled up through the trees. Zee and the boys clung to us, while Shurik were scattered, flung away. Higher, toward a wall of flame. I was blind with fear and pain, but I still felt a tingle—a brief warning—just as we were thrown through a Labyrinth door.

It was another nightmare of a world. My throat burned on the fumes of sulfur and blood. Red clouds scarred my eyes, red smoke drifting over red water running into a horizon full of spitting shadows that boiled and hissed like volcanic spit. The air tasted rank. I could hardly breathe, and the pain was so wild inside me, it was all I could do just to stay conscious.

The red sky disappeared behind writhing limbs of fire, rough and hoary. My skin crawled—heart pounding, light-headed. Grant began to sing, but the tentacles wrapped tighter around his body, burning him, squeezing his voice to silence. Squeezing even more, until a muffled cry escaped him, like he was screaming in his throat. The sound cut right through me. Our bond flickered, weakened.

And in its place, I felt the darkness rise. I felt the heat of the wyrm encircle my heart, and it felt so good and safe—for once, for the first time, it felt like me.

I'm yours, I said to the darkness, and I meant it, with all my soul.

I grabbed that fire with my good hand, and the flames burned, lit me up like an oiled match. I heard the *whumpf* as my body ignited, felt my hair rise, smelled my flesh cooking. I felt the pain, but I didn't care.

I was too hungry.

The fire was food, and so was the light. Power roared through me, over my skin. Fire flickered out, turned to ash. More tendrils swept down to grab me, but I soaked them into my body.

Still, the Aetar did not die.

A stout figure appeared at the corner of my eye. Jack. He ran toward us, holding the crystal skull. Shouting at the top of his lungs. I felt the entire weight of that flaming monster shift and turn.

"Wolf," whispered the Devourer, and the hunger in that one word almost rivaled mine. Grant and I were tossed down. Small hands wrapped around my arm as I flailed through the sky.

Zee, hugging me so tight I could hardly breathe.

We hit sand. Grant lay on his back, chest heaving. Zee was small and strong, bracing me against his shoulder. I followed his gaze, watching the fire hover over Jack, its writhing body sprawled across the red sky like a thundercloud, as far as the eye could see. An enormous face made of fire pushed free: cold, expressionless eyes staring down at my grandfather.

I heard nothing but my heartbeat in that roaring silence— and my heart pounded and my blood roared, and I sensed a great weight bear down upon my soul, as though I were the door holding back a heavy storm that railed against me, howling in my ear.

"Wolf," whispered the monster again. "How I've waited for you. I have such pleasures planned. A just gift for the one you gave me."

Jack didn't seem to be listening. He looked across the distance at me, holding my gaze, pouring into it grief and love.

"My dear girl," he whispered. "Follow me."

And on those words, he raised the crystal skull, and light poured from it, cutting through the other Aetar. I heard no cries of pain, but I imagined a cutting sound, like a saw. Light, slicing through the shell.

I tried to stand and almost blacked out.

Grant began dragging himself toward Jack, half on his hands and knees, pulling his bad leg behind him. I tried again to stand, half shut my eyes against the blinding pain, and breathed through my mouth. I stumbled toward my grandfather.

A tentacle batted at my grandfather, sending him flying. The crystal skull tumbled from his grip. The creature struck at it.

Raw reached the skull first, wrapping his body around it and rolling. The beast hit him, so hard his little body cracked the earth. I heard him cry out.

I started running. I forgot my wounds. I didn't feel them. All I could see was Raw and his body—so small, like a child.

My child. My boys.

The fire towered and smashed toward Raw, fighting for the skull. Zee and the others dove through flames, protecting their brother. I was right behind them. I forgot that my right arm was gone, but it didn't matter. Shadows gathered where it had been; a darkening pulse throbbed through my absent limb: a ghost.

Black light flickered in my eyes. The wyrm uncoiled in my chest, but when it began to rise through my throat, I stopped it.

Not like that, I said, and wrapped my heart around the presence, opened my heart, opened it so wide that I swallowed the darkness into my soul. Accepting it, taking it, possessing it in every way it had tried to possess me over the long years. I overwhelmed it with my embrace, and the darkness yielded.

I am yours, part of me whispered. *You are mine.*

We have waited so long, it replied, softly. *Only light can hold the darkness. And we have been hungry for a home.*

My heart was big enough. My heart, with room for demons and daughters, and old men who were crafty and silly—and even younger men who loved me—and my mother, and my father, and all who were yet to come. My heart was big enough for them all.

And ready to kill for them as well.

We will devastate stars for what is ours, said the darkness.

Yes, I replied. *But let's start with fire.*

I walked into the blaze and swallowed the heat into my skin. It was as natural as breathing. I dissolved the architecture of the flame, and this time, the Aetar could not escape.

Not until the last moment, when all that was left was a frail wisp of flesh, barely recognizable as human—the core of the flame, where the monster had stored its soul.

"Grant," I said. "He's weak now. Take what you need. Pull the cure from his mind."

And my husband cleared his throat and did just that.

Afterward, I killed the beast.

I ate his light.

CHAPTER 31

I was no longer human.

I'd never been human, not really, but at least I could pass. No more of that. My skin had burned black as obsidian, from head to toe. My eyes were dark as night, and so was my tongue.

I still had no arm, but sometimes a shadow gathered in its place. I could pretend. I could pretend that my body did not swallow light, or that I no longer hungered for food—only the sun, only stars, only everything that lived.

At least I had the boys. I had my daughter growing inside me. I could learn the rest as I went along.

But there was still a price.

GRANT was good with formulations of light. All the monster told him, he applied. The disease was a living thing, as much an extension of its creator as it was just a virus. By the time we arrived home, some of the demons had already begun to recover on their own—and for those who were still too sick, too close to death, the configuration of light, the pattern that could rearrange those cells to health—it worked.

But I didn't go home.

"I have new sympathy for you," said Jack, less than a week after we returned to earth. It was the right time, right place—our world had not changed too much. As far as everyone was concerned, we'd been gone less than a day.

"Your life, always being taken out of your hands. Terrible secrets inhabiting your past. Those who think they know better, keeping you in the dark." A weak smile touched his mouth. "I'm very sorry, my dear. For everything."

"Don't be," I said, which was sort of a lie, but I didn't know in what way. Just that a part of me still felt hurt, lost, though there was no point in dwelling on the matter. I had bigger problems. "Are you well? It didn't occur to me until afterward that killing *him* might take your life, too."

"It would have been a just sacrifice." Jack looked away, picking at the grass. We were back in Mongolia, where I'd found him; the sun was bright and shining, and the boys were sleeping. Fitful dreams. Nightmares, maybe. We had so much to explore together, to understand what we had become. I could still see them, even though my skin had turned black. Their scales were silver on me, gleaming in the sun.

"Perhaps it would be easier to be dead," he went on.

"You don't mean that."

"Don't I? But I suppose I must honor those I harmed in another life by bearing the truth as best I can." He started to reach for my hand but caught himself before he could clasp nothing but air. Pain lanced his features, remorse. "I did betray you."

"Oh, shut up," I said, giving him a faint smile to take away the sting. "Go get reincarnated for a thousand years. It'll make you feel better."

He almost smiled, for real. "And you? You're immortal now, I suspect."

"Yes," I said, touching my stomach. "Great."

Jack's smile faded. "That is the problem, isn't it? The boys are yours, my dear. They cannot be hers unless you die. And no matter what you are now, she might be just as mortal as any human."

You are the last. Wasn't that what I'd always been told? But I refused to believe that. Maybe I was the last of something. But not everything.

I stood. "Good-bye, Grandfather."

He gave me a startled, vulnerable look. "Ah."

"Yes." I bent and kissed the top of his head—but even that felt dangerous. I didn't trust myself, even with him.

A shudder passed through him—maybe he felt the danger.

"My dear girl," he whispered. "Remember your heart."

"It's here," I said, pressing my left hand above my breast, memorizing his face, his spirit. I could see *him* now. I'd never been able to, before. But my eyes were different now, and he was a storm of northern nights: dark green fighting with shimmers of blue, and around it all a white halo, a tremendous fire.

My grandfather. Made of light.

I turned my vision inward and focused on my husband. Our bond burned through the darkness. I clung to it.

And went to him.

⊰⊱

WE stood on the hill overlooking the farmhouse, beside my mother's grave. Shurik surrounded us, grazing through the grass. The Yorana were still bonded to Grant, but in the Labyrinth he had allowed them to go their own way, without his interference. Live or die, it was up to them. Good luck with that. Maybe we'd cross paths one day, but I sure as hell didn't miss them.

Grant, on the other hand, looked healthy, strong. Tearing

down the walls between him and the demons had not destroyed his spirit. Just made him stronger. Perhaps even immortal. Just like me. Just like the other demon lords.

We held hands. Sunset had already come and gone, but the last light was beautiful. Zee and the boys huddled close to us. Dek and Mal were stretched across both our shoulders, binding us close.

"Are you sure about this?" I asked him, watching as the Mahati climbed the hill. All that was left of a demon army, marching toward us, carrying their few belongings. Another exodus. I didn't give a shit if any human saw. We were past that. The Osul were with them, their cubs pouncing through the grass. The adults were more solemn. I saw Mary amongst them, and the Messenger.

"Yes," he said, and the look in his eye was not entirely human, either. "I made arrangements with Rex and Byron, and some of our other friends. The ones we can trust. Blood Mama, even. You know *she's* not leaving. They'll take care of everything. And they'll be here when we get back."

The funny thing was, they *would* be here. All of them, immortal in their own way.

"I'm sorry," I said, unable to help myself.

Grant studied me. "I still love you. No matter what."

"I know." I kissed his mouth, gently. "But I don't know what I am anymore. Maybe I'm a monster, maybe I'm . . . something more . . . but the answers won't be here. There's no truth in standing still, and the demons can't stay here, either. They need a new home." Where that might lead us, I could not begin to imagine. Who I might become, out there, as much a mystery.

I hesitated. "You don't have to come."

"Oh, be quiet, wretch." He flashed me his old smile, and it took my breath away, even while making me laugh. "Remember when we first met?"

"I loved you from the moment I saw you," I said, close to tears. "And I've loved you more every day since then. You are my light, Grant."

He was still smiling, unguarded and strong. "Both of us together. We can make anything happen."

"I hope so." I was afraid that was a lie; but then I touched my stomach, and hope swelled inside me, and determination. "For her, yes. We'll figure it out."

He took my hand. I drew in a deep breath and looked at the demons gathering around us. I felt Oturu close by. Tracker was nowhere in sight. Perhaps, in his prison. I would take care of that later.

"Young Queen," said Lord Ha'an, bowing his head. Dek and Mal let out a sad trill, while Raw and Aaz drank their last beers for a long time to come. Zee leaned against my legs, sighing.

I looked at my husband and placed his hand on my stomach. I drank in his face, bathed in the last glow of light; then looked from him to my mother's grave. For a moment I thought I heard my name called, and turned. Far away, so far from us it seemed to be another world—and maybe it was—I saw a figure standing alone, waving.

Her hand stilled. A greeting, or good-bye.

I blinked, and she was gone.

FROM *NEW YORK TIMES* BESTSELLING AUTHOR

MARJORIE M. LIU

THE MORTAL BONE

⇥ **A Hunter Kiss Novel** ⇤

When the bond Maxine Kiss shares with the demons tattooed on her skin is deliberately severed, the hunter is left vulnerable and unprotected. For the first time in ten thousand years, the demons have a taste of freedom. And as they grow more violent and unpredictable, Maxine starts to fear they will lose their minds without her. But reuniting won't be easy, as a great temptation waits for her little demons: a chance to return to their lives as Reaper Kings and unleash hell on earth.

"The boundlessness of Liu's imagination never ceases to amaze."
—*Booklist*

"Readers of early Laurell K. Hamilton [and] Charlaine Harris…should try Liu now and catch a rising star."
—*Publishers Weekly*

marjoriemliu.com
penguin.com

Two Stunning Works
From *New York Times* Bestselling Author
MARJORIE M. LIU

ARMOR OF ROSES

⊱ **A Hunter Kiss Novella** ⊰

When demon slayer Maxine Kiss investigates a grisly murder, she finds herself involved in a conspiracy dating back to World War II—and a secret mission that her grandmother may have carried out for the US government, one that involves the mysterious armor of roses . . .

THE SILVER VOICE

⊱ **A never-before-published Hunter Kiss short story** ⊰

On their honeymoon, Maxine helps Grant explore his heritage through memories locked inside a mysterious seed ring, leading him to the silver voice and secrets his mother kept hidden from him—until now.

Available together online!
Also includes a letter from Marjorie!

M992AS1011

From *New York Times* Bestselling Author
MARJORIE M. LIU

A WILD LIGHT
⊰ **A Hunter Kiss Novel** ⊱

Obsidian shadows of the flesh . . . tattoos with
hearts, minds, and dreams. By day, they are my
armor. By night, they unwind from my body
to take on forms of their own—demons of the
flesh, turned into flesh.

"I adore the Hunter Kiss series! Marjorie Liu's writing
is both lyrical and action packed, which is a very rare
combination."
                    —Angela Knight, *New York Times* bestselling author

"Readers of early Laurell K. Hamilton [and] Charlaine
Harris . . . should try Liu now and catch a rising star."
                    —*Publishers Weekly*

M935T0811